Seeking Grace in Beulah Land

A Novel

By

Lu Clifton

First Edition, First Printing April 2019
Cover image courtesy of Pixabay

Summary: Seeking Grace in Beulah Land is a tale about a small Oklahoma community and the mystery that has haunted its residents for decades. In the days following WWII, residents of rural Pittsburg County Oklahoma were mystified by the sudden disappearance of Grace Barlow, a young wife and mother of two daughters. When Grover Cleveland Barlow, her veteran husband, did not file a missing person's report or treat her disappearance with suspicion, assumptions were made that Grace had left of her own free will; she was known to be a free-spirited woman with high aspirations. Grover Cleveland Barlow carried on quietly, working as a sharecropper to raise his two daughters. Over the next sixty years, he spoke Grace's name not once. Until now.

At an urgent request from his mother, Mack Barlow, has returned to Pittsburg County to deal with his grandfather's eccentric behavior and end-of-life requests. What Mack discovers about the night Grace disappeared is more astonishing than anyone could have imagined. Stirring up long-dead memories creates a domino effect, causing several others to come to terms with long-held resentments and guilt. Piece by piece, what emerges is a story of dashed hopes, impulsive acts, and a series of extenuating circumstances that demand an old man receive forgiveness.

Filled with down-to-earth characters, Seeking Grace in Beulah Land is a mesmerizing tale that will speak to those who struggle with long-buried emotions and fears. It's a tale that speaks to all of us.

ISBN: 978-0-9985284-4-1 (pbk)
ISBN: 978-0-9985284-5-8 (e-book)

1.Fiction—General 2.FamilyLife—Fiction 3.Literary--Fiction 4.Small Town & Rural--Fiction…Oklahoma--Fiction
Two Shadows
P.O. Box 154
Davis, IL 61019

For Christopher and Jeffrey

ALSO BY LU CLIFTON

Freaky Fast Frankie Joe
Immortal Max
Seeking Cassandra
Scalp Dance, A Sam Chitto Mystery
The Bone Picker, A Sam Chitto Mysery
The Horned Owl, A Sam Chitto Mystery

"I reached some plains so vast, that I did not find their limit anywhere I went, although I travelled over them for more than 300 leagues . . . with no more land marks than if we had been swallowed up by the sea . . . there was not a stone, nor bit of rising ground, nor a tree, nor a shrub, nor anything to go by."

Francisco Vasquez de Coronado 1541

CHAPTER ONE

Mack Barlow swore under his breath as he glanced at the clock on the dash. A quarter to eight and the sun just now rising. Days were short and would get shorter yet as the planet inched toward the winter solstice. Short, dark days did not sit well with him. They forecast dry spells for anyone in the construction trade. And when you threw a bum economy into the mix . . . Well, empty days eliminated excuses for taking care of family business.

The windswept land along I-40 flew past as he pushed his Bronco to the speed limit. He frowned, wondering if the sun had reached the ground in the short-leaf pine country where he was headed. There, forests and thickets so dense you needed a brush hog to clear them robbed the days of even more sunlight, which made for even shorter, darker days.

For years now, he'd made a practice of avoiding densely wooded country. He'd chosen to live in the Texas Panhandle for a reason. Spanish explorers had called the place *Llano Estacado*, Translated, *Llano Estacado* meant the staked plains. The land was flat and empty of vegetation for the most part with few landmarks. So large and barren was the expanse that early travelers drove stakes in the ground to find their way across and back again. But the empty country fit him to a T. There was nothing to interfere with a man's vision there. It was safe ground.

He turned off the radio as it morphed to static, content with arrow-straight roads and his stoic road companions: pumpjacks sucking oil from the ground like giant metal grasshoppers and scrawny cows sucking water from stock tanks. Oil and water, he thought, liquid gold and liquid grace. Pumped from deep below ground made both commodities hard to get, and scarcity made them priceless.

An hour or so later, the land began to slope downward. Here, the North Fork of the Red River and Sweetwater Creek carved the earth deep, bringing forth enough moisture for scrub brush and cottonwoods to take hold. He slowed a bit, taking in the fall colors and the way the leaves danced in the breeze. But as he passed through a thick stand of juniper bush shadowing the road, the skin behind his ears began to crawl. Quickly, he looked into the rearview mirror, feeling an urgent need to check his six for snipers in the bush. As long-buried memories flooded back, he felt anger fill his chest, flush his face.

Why the hell was he making this trip, he thought, berating himself. His mother always did blow things out of proportion. But she'd been hounding him for a month or better, telling him, "You got to come home, it's your grandfather. There's a matter needs to be handled right away."

"Is he about to kick the bucket?" he'd asked.

"No—yes . . . Well, he's not dying at this exact minute, but that's what's causing the problem."

"What problem?"

She had paused. "I'd rather explain in person."

He'd pushed. "What? He got one of the nurses there at the home knocked up?"

"Oh, Mack, this is serious." Her voice had cracked.

"Give me a reason, Mama. I'm a working man." Not exactly a lie, but damn close.

"I just can't explain it on the phone. I've tried talking sense to him but he won't listen to me." Her voice had cracked again. She could not go on.

He hated it when she ended things that way. It was like waiting for the other shoe to drop.

No matter, he thought now, pressing on the gas pedal. On this trip, he was going to fix any and all problems for good, and the sooner he got there, the sooner he could leave. By the time he got back to Amarillo, work would have picked up and things would go back to normal.

But a few miles down the road, a sign announcing an exit to a town caught his eye. Shamrock, he thought, the last town before crossing into Oklahoma. Then, he spotted the other sign, a brightly painted one advertising a cafe. Easing off the gas, he exited the highway and eased to a stop in the U-Drop-Inn parking lot.

I'll have a cup of coffee, he thought, slamming the door shut on the Bronco. Maybe a short stack with some bacon on the side. A few minutes more or less wouldn't matter. Hell, what kind of problems could an eighty-seven-year-old man have?

CHAPTER TWO

Wynona Folsom, known as Nonny to those that called her friend or family, stood in front of a sorting case wedged in the back corner of the McAlester post office. She paused as she removed the last two pieces of mail, a postcard and an oversized envelope bearing a State of Oklahoma return address. Reading the name on the postcard, she turned to Claude Riley, a bandy-legged man working to her left.

"What do you make of this?" She handed the card to Claude, who was finishing up his sort.

"*Grace* Anderson," he said, reading aloud. "Now, there's a name I hadn't heard in a while."

"I didn't know she was from Marietta, Georgia. Did you?"

"Nope . . ." Claude handed the card back to Nonny. "But guess she could be, seeing this here's a high-school reunion notice."

"They need to update their alumni records." Nonny looked at the card again. "She's been dead a long time."

"Dead?" Claude contemplated this. "Well, I suppose she could be. Old man Anderson's way up in his eighties. Grace lit out so many years ago, couldn't say for sure. People figured she'd gone back home." He nodded at the card. "Most likely, that'd be Marietta."

"Isn't that funny," Nonny murmured. "I've known that family all my life and never heard a word about her running off. I just assumed she was dead." She hesitated, frowned, then turned toward Claude again. "Wouldn't they have her current address on record if she'd gone back to Marietta . . .?"

Looking around, Nonny realized she was talking to herself. Claude had finished packing up his mail and left, as had the other rural route carriers. Which she needed to do, too.

Hurriedly, she placed the manila envelope and postcard inside a faded cloth bag embroidered with the name BARLOW. Like a candle's flame, a memory flickered of Mack Barlow. A feeling, actually, the kind that causes internal organs to heat up. She snuffed it quickly and fitted the bag in a long, plastic tray loaded with similar bags. En route to the back door, she passed the postmaster.

The man was new to the job, having transferred from Oklahoma City three weeks before, and made it known on his first day that he believed in following the letter of the law. The law, that is, as laid out in the United States Postal Regulations. His pigeon-shaped body camouflaged a time when he had been military muscular, but that was before a Postal Service appointment had replaced his former rigorous regimen with a cushioned chair on rollers. He followed Nonny into the brisk, early-November air, his mouth running full out.

"Nowhere in the Regulations does it say mail needs to be put in bags," he said, watching Nonny load trays into an old postal jeep she had picked up at a government auction.

"Keeps the kids and old people from losing their mail," she said, talking over her shoulder.

"Never heard of such a thing."

"Well, now you have."

"City carriers don't put mail in bags," he said.

"City people don't walk a half mile to get their mail either. Besides which, I'm a contractor, not government."

The postmaster paused. "Slows you down—it's got to slow you down. That's costing more money."

She turned to face him. "How you figure that?"

"You're taking more time to case and deliver, that's how."

"Am I asking for more money because it takes me longer?" she asked, climbing into the driver's seat.

"Well no, but—"

"Then it's not costing the government more money, is it?"

He paused again. "Never heard of such a thing."

"Well, now you have." Nonny swung the door shut and revved the engine so hard, the jeep rocked on its wheels. As the postmaster retreated, she pulled out of the employee parking lot and aimed the jeep in the direction of the Walmart.

Locking the doors and trunk hatch at the Walmart, she made her way inside to the food aisles. Within ten minutes, she was checking out in the express lane with two gallon jars each of Welch's grape and strawberry jelly, two dozen pint canning jars, complete with lids, and a box of paraffin. Back at the jeep, she tucked her purchases under a blue poly tarp behind the front seat and took County Road 113 north, wending her way through hills crested with grass the color of spun gold and skirted with pin oak, pine, and scrub.

She made another detour along the way, stopping at a creek where she had spotted persimmons growing. A hard freeze ten days before would have made the fruit ripen, ready for picking. When she saw the persimmons glowing like ripe oranges in the crisp fall air, she smiled, knowing they would be soft and sweet and tart on the tongue. She gave a quick look in either direction to see if one of the Turners, the owners of most of the land in the area, was on the prowl. Like old-time vigilantes, they showed no mercy to those found trespassing on their property, even if the trespasser was one of their neighbors. The Turners were the only people on the route who didn't trust the post office to deliver their mail safely.

What's that tell you? she thought, then answered her own question. "Says they're not trustworthy themselves," she muttered.

Seeing no one, she pulled on rubber Wellingtons, waded through knee-high grass still wet with dew, and picked all the persimmons within reach. Back at the road, she packaged the fruit in a dozen or so recycled plastic bags and placed them in the front floorboard, on top of a box of jellies in pint jars.

Pausing to catch her breath, she climbed into the driver's seat and poured a cup of herbal tea from a quart-sized thermos. The liquid burned her tongue when she pulled the first draft, just the way she liked it. She closed her eyes, allowing the steam coming off the cup to moisten her face, and inhaled deeply. The aroma was healing, but her hands ached. The glycerin she used on her fingertips to sort the mail was drying, and the newsprint and sales flyers sucked the oil from her skin like a blotter.

Reaching into the glove box, she removed a jar wrapped with a blue label on which was the picture of a black-and-white cow and the words Udder Balm. She rubbed the thick unguent into her hands slowly, giving special attention to cracked and chapped knuckles. Finishing, she stowed the medicinal and started the jeep.

At long last, she was ready to begin the Friday mail run. Except this wasn't just any Friday mail run. It was the first-Friday-of-the-month mail run. She caught a glimpse of her image in the rearview mirror, noticed the sparkle in her yellow-brown eyes—"cat eyes" the kids at school had called them when she was growing up—and felt thankful she had something to look forward to. Right then, she wondered if the preachers who gave communion on the first Sunday derived as much pleasure from that act as she did from this one. She let out a snort, reflecting on the irony of her comparing the two acts, then set the thought aside and put her mind on her job.

She worked steadily, placing a bag with mail inside each mailbox, even if it was recycled junk mail, and retrieving the empty cloth bag inside to be used for the next day's delivery. Along with the mail, she left a treat. In some boxes, a jar of grape jelly. In others, a jar of strawberry. And for those that liked their fruit fresh, a bag of persimmons.

Just kids, she thought at one point. Old kids with a sweet tooth.

More than half of her patrons were waiting at their boxes, mostly elderly people bent over with stiff joints, many walking with the use of canes. She let those that were waiting select the treat of their choice and chatted a minute or two before moving on. Finally, she was down to her last few customers.

She smiled as she caught sight of the figure up the road, for the rust-skinned man wasn't just another patron. He stood leaning against the mailbox, his mouth spread so broad his toothless gums showed. Spying the brown-paper bag he'd carried with him, she winced.

"What'll it be today, Uncle George?" she said, pulling up beside him.

"Got any grape?" he asked, eyes twinkling. "Got a yen for a grape jelly sandwich, maybe a smear of peanut butter with it."

"Got you covered." She retrieved a pint jar of grape jelly from the box on the floor.

"You make the best jelly I ever ate, Nonny." He pulled the brown paper sack closer.

Eying the bag, she put a smile on her face. "What you got there, Uncle?"

"Swap you even!" Flashing his toothless grin again, he handed her the bag. "Jar of my special recipe for a jar of homemade jelly. I got a *good* bite on this batch."

George's "special recipe" translated to his version of moonshine. Raising the jar of homebrew to the light, she murmured, "I've never seen anything so pretty in all my life." She turned, giving the old man a cautious look. "Better make sure the law doesn't catch you making this hooch, Uncle George." She carefully tucked the quart jar out of sight. "Don't forget, we have our own slammer right outside town—a big one."

The old man returned the grin. "I'd like it you'd come in for a spell, Nonny."

"I'd like to, Uncle, but I'm running late." Reading the disappointment on his face, she quickly proposed they attend a dinner-on-the-grounds the next weekend. "I'll make a mac-

'n-cheese casserole and we'll catch up on the latest gossip. How's that sound?"

The toothless grin made another show. "I'll be looking for you. Not many friends left, family neither." The smile faded quickly as his eyes turned liquid. "Sure miss that daddy of yours. I'm the last of the line, you know."

"I know," she murmured.

"Guess you do, girl. You're the last of your daddy's line, too."

She exhaled slowly. "Sure looks that way."

"Your daddy was real proud when you went and got that college job, but to tell the truth, I'm right glad you come home, left those city ways behind to take over his route. He drove it better than forty years. It's been in the family a long time."

Dad *was* proud of me, Nonny thought. Mama, too. Lord, if they knew what had become of me, they'd turn over in their graves.

Forcing a smile, she said, "Coming home was the right thing to do. See you soon."

Nonny left the old man holding his jar of grape jelly, pulling away slowly so as not to stir up the powder-dry dust. As soon as he was out of sight, she edged the jeep off the road. Reaching behind the front seat, she retrieved the quart jar of homemade brew, pushed open the door, and walked to the barrow ditch. Wading through a patch of wild marigold, she dislodged sun-yellow pollen and its bitter scent. The odor brought back a memory of something else: the warm and soothing feel of a liquid with "good bite" to it.

Noticing the tremble in her hands, Nonny dumped the contents of the jar with one quick movement. The amber liquid spattered onto the red clay dirt, and as she caught a whiff, she was hit with a paralyzing ache in her cheekbones. Her head began to throb next, so hard she felt certain her eyeballs would pop from her head.

"Crap," she mumbled and bent her head low between her knees. As she got the heaves under control, she stared at the puke on the ground. A minute later, she smelled the odor of urine and became aware of dampness in her crotch.

"Well, hell," she mumbled, wondering if a dry hangover and weak sphincter muscles were fit-enough punishment for the sins of her youth.

Pulling upright, she mused on the way she'd taken to deconstructing her life in the same way she used to deconstruct language. What a profession she had chosen, picking apart words and the meaning behind those words to get at the truth of things long dead.

Like my life now? She sighed, wishing just once she could live in the moment, not focus on things past. Then something clicked in her head.

"Sins of my youth . . .?" She began to wonder when she had changed her terminology from *errors in judgment* to *sins of my youth*. Debating the difference between the two terms, she decided it had something to do with whether your shirt collar was white, or blue.

Wiping the spittle from her mouth on her sleeve, she studied the wet spot on the blue chambray. "There you go," she said. "I am now blue collar, and blue collars do not deconstruct their lives."

And with that, she was able to crawl back into the jeep, feeling enough recovered to finish her route. Somewhere along the way, without knowledge as to why, the Beatles song "Let It Be" came to mind, and she let it play.

CHAPTER THREE

Ruby Barlow turned off the radio as she heard the familiar fussing of her sister from down the hall. Quickly, she made her way to the pantry and retrieved the double-barrel shotgun from where it stood, day in and day out. Fitting two fresh shells into the barrels, she recalled the time she'd held an escaped convict at bay and felt her breath quicken. Will had been proud of her that day, Mack, too. In fact, she'd been the talk of the county. So long ago, she thought now.

She leaned the gun inside the pantry again and dropped two extra shells into her apron pocket. "Keep a close watch, Whitey," she whispered to the dog at her side. "There's escaped convicts on the run."

The snow-white dog, looking to be a blend of spaniel and hound, was crippled with arthritis, but picking up on Ruby's excitement, its eyes were bright with anticipation.

Hearing the sound of a car engine, she looked down the dirt track toward the county road and watched as a pickup drove past. She was expecting two people this day; her son Mack was driving in from the Texas Panhandle and Betty Winslow had a standing appointment for a permanent wave. Leaving the door ajar so Betty could walk in, she made it back into the kitchen just as her sister was getting seated at the table.

"Did you have a good rest, Sister?" she asked as she began setting up for Betty's permanent. Her own hair, more white than brown now, stuck in clumps to her forehead. Damp marks shaped like half moons stained the cotton shirt beneath her arms. "Maybe if you cut those afternoon naps short, you'd sleep better at night."

Sister's response had a sting to it. "Don't know how a body's supposed to sleep with all that noise on the roof!"

Sister's given name was Pearl Anderson, but she was known to everyone as Sister. She had made a good living as a seamstress until recent times. Places like Walmart had done away with her skill. A throwaway society didn't care about clothes that lasted. Six years Ruby's senior, Sister had never married and moved in with Ruby when Will Barlow died twenty-five years before. She still did piecework for locals, some mending too, and made enough to supplement her Social Security.

"Noise on the roof," Ruby repeated, feeling weary. She held her voice level, reaching deep for patience. "Those raccoons must be at it again. I'll have Mack trim some of those branches over the house so they can't climb up there."

Sister exhaled loudly. "If I told you once I told you a hundred times, it's not *coons*!"

Taking a measured breath, Ruby said, "Well now, I spotted what looks to be coon droppings in the garden so I know they're in the neighborhood—"

"Coons don't talk English! You need to call that sheriff again."

"Why you need to call the sheriff?" Betty Winslow walked into the kitchen, an anxious look on her face. "You seen those cons—"

"*Coons*," Ruby said quickly, hitching her eyebrows at Betty. "Sister's hearing coons on the roof."

"Oh, *coons*," Betty said, hitching her eyebrows, too.

"Mack's due in today," Ruby went on. "He'll trim those low branches off. That'll fix the problem."

"Coons . . . don't . . . talk . . . English—"

"C'mon Betty," Ruby said, cutting short Sister's reprimand. "I'm all set up." She welcomed Betty's intrusion on a conversation that had become a broken record.

As Betty sat down, she laid a zippered calico bag on the table with the name BARLOW stitched on the outside. "Brought your mail while I was at it. Nonny left a bag of persimmons, too."

"Oh, that girl." Ruby smiled as she examined the persimmons. "Nice and ripe. That hard freeze was just what they needed."

"There's something important inside the mailbag," Betty went on. "*Official* looking. Might need to take a look at it—" She stopped suddenly, her eyebrows knit. "And there's a postcard . . . addressed to your mama."

Ruby's jaws dropped. "My mama—" Pulling the postcard from the bag, she pitched it in the wastebasket, unread.

"Mama got mail?" Sister quickly retrieved the card. "Well, I swan. Her high school's having a homecoming." She made a clucking sound as she sat down again. "Someone needs to let them know she's gone."

"What's that other one say?" Betty asked, pointing her chin at the envelope Ruby pulled from the pouch.

Ruby put her attention on the oversized envelope. She hated the way Betty stuck her nose into her business, but what could she do? Betty was a steady customer and these days, she needed every one of those she could get.

"Oh, it's nothing," she said, tearing open the envelope. "Just the renewal of my beautician's license." She handed the document to her sister. "Here, make yourself useful. Replace that old license on the wall there with this here new one."

Ruby had hung two framed documents on the wall as someone would hang college degrees as proof of proficiency. One was her state beautician's license. The other was a yellowed fragment that read, *Oklahoma Law: Females are forbidden from doing their own hair without being licensed by the state.* Many years ago, she'd ripped the page from a magazine she found at the nursing home while visiting a friend. Lots of people dropped off magazines at the home. An attorney must have donated that particular one, she'd decided, probably one of those rich shysters who deducted donations of useless magazines off his income tax. Though Ruby considered herself as devout a Christian as the next, she felt no guilt in lifting the page. She told herself that someone whose heart was in the right place wouldn't take magazines to an old folk's home. Anyone with a grain of sense would know that old people's eyes were the first thing to go. Then it was their ears. And then, their minds. No, she'd decided, she was meant to find that magazine. A higher order had put it there. The Lord worked in mysterious ways.

"I'm done past useful," Sister said, making no effort to retrieve the outdated license from the wall.

Ruby sighed. There were days lately when she found her sister especially vexing. It looked like today was going to be one of those days.

"Don't talk nonsense," she urged, retrieving the framed certificate from the wall. "We need to show people we're legal. Besides, you forget I'm giving you a perm right after I finish up with Betty? Help me out here. Slip the back off this frame, put the new license on top of the old one."

"Oh, all right, but you ask me, it's a waste of time. Nobody's gonna come out here to make sure two old crows like us are doing things *legal.*"

Ruby sighed again. As Sister fussed with the frame, she began to shampoo Betty's bleached-out hair, noting the woman was in bad need of a tint.

"When can you color this stuff again?" Betty asked as if reading Ruby's mind. "I'm thinking of going a lighter shade of blonde for the holidays. Maybe that rosy platinum color. What do you call it? You know, the one you put on Tootsie Turner's hair?"

Lord help, Ruby thought, catching her breath. Tootsie would have a fit if she used Fawn Beige on someone else. Fawn Beige was *her* color.

Being a beautician required a good deal of diplomacy and Ruby was good at it. She couldn't recall the last time she had ruffled a customer's feathers. Recently, however, her patience had been taxed to the limit and she hoped she had enough left to appease Betty.

"Let me give some thought to the color, Betty. The *right* color." She wrapped a towel around Betty's head and walked her to the kitchen table. "Fawn Beige is all wrong for your complexion."

"Oh?" Betty picked up a hand mirror and studied her coloring. "Maybe a henna rinse then. I always wanted to be a redhead. You know, like Lucille Ball. Might as well do it today—"

"Two weeks," Ruby said, shutting down Betty's cinematic fantasies. "Have to wait two weeks after a perm before putting on color. It's a chemical thing." When Betty opened her mouth to protest again, Ruby pointed to the new license that Sister was working on. "They wouldn't have sent me that certificate, Betty Winslow, I didn't know what I was talking about."

Betty went silent, but within minutes found a new can of worms to kick over. "*Oh*, did I tell you I stopped to see your daddy on my way out? I think he's taken a liking to the home."

"Why, no such thing—" Ruby's back stiffened to a rod. "He hates that place and I hate like everything I put him away like that. I've been thinking about bringing him back home, just like he did when he took his sister Ida out of Vinita."

"Ida was crazy as a bedbug," Sister said, not looking up from her framing job. "That's why they put her there."

Ruby stiffened again. "No such thing," she repeated with emphasis. "Ida would just get withdrawn from time to time, what they call *depressed* these days. But other than that, not a thing wrong with her. Show me a body that doesn't get depressed from time to time."

"Well now," Betty said, sounding conciliatory. "All I was supposing is maybe that's why your daddy gets *detached* now and then."

"Detached . . ." There was a pause in Ruby's eyes. "Well, Pa's always been a quiet man. No supposing to it, that's just his way."

"Since the war," Sister said, nodding in agreement.

"What?" Ruby turned to look at Sister.

"I said, Pa's been that way . . . *since* . . . *the* . . . *war*," Sister said, voice elevating.

"And the way he keeps falling down." Betty made clucking noises.

Sister duplicated the clucking. "That's not good. Bones get brittle, older we get."

"It's called osteoporosis," Betty went on. "Course, it's worse for women than men. In any case, don't think that would account for him being . . . *detached*."

Ruby backed away from the table feeling as though she were listening to a conversation between strangers on a city bus, not two women she'd known all her life. "Well now, I thought that through." She spoke loudly, as if calling out to someone that was outdistancing her. "All he needed was a walker, that's all they've done for him at that home, give him a walker."

"But . . . what about those night spells?" Betty said, frowning. "Would you call them depression?"

Ruby paused again, trying to gather her thoughts. "Don't know what you'd call those, Betty, and those people at the home don't either. So I don't see any reason to leave him there."

"Still and all, I'd give it some more thought." Betty used the corner of her towel to funnel her voice away from Sister. "Sometimes things get passed on in the genes, and now that Sister's having night spells, too—"

"*What's that you said*?" Sister said, bristling. "You don't want me to hear your tittle-tattle, just say so and I'll leave the room!"

As the words blasted from Sister's mouth, Ruby knew she'd had enough. "It *is* time you left the room, Sister. Go watch TV or take a nap. Better yet, work on mailbags."

"But I'm not done with this license—"

"I'll finish it later. Christmas is gonna be here before we know it, and you know how folks look forward to getting a new mailbag every year. Besides which, Nonny pays us good money to make those bags and we got lots to go. C'mon, I'll help you get set up."

"Guess I might as well," Sister mumbled. "Almost time for my doctor show anyway." She pushed her chair away from the table. "Can't see as good as I used to, stitches show it, too. Everything's wearing out at the same time."

Ruby was overcome with guilt as she escorted Sister from the room. What's come over me? she thought. I'm known for having the patience of Job. Many have told me so.

"Your embroidery's still beautiful, Sister," she said, feeling contrite. "And your hearing might be going but your hand's still steady. Last time you was in, the doctor said you were healthy as a horse—"

"Like these young doctors know anything. I think maybe I caught sleep deprivation."

"Wha—what? Where do you come up with these things?"

"On the TV! Most illnesses these days aren't in the bones, they're in the head." Sister tapped her forehead. "That's why people can't sleep—though it doesn't help when people are walking around on the roof either."

Ruby's shoulders slumped. Wordlessly, she turned on the television and clicked through channels until she found one that satisfied her sister. Making her way back to the kitchen, she began twisting Betty's hair around plastic curlers. As the sound of the television went up several decibels, she let out a long sigh.

"What would we do without the TV," Betty said, talking over the blare. "I just can't stand to miss my favorite programs. Sounds like Sister's much the same way."

"Yeah, well," Ruby mumbled. "I'm afraid Sister's watching a program all her own these days."

Her family's business a sore spot, Ruby put her mind on other matters. "I heard on the radio, those escaped convicts are still loose. Report said nobody was killed though."

"That's right, on both accounts. I called Luther on my mobile phone on the way here. They're setting up roadblocks and bringing in the dogs. Said the cons are leaving a trail a fool could follow. Must be city boys. Country boys would know how to cover their tracks."

"No . . ." Ruby's voice faded, sounding distant. "They're just running scared. Don't matter if you're a city boy or country boy when you're scared. They'll bring them back covered in chiggers and ticks, give them a hot bath, add another year to their sentence and that'll be that. Things will go back to being dull as dishwater around here."

Swiveling, Betty looked up at her. "Why, that don't sound like you, Ruby. You having a bad day?"

"Course not." Ruby smoothed her hair from her face. "Just a lot on my mind, what with Daddy and all." The plastic curlers clicked as her hands wound Betty's hair around each one. Neat, symmetrical rows began to march across the woman's head.

As Ruby finished up, she frowned suddenly. "Pa still making noises about Bill and Jack?" she asked. "When you saw him today, I mean."

"Mentions it every time I go in." Betty paused as Ruby slipped a plastic cap over her head. "He's really got his shorts in a bundle this time, don't he? Think Mack will be able to talk any sense to him?"

With the mention of her son's name, Ruby's spirits lifted. "You can take it to the bank. Those two were always thick as thieves. Anyone can do it, Mack can."

"Thank Heaven for small blessings." Betty took a seat under a hairdryer in the corner. "Buried next to Bill and Jack—where'd he get such an idea. He wouldn't know any different if you buried him at the Hugh Low Cemetery. Once he's dead, you can put him anywhere you want."

Ruby's mouth dropped open. "I can *not*! He had a legal paper drawn up."

"You're not seriously considering—"

"The law's the law, Betty Winslow. I had Nonny Folsom check into it for me. It's as legal as it can be."

"You could just tear that paper up. Who's to know?"

Ruby puffed up like an adder. "Destroy my daddy's dying wish? Why, I'd never be able to live with myself, I did that."

"Well, that's what I'd do, it was me."

Starting the hairdryer, Ruby sighed. Turning on the radio, she listened closely for an update on the prison break. It was just as Betty had reported. The convicts were still on the loose but the law was closing in. Sighing again, she glanced out the window toward the crossroads, hoping to see Mack's car. But the road was quiet.

Becoming aware of an ache in her hands, she noticed the setting lotion had roughened them to an angry red. She reached for a jar on the counter, and as she massaged balm into the chemical-burned skin, she whispered, "Yeah, well, I'm not you, Betty Winslow."

*****

The kitchen smelled of permanent wave lotion and pinto beans. A misty glow filled the room as heat from chemicals and the boiling pot on the stove steamed the evening air. The room's only light fixture barely made a dent in the darkness. Pink- and blue-plastic curlers clinked as Ruby unwound them from Sister's hair.

"How's it look?" Sister ran thin fingers through the damp white curls on her head.

"Nice and soft, just the way you like it. Let's dry you quick and set it tomorrow. Right now, it's bedtime."

"I won't be able to sleep. I know I won't."

"Yes, you will." Ruby handed her sister a juice glass. "I fixed you a toddy, just the way you like it. Three fingers, straight up. You'll sleep good tonight."

"*Oh.*" Sister sniffed the contents of the glass. "Thought we was out of blackberry brandy."

"I had Betty pick up another case when she drove up to Muskogee last week."

"Muskogee— Why don't you go into town and buy it yourself? Nothing to be ashamed of. Lots of people drink for their health. Brandy's medicinal, red wine, too. I saw it on the TV."

Ruby debated responding at all. She'd had this conversation with Sister many times before. Medicinal or not, hardcore types would stop frequenting her beauty shop if they knew a drop of alcohol was in the house. They were in my shoes, she thought, they'd buy it by the boxcar.

"I'm a little tied down here in case you hadn't noticed," Ruby said, resorting to her stock response. "Besides, Betty doesn't work for a living and it's not out of her way to bring it out when she gets her hair done." She set the timer on the hairdryer for fifteen minutes and turned it on HIGH, shutting down any further comment from Sister.

Busying herself, Ruby cleaned the kitchen. By the time she finished, Sister had finished her brandy and was nodding. Ruby led her to the bedroom and helped her into a nightgown.

"You going to bed now?" Sister asked. "If you're a mind, you can crawl in next to me. Be nice if you were here, in case those people climb back up on the roof again."

Ruby forced a smile. "Can't tonight. Mack's due in, remember? He's running late and I'm a little worried so I'm gonna wait up." She pulled the covers over Sister as if tucking in a child.

Hurrying back to the kitchen, Ruby retrieved the shotgun from the pantry and made her way to the front room. Propping the shotgun against the arm of a rocker, she went to the door to let Whitey out for his evening constitutional. She paused, taking in the crisp fall air, heavy and raucous with the hum of insects, and smiled.

"I'm half a mind to sit out here with you, Whitey," she murmured. Instead, she closed the door on the old dog and eased into the chair. Picking up a brightly-colored cloth bag from a stack lying on the side table, she checked for the next name on a list and began to sew.

She rocked slowly as she stitched and listened closely to night sounds. She heard a dry limb scrape across the roof once and hoped it did not wake Sister. Between her father and sister, she hadn't gotten a full night's sleep in a year or better and she let the thought enter her mind that maybe there was something to what Betty had said about genes. She pushed the thought aside and willed herself to wind down, but the conversations of the day still roiled her mind. It was sometime later that she began to murmur a quiet prayer.

"Now Lord, you know I'm as anxious as the next to cross over to Beulah Land . . ." She paused to listen to noise on the roof, decided it was the tree limb again, then resumed her prayer. "And you know I don't ask for much, but I'm right content with this life I got, at least for the time being. Besides which, there's those depending on me." She paused again, sighing deeply. "But Lord when my time does come, please let me leave this earth with all my faculties intact. I don't mean to sound critical, but you might want to rethink this gene business. I know you place a lot of importance on who begat who, but to my thinking, there's some of those genes we could just as well leave go with the ashes and the dust."

Finishing with a quick "Amen," she checked the clock on the wall and frowned. Time had passed more quickly than she'd supposed, and she began to wonder what stretch of highway her son was on and why he was running so late.

CHAPTER FOUR

It was near dark when Mack exited the Indian Nation Turnpike and drove into the town of McAlester. The seven-hour drive from Amarillo had taken ten, due to many stops. Most of them unnecessary. The smell of Popeye's fried chicken drifting through the air vents triggered a hungry growl in his stomach and he debated about stopping one more time. But he knew his mother would be waiting up. Like she always did. And would have cooked. Like she always did. So he drove straight through town and out again, veering north onto a narrow two-lane road leading into low hills.

His headlights scraped across oak trees with leaves the color of rust, hickory trees cloaked in gold, and state road signs that read, CAUTION: HITCHHIKERS COULD BE ESCAPED INMATES. Rounding a bend, Mack saw Oklahoma's state penitentiary come into view. Just as he remembered, Big Mac was lit up like a giant Christmas tree, one skirted with guard towers and security fences.

Long before he'd been born, the town fathers had been given a choice: to have the state university there, or the state pen. In his growing-up years, he'd tried to figure out why they had decided on the pen. Right then, he began to wonder if his father might still be alive if they had chosen differently. He grew suddenly angry, thinking how his father had died prematurely.

"If you were still alive," he told the man who had been in the ground twenty-five years, "I wouldn't have to make the decisions I'm making."

He braked hard as he realized some of the lights ahead were from police cruisers blocking the road. His heartbeat speeded up as he mentally ran through the implications of the roadblock, none of them good. For a half-second, his mind backtracked to another period in his life. A time and place where night occurrences meant you had someone's ass in your scope—or maybe that someone, better at jungle warfare than you, had already pulled the trigger on yours. He wiped the sweat from his eyes, thinking there must have been a time before then. But if there was, he couldn't pull it from his memory.

Hell, he thought. Scientists had found that the earth had experienced many time periods. Why had he been limited to two? That time when he didn't drench his clothes at the drop of a hat . . . and now. But those sweet moments of grace were gone for good.

He eased to a full stop and watched two uniformed men walk his way. They stopped briefly, scrutinizing the Texas plates on his Bronco. When the older man walked to the driver's side, the other man to the passenger, Mack rolled down both windows.

"Howdy, Mack. Heard you was coming in tonight."

"That so?" Mack shook the hand that Luther Winslow extended. The man had reported to his father years ago when he was the prison farm supervisor. Judging from the patch on his khaki shirt, Luther had worked his way up through the ranks.

"Yeah, Betty was due a perm. She left your place 'bout five. Called me soon as she got home, told me to keep an eye out. Ruby and Sister were okay when she left."

"That's a relief." Mack tilted his head toward the prison's location. "Riot or break?"

"Break."

"In a maximum-security prison? How the hell could that happen, Luther?"

The man shrugged. "Two sons-of-bitches kayoed a greenhorn guard out in the fields."

"Anyone killed?"

"No. This idn't a repeat of your daddy's story—thank the Lord."

Mack eyed the roadblock and cruiser ahead, lights flashing. "But you haven't caught them yet."

"No, but getting close. Looks like they headed west, not north towards your place. Hounds picked up their trail, hot on their heels as we speak. Your women aren't in any danger, Mack. They were, I'd move them outta there myself. You know I would."

"Yeah, well . . ." Mack did not finish saying what he was thinking. He would be taking care of any further danger to his mother and aunt soon enough.

"What'cha doin' home this time of the year, Mack?"

Mack eyed the overweight man leaning on the passenger-side door. He and Billy Joe Turner had been high school classmates, but never friends. The friction between them was generational, a shared sentiment carried forward with resolve. Billy Joe's father, Washburn Turner Jr., called

Junior for short, had been on duty the day Mack's father was killed.

Mack had harbored gut resentment ever since, sensing the wrong man had died that day. When the Turners took an uncommon interest in him and his mother after his father's funeral, it seemed only natural to tell them to get lost and stay lost. His mother had scolded him for his unchristian conduct. When he expressed suspicions about his father's death, she had ridiculed the idea, telling him he shouldn't second-guess the Lord's intent. "Not the Lord's intent I'm questioning," he'd told her. "All I know is a leopard doesn't change its spots. Those Turners are hiding something—I don't know what, but something."

Mack pulled his thoughts back to the present. "So, your dad still working at the pen, Billy Joe?"

"Well, hell no—not for a long time. Grandpa's accumulated a good bit of land hereabouts and Daddy quit the pen to manage the business. Given he's not a spring chicken, looks like I'll be taking over soon." Billy Joe grinned big. "We got quite an enterprise going here. Figured you'd know that, Mack. What? You don't keep up with the homeboys no more?"

Mack stifled a snort. "I keep up with the important things."

After high school, Mack and Billy Joe split ways. Billy Joe followed in his father's footsteps, going to work at the prison, and he had joined the Marines, putting an end to the generational animosity. Or so he thought. He hadn't given a thought to Billy Joe Turner in more than twenty years, but when he locked eyes with him right then, time dissolved.

Noticing Billy Joe zeroing in on a manila envelope on the dash, Mack quickly shoved it under the front seat. Billy

Joe moved his attention to the sleeping bag, portable camp stove, and toolbox in the back end of his Bronco.

"Well, now," Billy Joe said, eying the gear. "I heard building had slowed down considerable in the Panhandle. From the looks of this rig, it's gone to hell in a handbasket. You living in this thing, Mack? It's a doggone pigsty. You moving back home, that why you're here?"

"Family business," Mack said stiffly. Never in his wildest dreams did he imagine that he would have to account to Billy Joe Turner for anything. "My work keeps me on the move, so I haul my tools with me."

"I'd hire you in a minute, you were so inclined." Luther Winslow laid a hand on Mack's shoulder. "You know that, don't you, son?"

Mack turned to the older man. "Thanks, Luther. But like you said, this isn't a repeat of my daddy's story. Besides, Amarillo suits me. You can see what's coming at you out there in the big and wide."

"That's what I hear." Luther grinned. "How's that old saying go? Ain't nothing between Amarillo and the North Pole but a bob-wire fence and it blew down last winter."

"Just the way I like it," Mack said, nodding.

"Family business, huh?" Billy Joe said, working his way back to Mack's earlier comment. "Yeah, I hear that grandpa of yours is giving your Mama the dickens."

"You have, have you?" Mack muttered, wondering how the jackass at his elbow had learned of his family's business.

"I'd do it, was me," Luther said, chuckling.

Mack wished he knew what the two men were talking about. All his mother had said when she called him to come home was that he needed to talk some sense into his grandfather. He downshifted quickly. "Better get on down the road, check on Mama and Sister."

Nodding, Luther motioned Billy Joe toward the barricade. "Open 'er up."

As Billy Joe began dragging the roadblocks to the side of the road, Luther bent close. "I'm sure your womenfolk are fine, but I'd bet a dollar to a donut that Ruby is waiting up with her double barrel loaded and cocked. So hail the house before you walk up."

Mack pulled through the roadblock, recalling the time his father was working night duty at the pen and an escaped convict found his way to their house. He had stayed up to keep his mother company that night. First, they had heard a squeak on the front porch, then seen the doorknob turn. Cool as a cucumber, his mother had called out her warning. "Open that door and I'll unload both barrels." The convict never tried the door again, but he had stayed around the rest of the night, scratching on windowpanes and throwing rocks on the roof. His father had captured the escapee when he got home, figuring something was amiss when he found the house lit up brighter than the state pen. He had a phone line run to the house right after that and kept a fresh box of shotgun shells handy for Ruby at all times.

"Bet she would've pulled that trigger," Mack said, grinning. Then his face took on a grim set. "But that was then. This is now."

Asphalt turned to fifteen miles of gravel road. Mack drove fast, thinking of all kinds of ways an escaped convict could evade searchers, even hounds. Whiteface Herefords, bedded down in shadowed pastures, were the only living things he came across. At least, any living thing that he could see. He swung right at a T in the road and drove past a cluster of old farmhouses and single-wide trailers. Diehards left over from days when it paid to grow cotton and peanuts and sweet onions.

A couple of miles on, he pulled into a narrow tunnel of oak and hickory trees at the end of which sat a Craftsman-style house. He killed the engine and lights and coasted the last fifty yards, running surveillance on the place. Pulling to a stop, he sat staring at a front porch lit by a bald 40-Watt bulb. The place had not changed much from when he bought it with his mustering-out pay for his mother, aunt, and grandfather to live in.

And Whitey.

Mack rolled the window down and grinned at the scrawny dog panting outside the car door. "Some watchdog you are." He reached out and scratched the old dog's ears. "What'd you do, recognize the sound of the Bronco? Legs might be gone, but there's nothing wrong with your ears."

Through the front window, Mack could see a stooped woman sitting in a chair, looking like a ghost floating behind the lace curtain. The long, stick-shaped object next to her could be mistaken for nothing other than what it was. He sighed, thinking that an intruder would be on his mother before she had time to take hold of the gun. Wrestling his duffle bag from the backend, he opened the car door quietly.

He took a minute before going inside, letting the night enfold him. The racket of katydids, crickets, and frogs bombarded his ears, sounding like a discordant gospel choir. Like flickering specters, fireflies hovering in low boggy places moved *en masse* when the slightest breeze stirred. Standing water and rotting oak leaves in the creek back of the house gave the heavy night air the smell of a sweet-sour mash.

"A jungle," he mumbled. "A goddamn fucking jungle." Rubbing away the smell of sweat in his nose, he shouldered his duffle and walked toward the door.

CHAPTER FIVE

Mack took the shotgun from his mother and gave her a hug. Feeling her softness under his hands, he remembered a time when her muscles had been taut as bedsprings. She said something about fixing him a plate and he did feel hungry enough to eat. He followed her to the kitchen, carrying the shotgun with him and taking stock of the house as he went.

He'd put some work into the place after he bought it. Jacking up a sagging foundation on the south side, putting forty-year shingles on the roof, modernizing the kitchen and bathroom. But the original builder had been a good one, using prime lumber throughout, setting the studs on twelve-inch centers, and finishing off with red oak trim. Though showing wear, the house's bones were solid as the Rock of Gibraltar. One of a kind, he thought, comparing it to the cloned cracker boxes he now worked on.

He picked up a postcard on a table in passing, and his mind stumbled as he noted the addressee. "*Grace* Anderson? What's this, Mama?"

"*Lord help—* Sister must've carried that thing in here." Jerking the card from his hand, she ripped it to pieces and stuffed it into her pocket.

"Why's Grace getting mail here? She's been gone long as I can remember."

"Don't know and don't care."

Reading his mother's mood, Mack dropped the subject. As he followed behind, he noticed a stack of cloth bags in various stages of construction. Some things never change, he thought, then frowned, thinking some things should have. For one thing, the sparse, dated furnishings in the front room.

In the kitchen, Mack made sure the safety was set on the gun and stood it by the back door. Turning the radio on, he watched his mother's waddling gait as she bustled around the kitchen. She had looked the same to him since he could hold a memory and shouldered responsibility for that. He'd been a big baby, too large for the slender-framed woman who bore him. Even today, he held himself personally accountable for the rupture that had weakened her abdominal muscles and caused her stomach to protrude. She had never complained in his forty years on the earth of the discomfort such an imbalance to her spine must cause, or of the mental anguish from never being able to bear another child. How was a son supposed to make up for such a sacrifice?

"Didn't I send you money for some new furniture last Christmas, Mama?"

She talked as she dished up food and filled a glass with sweet ice tea. "Yes, you did, but the car needed new tires."

"Tires don't cost that much," he said, taking a seat at the table.

"Well, I got good ones, what with the need to run back and forth now to check on Pa. You know, ones with deep treads to handle the ice storms we get here in the winter."

He remembered well the storms that turned the narrow roads into sheets of black ice. "How much they cost?"

"Eight-hundred dollars."

He let out a low whistle. "Those would be good ones, all right."

She paused to look at him. "You think I should've bought cheaper ones?"

"Water under the bridge now. You could've let me know. I would've sent more money."

She carried the food to the table. "New furniture would just make the taxes go up on this place. Don't need more taxes."

"Damn, I forgot about that tax on personal property here." He thought a bit. "Still wouldn't matter. The hay on that back pasture would cover it. A new sofa couldn't add that much to the tax bill."

"No need to swear. Besides, nothing wrong with the davenport we got. It's old but serviceable." She gave him a look. "And I heard that building's in a slump in the Panhandle."

Mack felt his muscles tense. "Where'd you hear that?" He ate as he waited for her response, knowing full well where she'd heard the rumor. When she didn't answer right away, he looked at her. "Old man Turner and Junior still hanging around here?"

"No," she said after a pause. "Tootsie Turner gets her hair done on Fridays. You remember Tootsie, Billy Joe's grandma?"

"Damn—all them Turners are nosy sons-a-bitches."

"Now Mack, people around here look out for one another. You know they do."

"Some more than they should. I thought we discussed a sleeper sofa. You said you'd like one for company."

"That's right, I did. But it didn't make much sense after your grandpa went to the home. You're the only one sleeps over these days and you can have his room now. And when we get him out of that place, you can have my bed and I'll sleep in with Sister, like I did before."

Mack wiped his mouth with a paper napkin. "What do you mean, 'get him out'? I thought you wanted me to come home so I could talk to him about his final arrangements."

"Well, it does, in a way. You see, he drew up this paper saying where he wants to be buried—that's what I want you to talk to him about. But here lately, I've been thinking he's not as bad off as I thought. He could last a good while yet if I can get him back home."

"Mama . . ." He pushed his plate away and talked slowly. "Pa hurt you, hurt you bad."

"But he didn't mean to. He was just out of his head and I shouldn't have grabbed hold of him like that." She set her eyes on his. "I'm just trying to do the right thing here, Mack. I'd like to bring him back home."

"Hold the phone now, let's not get ahead of ourselves—"

"*Shhh*, listen." Ruby turned an ear to the radio

Mack followed suit, and together they listened to the news bulletin about two convicts being captured and returned to the state penitentiary at McAlester.

"Well now," she sighed. "Guess we can put this thing away." She picked up the heavy shotgun and walked to the pantry.

Mack watched as his mother removed two shells from the gun's chambers, then two more from her pocket, and made a mental note to check the date stamp on the ammunition. Shells that got old could cause a misfire. She wouldn't think about things like that. Then he pushed that kind of thinking aside, reminding himself of the real business that had brought him back. Soon, old ammunition would no longer be a concern.

"Looks like it'll be an uneventful night after all." Ruby sighed again as she made her way back to the table. "Guess we can all sleep quiet."

Mack hoped he was tired enough to sleep quiet. What he wouldn't give for just one full night's rest. One without dreams. Night sweats. He watched his mother place leftovers in plastic containers and store them in the refrigerator. She looked tired to the bone and the deep circles under her eyes were an indication that she also suffered sleepless nights. One thing for sure, he thought. I'm on the right track with the business I come home to handle.

"Maybe it would be better to talk in the morning," he said. "Let's get on to bed now. Got some business to tend to early, but I'll talk to Pa after that."

She looked at him. "What kind of business?"

"Nothing to worry your head about." He switched off the kitchen light as they headed for the bedrooms down the hall. Recalling his conversation with Luther Winslow and Billy Jo Turner at the roadblock, he paused. "You haven't said yet just what it was Pa was wanting."

"Oh. Well, you're not gonna believe this . . ." She rubbed fingertips across her forehead. "But he wants to be buried next to Bill and Jack."

"Bill and Jack . . ." Mack stared at his mother, her meaning sinking in slowly. "You don't mean *that* Bill and Jack."

"Yes, I do, I mean *exactly* that. The legal paper he had drawn up directs the manner his body's to be disposed of. It's a sworn affidavit, as legal as it can get. If you can't talk some sense into him, I don't know what we're gonna do."

"Well, hell." Mack laughed softly. "I don't have a problem with it. Do you?"

Redness crept up Ruby's neck. "Well, of course I do! Folks around here wouldn't think it proper. Why, it might even affect my business."

"To hell with what folks think."

Ruby's face reddened to scarlet. "Wouldn't be a Christian burial. Folks would think we were . . . *heathens*."

"To hell with what folks think," he repeated.

She paused, wetting her lips with her tongue. "Then there's this other problem."

"Other problem?" Uneasiness settled along Mack's spine.

"He can't remember where they're buried."

The tension along Mack's spine burst like a balloon as his laughter exploded into the air.

"Well, think on it, Mack." Ruby's voice took on a scolding tone. "Pa sharecropped all his life. He worked different pieces of land, 'specially in those early years."

Still, he could not keep from laughing.

"Mack Barlow, this is *not* funny!"

The sound of a door opening put an end to Mack's laughter.

"They're on the roof again," Sister said. "And they're talking English!"

Mack faced Ruby. "What's Sister talking about? Someone been on the roof?"

"No, she's just been imagining things." Irritation edged Ruby's voice. "We'll talk in the morning. I have to get Sister to bed—again."

Ruby looped her arm through that of the frizzy-headed woman standing in the doorway. "C'mon Sister, it's just Mack come home. Let's get you back to bed. Tell you what, I'll rest with you a bit. You'd like that, wouldn't you?"

As Mack watched the two women disappear behind the bedroom door, a hollowness filled his chest. "You're right, Mama," he murmured. "This isn't funny."

CHAPTER SIX

Rising early, Ruby carried her going-to-town clothes to the kitchen so she wouldn't wake the house and put the coffee pot on to perk. She dressed quickly. Tying an apron over her navy-blue slack suit, she dabbed on some makeup, then put a curling iron on her hair. Taking a quick look in the mirror, she was satisfied with her looks. Appearing professional was important when you owned your own business. She always ran into customers in town and, sometimes, one of those uppity salon owners.

Readying things for Mack, she laid the legal affidavit between the dinner plate and his coffee cup, the telephone book right next to the affidavit, then got ready to set Sister's hair. She propped the hot curling iron on a tablespoon so it wouldn't burn the Formica countertop and set a can of AquaNet next to it.

She had slept well, better than she had in a year, and credited the restful night to Mack being home. As she lay under the covers after waking, she ordered their day. First, they would go see Pa. As soon as Mack explained things, her father would come around, give up this idea about Bill and Jack. Then they would talk to the Administrator there at the nursing home. Those people there used language that was hard to follow. Nonny Folsom could understand them fine, but Nonny wasn't family.

Though Lord knows, she should've been. Sidetracking briefly, Ruby wondered again, as she'd done a thousand times before, what had happened between Nonny and Mack those many years ago. She forced her thinking back to the present, to the mental list she'd created.

After talking to the Administrator, they would talk to the doctor. Ask him about the medication Pa would need once they got him home, about the cause of those night spells. Together, we'll figure it out, she thought. Then we'll load up Pa and haul him home, and tonight, we'll sit down to supper, just the way a family should.

"Why, maybe I'll call Nonny, invite her over, too," she murmured. "Wouldn't that be just the perfect ending to this day? Get Mack and Nonny back together again after all these years."

Hearing someone coming down the hallway, she debated whether it was Sister or Mack. She sipped coffee while she waited, ready for whichever one walked through the door. Not prepared to see both of them enter the room at the same time, she stared at the spectacle they made: Sister clinging to Mack's arm, barely standing above his waistline and looking up at him like a love-struck girl, and Mack taking baby steps, pacing himself to his aunt's gait like an awkward teenager.

In the full light, Ruby noticed that Mack's sandy hair was graying at the temple now and his tanned face was showing the deep wrinkling of a man who worked out of doors. And, of course, there was his nose, which had not been the same since he got out of the service. She often wondered what had happened to him over there, but he had refused to talk about his military years.

Still, he's a handsome man . . .

Ruby caught her breath then, noticing Mack's resemblance to his father. Simultaneously, she realized he would be the same age her Will had been twenty-five years ago when that prison riot took his life. Mack was no longer that fifteen-year-old boy she wished him to be but a grown man, and the vision of him right then brought both a gladness and an ache to her heart.

"Look who came to get me for breakfast," Sister said.

"I see that." Ruby gave her sister an up-and-down look. "Why'd you pick that dress?"

Sister pulled at the pink cotton dress to straighten it. "Mack picked it out."

"But it's a summer dress."

"He said it was my color, even helped me into it." Sister laid a hand on her head. "My hair frizzed, I seen it in the mirror."

Ruby looked toward Mack. "You dressed Sister?"

"Don't worry, I turned my back at the appropriate times." Grinning, he led Sister to a chair next to the counter. "Looks like Mama's all set up for you." As soon as Sister was seated, he started for the back door. "I'll get outta here so you two can get on with your business."

"Hold on—" Ruby's thinking became tangled. She had assumed Mack would have planned for them to spend the day together, that he would want to spend as much time with her as she did with him. When Mack turned to look at her, she spoke hurriedly. "Well now, I thought I might go to town with you. I cleared my appointments already."

"I see . . ."

Ruby watched her son rub his fingers across his mouth and knew he was mulling things over. He had developed that mannerism as a boy, was always prone to thinking things through before speaking. Who had he gotten that from? she wondered now. Will, maybe. She tried to remember if her husband had done that, too. Dear Lord, she thought, how quickly memories fade once someone was gone.

"What about Sister?" Mack said. "You don't leave her out here all alone, do you?"

"Well, for short trips, I do," Ruby said, puzzled by the question. "I go in the afternoons when she naps, but I leave Whitey in the house with her. When I go on longer trips, she goes with me. Like when we go to the home to see Pa or to the Walmart. She likes to ride in those chair-carts when we shop, the motorized ones." She paused. "I thought she'd like to go with us today. There's a lot to do, a lot to take care of."

"I wouldn't be caught dead at a dogfight, my hair looking like this." Sister ran a hand through her hair, trying to smooth the tangles with her fingertips.

Mack rubbed his mouth again. "How 'bout I meet up with you later, Mama. I got that appointment and you *do* need to fix Sister's hair."

"Doesn't take but a half hour to drive into McAlester and Sister's hair won't take but a few minutes." Seeing Mack look at the watch on his wrist, she grew uneasy. "Why you need to leave so early, Mack?"

He rubbed his mouth again, then took a seat at the table. "Aw hell, guess I got time for coffee. I slept longer than I should've, that's all. Couldn't go to sleep, kept hearing something on the roof."

Perking up at this announcement, Sister said, "Did they speak English?"

"*Hush*, Sister." Quickly, Ruby filled Mack's coffee cup. "It's just branches on that old tree. Thought you might do some trimming while you were home."

"Guess I can do that." Mack nodded toward the materials Ruby had placed on the table. "What's this?"

"Oh. That one there's a copy of the affidavit I told you about, the one your grandpa had drawn up, and . . ." She pointed to the telephone book next. "That's the phone book."

"Yeah," he said, looking at Ruby questioningly. "I can see that."

She exhaled loudly. "Well, look at that list Pa made on it! He did that the night before he had that bad spell. I've been giving it some thought and I think it's what set him off."

Mack studied the scribbling on the front cover of the phone book. "Looks like a list of names to me."

"I *know* what it is, Mack. I don't recognize a name on that list, not a single one. Who are those people?"

"Hell if I know," he said after looking over the list. Handing the phone book to Sister, he said, "You know any of these people?"

"Oh, *Mack*," Ruby said. "I already showed it to her. She doesn't know who they are either."

He shrugged. "thought they might be someone Grandpa knew before you were born. Sister's a good bit older than you."

Ruby stared at him, hands on her hips.

He turned his hands palm up. "I'm just trying to help here, Mama."

"Who are these men?" Sister said, deciding to put in her two-cents worth. "Am I supposed to know them?"

Ruby's shoulders drooped. "I swear, you two are enough to put anyone in Vinita!" She took the phone book from her sister's hands and pitched it into a kitchen drawer. The next thing she knew, she was pointing a finger in her son's face. "Well, I tell you what, Mack Barlow. There's some connection between that list and your grandpa's spell—I *know* there is."

"Easy now, Mama. I'm not saying there's not. But if you and Sister don't know who those guys are, I sure wouldn't. Hell, I've been gone better than twenty years. Just let me look at this affidavit. Okay?"

Ruby breathed deep to calm her ragged mind. She watched as Mack picked up the legal document, telling herself that, of course, he was right. They needed to focus on that legal paper, talk some sense into Pa. They could figure out that list of names later. And once Pa got better, he could just explain that list himself. She resumed working Sister's hair, keeping one eye on her son's face to see what his reaction might be. Within a couple of minutes, she saw Mack set the affidavit aside.

"That didn't take long."

He shrugged. "It's short and sweet. Says he wants to be buried next to Bill and Jack. Made you the Assignee."

Ruby felt anxious again. "Do you see any loopholes? Ways we can get around it?"

He shrugged. "I'm a carpenter, Mama, not an attorney."

What's happening? Ruby wondered. Things aren't going at all like I planned.

"Well then," she said, "you got to talk some sense into your grandpa. I'll not have this . . . this *travesty*. It just wouldn't be seemly."

Slipping the affidavit into his shirt pocket, he said, "Let me think on it." Rising from his chair, he walked around the table to where Sister sat. "See you later, gorgeous." He gave her a kiss on the head, then stepped up beside Ruby. "I think you're making too much out of this, Mama."

"Just do this for me, son. *Please*?"

Ruby savored the long hug her son gave her, wishing she could tuck him into her apron pocket so she could keep him close forever. But her boy had taken the wanderlust after he gotten out of the service. Fleetingly, she wondered if he had inherited his grandmother's genes, for Grace had turned out to be a wanderer, too. She pushed the thought away quickly, reminding herself that Mack had a good reason for leaving home. He had to go where the job took him. Grace had left for no good reason at all.

"How about I meet up with you and Sister for lunch at the Hometown Buffet? Say, twelve o'clock?"

Ruby crossed her arms over her chest. "I just don't understand why we can't all go together."

"I'm just thinking I could talk to Pa better if I was alone. It might confuse things, we double team him."

"Well . . ." Though she did not agree, Ruby said, "If you think it's best."

But as Ruby followed Mack to the living room, she came around to his way of thinking. Pa was on a short fuse these days and Mack understood Pa better than anyone did. They were two peas in a pod. Mack would lay the groundwork and it would all work out in the end—for the better.

"C'mon, Whitey," Ruby said when they reached the front room. The old white dog struggled to get up from his blanket beside the rocking chair. "It's time for your morning constitutional." She opened the front door and let the old dog out with Mack.

Breathing in the crisp air, she let it cleanse the smell of setting lotion and heated hair from her lungs before she closed the door again. She watched through the front curtain as Whitey flopped down on the front porch and Mack got into his Bronco. She continued to follow him with her eyes as he backed around and drove toward the county road, then hurried back to the kitchen so she could watch some more.

It was always the same when Mack came to visit. She wanted to fill her eyes with as much of him as she could for as long as she could. From the kitchen, she would be able to see the dirt trail his car would stir up as he made the crossroad and veered south toward McAlester.

She stood at the kitchen window now, looking. She had watched her son depart in this same way for over twenty years now, on his way to somewhere else, and it pleased her to know that at the end of the day, he would be returning home. This was the day when things would change, when things would go back to normal . . .

A puzzled look crossed Ruby's face as she watched the dust trail at the crossroad veer north rather than south. "Mack. . .?" she whispered.

CHAPTER SEVEN

Mack drove faster than he should have down the backcountry roads but made good time. When he reached the Indian Nation Turnpike, he headed north toward the town of Henryetta, wending his way through river valleys and rolling hills decked out in every fall hue known to mankind. Looking over the country, he could almost understand why his father had called this part of the country "Heaven on Earth" after he finished his stint in Korea.

One man's heaven could be another man's hell, he reflected.

His route took Mack past Lake Eufaula, the largest manmade lake in Oklahoma. One-hundred-thousand acres large. And to the south was another manmade lake almost as big. Lake Texoma. He had read once that there were over two hundred lakes in Oklahoma. Rimmed by the Ozark Mountains to the north, the Ouachitas to the east, and the Arbuckles to the southwest, the region became a stewpot in the summer—a hot, humid cauldron dense with trees and undergrowth that concealed things from view and set his nerve endings tingling.

"A jungle," he mumbled. Aware that he was sweating in his clothes, he trained his eyes on the broken stripes in the middle of the highway.

He reached the realtor's office only fifteen minutes late. As he eyed the one-story yellow-brick building, he questioned the realtors' inclination toward building materials. Brick was good, he supposed. It tolerated the elements well enough, but he was a wood man himself. The trouble was, good lumber was getting hard to find. Even then, it wasn't allowed to cure long enough, was sent to building sites too green. Studs were so green the sap ran, which made it twist and bow as bad as a swayback nag. That's why builders were going to metal studs nowadays, replacing wood with metal. It made no sense to Mack. With all the trees in eastern Oklahoma, there was no excuse to resort to metal. To his thinking, it wouldn't be a great loss to clear-cut the entire state, turn it into prairie, just like the Panhandle.

Panhandle. That one word helped clear Mack's thinking. Pulling the manila envelope from beneath the front seat, he went inside to find the woman he had been conversing with for the past several weeks. He introduced himself to the receptionist, informing her that he had an appointment with Roxie Komenski.

"That would be me."

Mack turned toward the voice and saw a tall, middle-aged woman thin as a broomstick with platinum blonde hair, cut and combed in a short burr. Her accent was definitely not homegrown.

Roxie Komenski extended her hand. "Good to finally meet you, Mr. Barlow."

"I go by Mack."

"Roxie will work for me. I have a number of places lined up to show you, the ones I sent descriptions on. And I put together the listing for your place." She pulled a packet of papers from a portfolio. "Might as well get it out of the way now. Just sign on the line marked with an X."

Efficient, Mack thought, nodding with satisfaction. All business and that's what I'm here to do. Tend to business.

He took the thick packet of papers and noted the place with an X was on the last page. "I'll just look the rest of this over first—"

"They're standard terms. I put together the asking price based on my inspection."

"Inspection?" He paused. "Thought I told you not to do that, Roxie"

"I had to get some idea of its worth, Mack."

He paused. "Mama didn't mention it."

"We waited until we saw her drive off."

Mack rubbed his mouth. "You staked out the place?"

"Sometimes we have to get inventive. No one will be the wiser. An old dog in the front room barked a little, nothing more. We weren't there long."

"We?"

"I took another realtor with me. He climbed up on the roof."

Mack was slow to respond, but his eyes indicated he was chewing on the realtor's words. Suddenly, the light switch flipped. "Did he speak English?" he snapped.

"What?"

"Never mind."

Roxie moved on. "He said the roof needs replacing."

"No way, Jose— That's a forty-year roof, just had it put on six, seven years ago."

"Marketing hype's not a guarantee. Shingles typically last through the warranty, then give out. Bet if you read the warranty on those shingles, it was for seven years. House will also need some updating before I can flip it."

Mack paused again, letting his mind catch up with the woman's words. He had met people like her in the military, people from back east that talked fast. People from places like New Jersey. New York. New Hampshire. States with New in their names that were the oldest states in the union. For some reason, he found that thought incongruent. Then he started wondering what someone from back east would find appealing about Oklahoma. Then he caught up.

"Flip it," he said. "You mean, fix it up to sell it. Think that would pay off?"

She shrugged. "Sometimes you have to spend money to make money. It's that or sell it for the land. Was me, that's what I'd do. Probably get as much for the land alone as you would for it and the house. Old houses in the country aren't worth a damn these days. You follow CNN? Real estate market's in the tank."

"Yeah," Mack said slowly. "I heard that rumor." He stared at the listing in his hand, then placed it in the envelope with the other papers she'd sent. "I'll just take this with me, give it a quick once over."

The stare she gave him was icy. "You said you needed to move that place to get money to resettle your mother."

"Yes ma'am, I do, but I'd like to see these offerings you told me about first." He tapped the packet of papers. "I'll get back to you with the listing soon enough." The room grew so quiet, he could hear the clock on the wall ticking.

She paused, exhaled deeply. "It'll be faster if you ride with me." She walked away, her stride long.

"Hold up," Mack called out. "I'm meeting some folks for lunch in McAlester. I'll follow you."

"Suit yourself," she said, not breaking her stride. "If you lose sight of me, I'll be at the Seven-Eleven on the highway."

Mack revisited his conversation with Roxie Komenski as he walked to his car, his mind crimping on something else she'd said. He was certain he had told her that he was a carpenter. If the real estate market was on the skids, wouldn't it follow that the building trade was, too?

"Don't need CNN to tell us the country's in deep doo-doo," he mumbled. "Just look out the window."

The new Cadillac sedan the realtor had revved up and waiting gave him pause, and he considered that maybe his last thought wasn't entirely true. Some people didn't seem to be hurting all that bad.

Within minutes, Mack was back on the Indian Nation Turnpike, steering his ten-year-old, secondhand Bronco with one hand and drumming his fingers on the armrest with the other. What Roxie Komenski had said about getting inventive troubled him. Architects were the inventive ones in his business. He just followed their plans and the simpler the plans, the better. Inventive led to delayed schedules. Higher costs. Compromises in quality. Inventive wasn't always good.

Mack stepped on the gas pedal to keep the realtor in sight. He followed the Caddy down remote county roads and finally stopped in front of a sign that read GOOD SAMARITAN RETIREMENT HOME. He sat in the car, calculating the distance from where they sat into town and figured it was ten miles, at the least.

"This is pretty far out in the sticks," he called through his open window. "Why'd they build a retirement home way out here?"

"Cheap land," she called back.

"Don't doubt that." The land he looked at right then would turn into a swamp in a heavy rain. Mosquito heaven. He took in the austere-looking building again, noticed the realtor was staring at him, and got the feeling he was supposed to fill the space with words. "Brick is good," he said, "doesn't need a lot of maintenance, but . . ."

"But . . . what?" She paused, blinking. "You said safety was top priority."

"Yes ma'am, I do want my mother and aunt to be safe, no two ways about it."

"Well, it doesn't get any safer than that." She aimed her index finger at the tall building. "Same contractor built this as put that new wing on the prison."

Mack sucked the spit from between his teeth. "What say let's take a look at second best."

She blew the air from her lungs and looked at her listing sheet. "That would be the senior apartment building. The residents need to be able to care for themselves. That's a requirement."

"Let's take a look."

The engine on the Cadillac revved to life. Again, Mack took a tandem position.

"Note that it's brick," the realtor said twenty minutes later. They stood in front of another complex set in a square and surrounded by an asphalt parking lot.

"Where's the yard?" he asked. Patched asphalt ran right up to the sidewalk and overgrown evergreens hugged the narrow space next to the walls.

"Yard?"

"You know, grass and trees. Someplace to walk around, maybe do a little gardening."

She raised pencil-thin eyebrows. "Balconies look down on a courtyard. They can sit on the balcony or in the courtyard. Old people sit a lot. There's something special I want you to see. Follow me."

Mack followed the realtor and a plump woman guide whose name escaped him into an elevator. They exited six floors up into a long, dark hallway. Mack extended his arms as he walked and found he could touch both walls without straightening his elbow. As he took a quick look down each end of the hallway, where EXIT signs indicated stairs at the far end of each, the image of a panicked herd of cattle being run through a de-ticking chute flicked through his mind.

"This is a *very* safe building," Roxie said as if reading his thoughts. "Look at that."

Inside the small apartment, the woman guide pointed to a red panic button that residents could push if they needed help. "The residents can get help fast. You know, in case they fall."

Mack eyeballed the distance between the button and the floor. "No way a person could reach that button, they're on the floor."

Roxie's pencil-thin eyebrows took another hike. "You said your mother and sister would be living together."

Mack cocked his head, frowning. "You lost me."

"The one not laying on the floor could push the button." She sounded impatient.

He cleared his throat and turned in a circle in the living room. A small bathroom was wedged between two closet-sized bedrooms and a sliding glass door led onto a balcony that looked to be four by eight.

"Well?" the realtor said.

"Kind of small for two people. How 'bout—"

"Let me guess," she snapped. "You want to look at third best." Without a word, she spun on her heels and headed down the dark narrow hallway.

Mack left the plump woman guide standing next to the panic button and caught up with the realtor, who was already in her car. Through her opened window, she informed him the next stop was a gated community north of town.

He drove hard to keep the Cadillac in sight. At a covered entrance landscaped with flowers and shrubs, he watched Roxie converse with guards, then pulled up next to her in a parking lot. She motioned him to join her, mouthing, *Get in!* He was barely seated when she took off.

"You wanted a safe place for your mother and aunt. Well. this one costs more but it's as good as it gets. You notice the gate?"

"I did—"

"There's also security officers that drive around on a regular basis."

"That sounds pretty good—"

"That's the clubhouse." Pointing through the windshield at a building in the distance, she read from a marketing brochure propped on the dash. "Woman's Club meets the first Tuesday of the month, Coffee Hour on the second Tuesday, cards every Friday afternoon, plus there's a quilting club, a Gram's Club—"

"Gram's Club?"

"For women with grandchildren."

"Mama and Sister don't have grandchildren—"

"Square dance on weekends, a couple of book groups—*lots* to keep them busy." She pulled into a parking lot next to a chalet-looking structure, put the car into PARK, and opened her car door.

Mack did not move.

"Well?" she said. "Don't you want to check out the activities going on inside the clubhouse?"

"I'll take your word on it."

She closed her car door and stared out the windshield. "I'm getting the feeling you don't like this place either."

"I didn't say that. It's better than the other two. Not overgrown, you know, like a jungle, but it's got yards."

"They're called green spaces."

Mack stared at her.

"They're supposed to be healthy. Something to do with the exchange of oxygen and carbon dioxide."

"Well, then," he said, "let's drive around those green spaces, look at the perimeter fencing."

"Look at fencing . . .?"

"And one of those duplexes."

"They're called patio homes. There's two built together with an adjoining wall."

"Okay. Let's take a look at one of those patio homes."

"Now we're getting somewhere." She drove back toward the front gate where a model home was open for viewing. "They're two-bedroom units."

"That'd work," he said. "Could put a sleeper sofa in the living room for company."

"If your mother or aunt needed help, they could bang on the adjoining wall."

He grunted softly. "Better than nothing, I guess."

"There's a combination living room and dining area, kitchen comes with appliances, including a combo washer/dryer, and a cement patio—lined with trees and grass."

"No garden spot?"

She gave Mack a sideways look. "There called patio homes for a reason. People garden on their patios. Container gardening's big these days." The realtor glanced at the brochure again. "Did I mention there's a Garden Club?"

"Garden Club?" He frowned. "What do they do, look at each other's pots?"

He got no response. Their route took them past new construction near the back of the subdivision and the perimeter fence. The realtor slowed the Cadillac so Mack could get a close look.

"Hell, that's nothing but bob wire," he mumbled.

"Barbwire's good fencing."

"For keeping livestock in or out, depending on which side of the fence you're on. Not worth a damn for perverts and escaped convicts."

"You know of another place around here that has its own security patrols?"

"You make a good point." He paused. "We can skip the duplex."

"What? Thought you wanted to look at the model home."

"No need. Could tell from a distance they're shooting the shingles on with staples and putting the studs on sixteen-inch centers."

"Sixteen-inch centers satisfies standards—"

"This is tornado alley, *lady*. I had twelve-inch centers in mind."

She paused. “Let me get this straight. You’re *not* going to look at the model home.”

“Let’s move to the next thing on the list.”

The burr-headed woman hit the brake hard and stared at him. “This isn’t Oklahoma City, *buddy*. These are your choices.”

“Well, they’re slim pickings.”

“They’re filling up fast.”

He paused, exhaling slowly. “I’ll think on it.”

Stomping the gas, Roxie drove to Mack’s car, shifted into PARK, and stared out the windshield.

Mack rubbed his fingers across his mouth, then sighed. “Any chance of changing the specs on one of these places. I work in construction, maybe I could oversee the building of it.”

“I’m not a miracle worker . . .”

He reached for the door handle.

“But I could try.”

“You could make it happen, we’d be getting closer to what I had in mind.”

“Might have to put your money where your mouth is, Barlow.”

“Balls in your court, Komenski. I’ll give you a call in a couple days.”

“And you need to sign that listing agreement,” she said as Mack was closing the door. “Given the remote location and shape it’s in, it’ll take a while for me to flip your place.”

“Couple days,” he repeated.

CHAPTER EIGHT

The nursing home was a rambling single-story building in a neighborhood lined with older-style homes considered affluent in a different time. The appointment with the realtor had taken longer than Mack expected. He was supposed to meet his mother at the Home Town Buffet at twelve o'clock. "Damn," he mumbled, glancing at his watch. Eleven thirty.

He tugged on the heavy-duty glass door but it refused to open. Inside, a grizzled old man sitting in a wheelchair smiled at him.

"I can't get in" Mack called to him.

"It's locked."

"Yes sir. Can you open it?"

"They won't let me." The old man turned a permanently bent neck toward a nurse's aide hurrying to the front door.

Mack watched the aide push some numbers into a keypad, listened to an irritating buzz, and watched the door snap open. Walking in, he said, "I'm sure you got a reason for that."

"Yes. To keep our people safe."

"Safe?"

"They tend to wander off. Can I help you?"

"Just point me to Room 32." He walked in the direction the aide pointed, passed white-haired men and women in wheelchairs or using walkers, and smelled the odor of vitamins, bedpans, and floral-scented room deodorants. In Room 32, he found his grandfather strapped into a hospital bed with a metal rail around it like a child's playpen. He stood beside the bed, staring at the man.

"He's sleeping."

Mack turned to where the voice came from and found an elderly black man sitting in a recliner with his legs elevated, holding a book. His feet looked oversized for the rest of his body.

"I see that." Mack studied the man more closely. "Don't I know you?"

"I'm your grandfather's roommate. Name's Carter, Henry Carter. You might remember me from the state pen. I worked at Big Mac for many a year. Knew your father well. Tragedy, what happened to him."

"I remember you now." Mack extended his hand. "How you doing, Mr. Carter?"

"Can't complain." The man gripped Mack's hand. "Diabetes gives me fits but could be worse. I got a granddaughter works here. She keeps a good eye on me and my comfort. And a friend comes by to see me now and then, sneaks me gumdrops. Got a bag hid away down there." He indicated the bottom drawer of his nightstand then looked at Mack quickly. "You won't tell on me, will you?" A look of concern appeared in his eyes. "They'll take my gumdrops away, you tell on me."

"I won't tell, but I got a feeling gumdrops would make those legs worse than they are."

"There's worse things than a little pain. Sometimes, a gumdrop helps take the edge off."

"I see," Mack said, not at all sure that he did. Sitting down next to his grandfather's bed, he took in the beige-painted walls, scuffed woodwork, and plastic flowers. Multiple vases of fake flowers lined windowsills, bedside tables, and tops of dressers. His observations took him again to the old man sitting in the recliner, who had left his book lay and was studying him.

"How's Pa doing, Mr. Carter?" he asked, figuring the old man wanted some company. "Seems to be sleeping awful hard."

"Yeah, they got him doped up."

Mack studied his grandfather's slow deep breathing. "Had another one of his spells then?"

"Spells? Oh, yeah, that's what they call them." He paused. "Your grandpa did have a bad night last night. That blamed fool next door heard him and rang for the orderly. They don't understand, you see, so they dope him up."

Mack stared at his grandfather some more, then turned to Carter again. "More than likely, it's to keep him from hurting himself . . . or maybe, someone else." Noting the question in Carter's eyes, he said, "He hurt her, you know, during one of those spells."

"Yes, he told me about that. Grace didn't understand his bad nights. I figure she used it as an excuse to cut out."

Mack paused. "Grace?"

"Your grandma."

Mack paused again. "I was talking about my mother, Mr. Carter. He hurt Mama during one of those spells."

"Oh." The old man took a Kleenex from a box sitting on a table next to him and wiped spittle from the corners of his mouth. "You can call me Henry. We both saw service, your grandpa and me. Same war but different units. I was with the Tuscaloosa bunch. Grover there survived Normandy. No small feat, surviving Normandy."

"You got that right." Mack hesitated, "You sure he said Grace? I never heard much about her." He turned toward a sudden movement on the bed before Carter could answer.

"Who's there? That you, Grace?"

Mack looked into pale blue eyes, sunken now into a face that had shriveled in on itself like a dried apple. "How you doing, Pa? It's me, Mack."

"Mack—you come to take me home? It's time to bale that hay."

He swallowed hard. "No sir. I come to talk to you about this piece of paper." He pulled the affidavit from his shirt pocket and fitted it into his grandfather's hands.

The old man's hands trembled as he looked over the document. "Oh, I read this a'ready. You come to help me find them boys, that's good."

"No sir, I come to understand your reasons for requesting such a thing. Mama doesn't understand."

"What's to understand." The old man's head began to nod, then his eyes took on a distant look and his chin settled slowly onto his chest. "Just need to find them, that's all. You see, we misplaced those graves . . ."

"Pa?" Mack reached for the document as it fell from his grandfather's hands. "Pa . . .?"

"He's out again." Henry looked at Mack over the top of his book. "Probably be in and out most of the day."

Mack stared at his grandfather, listened to the ticking of a clock, then looked across the room. "What don't they understand, Henry?"

"What's that?" Carter laid his book aside.

"You said, 'They don't understand.'"

"Oh." The old man looked at Mack as though sizing him up for a suit of clothes. "You saw military duty, didn't you son. I can see it in your eyes, the way you carry yourself. I figure the Scouts, what they call Special Forces these days."

Though confused, Mack nodded. "I did a couple of tours."

"*Two* tours? What's wrong with you, boy?"

Mack laughed softly. "Got a hard head, I guess. Took a while to come to my senses."

The old man laughed, then turned serious. "You ever get memories in the night, when you're least expecting them? You know, *bad* memories?"

The skin on the back of Mack's neck felt as though it were crawling off his body. "Yes sir," he said slowly. "Guess I do at that."

"You know what's so hard about growing old, son? The less we're able to do, the more time we got to remember things. Things we done we ought not've done, leastways no God-fearing man should've done."

Mack stared at Henry Carter, then said, "Aw, hell . . ." He turned to look at the frail body on the bed, held down with reinforced straps and penned in with an iron bar on all sides, and began to shake. Leaning his head between his legs, he gasped, trying to control the convulsions in his stomach and the taste of stomach acid in his throat.

"Haunts you to your dying day, losing sight of God," Carter said. He released the handle the recliner and moaned as the blood pulsed through his swollen legs. Then he tugged open the bottom drawer of his bedside table and began to rummage through socks and underwear.

Pulling himself together, Mack helped Henry Carter find his bag of gumdrops.

CHAPTER NINE

Ruby had parked as close to the Hometown Buffet's front door as she could get and chatted idly with Sister to pass the time. She had driven the gas tank in her car almost dry that morning. First, she had stopped at the Walmart just to kill time, then driven past the nursing home twice, looking for Mack's Bronco. When the gas gauge reached a quarter of a tank, she proceeded to the cafeteria.

She had speculated on her son's behavior as they waited. What was this appointment that he needed to take care of? Why had he gone north at the crossroad? Could she have mistaken his car for another one passing?

She wanted that last thought to ease her mind, to lessen the tension that knotted her neck muscles, but it hadn't. The clock on the dash read twelve twenty-five. She had expected Mack to be there no later than twelve fifteen. Fifteen minutes late was acceptable in her mind. Twenty-five was not. She looked into her rearview mirror, hoping to catch a glimpse of her son's car.

"We'll probably need to get you a wheelchair, Sister," she mused idly. "It's Saturday so the line will be long, 'specially as Mack's running late."

"Don't need a chair. Been sitting on my butt all morning—"

"Look, I believe that's Mack. Yes, here he comes." Ruby simultaneously breathed a sigh of relief and felt anxiety building in her chest. She wondered what kind of luck her son had had with his grandfather. "You wait there, Sister. I'll have him get you a chair."

"I said I *don't* want a chair." Sister opened her door and took off for the front door.

Ruby struggled to get out of the car so she could catch Sister, calling, "Wait, you'll need help."

"Looks like she's motoring just fine on her own, Mama." Mack looped his arm through Ruby's. "Sorry I'm a little late."

"Well, you're here now," Ruby said, holding his arm close. "You don't think we need to get Sister a chair? Looks like we might have to stand in line a bit."

"I think Sister's capable of doing more than you think." Mack nodded at his aunt, who was two lengths ahead of them. "Maybe you shouldn't wait on her so much."

Ruby pulled to a stop. "Why, she was to fall and break a hip, I'd never forgive myself. Broke hips lead to an early grave."

"And some people worry themselves into an early grave."

Ruby gave her son a scolding but affectionate glance and joined Sister at the back of cafeteria line. Looking around to see if anyone was listening, she leaned close to Mack and whispered, "Well? How'd it go with Pa?"

"Pa wasn't having a good day. Couldn't stay awake."

Ruby felt anxiousness building in her chest again. "But he's always wide awake in the morning, doesn't get sleepy till after lunch." She shook her head, forehead creased. "That doesn't sound like Pa at all. I'm a mind to just have you help me load him up and bring him home today. That's it, we'll eat a bite, then go get him—"

"*Whoa* right there." Mack tapped the affidavit folded up in his shirt pocket. "I came here to talk to Pa about this paper, not kidnap him out of a nursing home." He paused. "Besides which, I don't think that's such a good idea."

"He'd do better back home, I know he would." Ruby waited for a reply. Though none came, the look on his face indicated he was not of the same opinion. She glanced around the packed cafeteria, spotted many of her regular customers, and decided to postpone that particular conversation until they had more privacy.

"Well then," she said, moving to the next item on her list. "Did you at least talk to him about that paper?"

"Yes ma'am, I did."

Feeling the tightness in her chest ease, Ruby let out a long breath. "I *knew* you could talk sense into him." She nodded at the paper in Mack's pocket again. "What do we have to do, see a lawyer to cancel it out? Lord, I hate to have to put more money out to a lawyer. Had to sign Pa's Social Security over to the home and doubt we could get it back—but no, we'd better make it legal just so there's no hitches when it comes time to lay him out—"

"Slow down now," Mack said. "I didn't say I'd changed his mind."

Ruby watched as Mack began to rub at his mouth, the worry resurfacing. "Just what *are* you saying, Mack?"

"Aw hell, Mama." He blew the air from his lungs. "I didn't see anything wrong with laying him out with Bill and Jack in the first place. You're the one with the bee in her bonnet about this business." He paused. "And by the way, what's the deal with Grace?"

"Grace?" Ruby said. "You mean my mother Grace?"

"How many Graces we got in the family? You know, most men want to be buried next to their wives. Why doesn't Pa want to be buried with his? Just where is she, anyway?"

"Grace's in Beulah Land," Sister said over her shoulder.

"Where?" Mack caught up with the little woman who had been quietly inching her way forward in the line.

"I said, *Grace . . . is . . . in . . . Beulah Land—"*

"Hush now, Sister." Ruby watched heads turning their direction. As Sister moved forward a few more inches, she pulled Mack aside. "All Sister's saying is that Grace is in Heaven, Mack. Beulah Land's just another name for Heaven. You haven't forgot everything you learned, have you?" She laughed, humorlessly. "Though there's little chance of her being in Heaven, you ask me."

Sister let out a chuckle. "Grace *was* a tart," she said, moving forward again.

"My grandma was a tart?" Mack looked between Ruby and Sister. "One of you want to explain what that means?"

"You can't put stock in what Sister says these days," Ruby whispered, moving closer. "I'm afraid there might be something to this gene business."

"I'm not following you," Mack said, frowning.

Ruby raised her eyebrows and simultaneously tapped her head. "Pa and Ida? And now, Sister? You know . . . *genetic*?" Getting a blank stare, she moved even closer. "Pa's sister, Ida, was put in Vinita. She suffered from depression or some such thing. Now with Pa's spells and . . ." She paused, glancing at Sister. "Well, I'm afraid some of the family's strangeness might have got passed on."

Mack snorted. "Can't speak for Ida, but genes don't have anything to do with what's wrong with Pa." He paused, shaking his head. "And the same goes for Sister. There's an explanation for what she was hearing on the roof."

"Well, think what you want," Ruby snapped. "You don't have to live with it day in and day out!"

"Now, Mama—"

"Can we get back to that paper in your pocket?"

She pointed to the folded affidavit in Mack's pocket again, then watched as he studied the tiles on the floor. Mack had grown harder to talk to in the last year, ever since she'd called him about the incident with his grandfather. Irritable. Touchy. She could tell that he was in one of those moods right then. As they moved up another foot in the line, she found him looking at her intently. Whatever was on his mind was about to leave his mouth, and she felt a knot in her stomach tighten.

"Mama, I'm gonna find Bill and Jack, bury Pa where he wants."

Ruby's felt a dizzying spin in her head. "You're *what?*" she mumbled.

"He's earned the right to his last request."

"You would shame this family?"

"Shame or not," Mack said. "I'm doing it."

"Pa's lived through enough shame," she said. "What with Grace deserting him and his . . . condition. He doesn't need to suffer any more than he already has."

"I grant you, he's suffered more than his share." Mack paused. "I don't want to hurt you, Mama, but I plan on looking for Bill and Jack. Pa's in his right mind."

"Grace was a Georgia peach," Sister said out of the blue.

"*Sister!*" Ruby tugged on her sister's sleeve. "Hush now. We're talking business here." Reeling with the import of Mack's words, Ruby searched for a way to gain control of the situation. "What about your job, Mack? I thought you could only stay the weekend. You don't have time for this nonsense."

"I can take a couple more days. Need to spruce the house up a bit anyway, trim those tree limbs you mentioned. In between, I'll look for Bill and Jack."

"They're in Beulah Land," Sister said impromptu. "With Grace."

Ruby rolled her eyes. "Tell me *that* sounds like a person in their right mind."

Mack grinned. "Who's to say Sister's not right. Maybe it's just one big happy family in Beulah Land."

Instantaneously, the anxiousness for her father and her annoyance with her son and the worry over her sister's mental condition collided within Ruby and burst forth with a zeal the likes of which would have made an evangelical preacher envious.

"Mack Barlow," she shouted, raising one hand heavenward. "Are you telling me a couple of long-eared, braying mules went to Heaven? Only those with *souls* go to Heaven!"

You could have heard a pin drop in the Hometown Buffet. Ruby saw heads turning her way. Some belonging to people she knew, some to others she recognized but could not put a name to, some to total strangers. With certainty, they would all remember who she was from this day forward.

"You saying Whitey doesn't have a soul, Mama?" Mack grinned. "I always figured I'd run into him one of these days

. . ." He pointed toward the ceiling of the Hometown Buffet. "Up there."

"Oh, *Mack*." Feeling tears brim her eyes, Ruby blinked hard.

Walking up close, he put his arm around her shoulders. "Where do you suppose I should start looking, Mama? Where's the last place you lived when Pa was still farming with mules? Was it before he got back from the war? Or after?"

"I'll not help you one bit!" Ruby crossed her arms over her chest and turned her face from him, turned away from everyone in The Hometown Buffet to stare at a wall the color of putty.

"Was me," Sister said unprompted, "I'd look in Beulah Land."

"*Sister*!" Ruby hissed. Seeing Mack grin again, she elbowed him in the ribs for good measure.

"Was right after the war," Sister went on, inching her way forward. "That's when he bought that second-hand tractor. Used it to dig the hole to bury Bill and Jack in. Biggest hole I ever saw."

Mack stopped smiling. "Are you saying both those mules died at the same time?"

Sister hesitated. "Well, I guess they must have, seeing Pa buried them in the same hole."

Ruby shook her head, drained of energy. "Mack, you 're not putting any stock into any of this nonsense—"

"Where was that, Sister," Mack said. "Where *are* Bill and Jack?"

"I swear," Sister mumbled, irritably, "the whole world's gone deaf." She pulled Mack's head close, put her mouth next to his ear, and yelled, "*Bill . . . and . . . Jack's . . . in . . . Beulah . . . Land.*"

Without any thought to locality or those present, Mack let out a guffaw that could be heard the next county over. A startled busboy dropped a tray of dishes causing cafeteria workers and customers to stare, Sister reached the front of the line and demanded her senior citizen's discount, and Ruby turned her burning face to the putty-colored wall, making no attempt to push genes from her mind.

CHAPTER TEN

It was late in the day when Mack pulled up to the mailbox. The oak and hickory were throwing long shadows by then and the air had cooled considerably. He made a mental note to check out the furnace while he was home. His mother and aunt would be running it full blast before long.

"What the hell am I thinking," he mumbled. "They'll be in a house with a new furnace before then and have a maintenance man to make sure it runs right."

He laughed quietly then, thinking of what else that meant. No more worrying about prison breaks. No more watching the TV, wondering where the latest rash of tornados would be touching down. There would be warning signals in town, time to get to safety.

Opening the box, he removed the mailbag and placed it on the front seat, next to the packet of information from Roxie Komenski. In so doing, he remembered that he had not yet looked over the listing agreement she'd drawn up.

He figured the burr-headed realtor to be a steamroller when it came to persuading someone to her point of view. People with Cadillac appetites were turned that way. She had probably pitched his idea to the builder at the gated community that very day, which meant he needed to look at that agreement fast. But time was on his side as Mama and Sister planned to visit Pa after they left the Hometown Buffet, then stop at the filling station to gas up. He had a good hour, maybe more.

He carried the envelope and mailbag inside, letting Whitey in while he was about it. The house seemed unnaturally quiet, with only the hum of the Frigidaire and the *poof* of the gas flame on the water heater filling the void. Hearing a roof joist crack as the house began to cool, he paused to listen. Old houses did that, but he knew it didn't mean the house wasn't sound. He wondered if Roxie Komenski had heard those sounds when she had made her guerrilla run on the place. If that was the reason she had determined the house needed fixing up before she could flip it.

A Walmart Christmas ad and a church flyer were the only things in the mailbag, so Mack laid them on the kitchen table. He opened the refrigerator in hopes of finding a Bud or Coors. He settled for a 12-ounce bottle of Pepsi, telling himself he should've known better than to find alcohol in the house. He was knee-deep in the Bible Belt. Besides which, his mother and aunt were teetotalers, had been since he could hold a memory.

Abruptly, he felt a dryness in his throat, then a longing, and his mind wandered to taverns he frequented in Amarillo and Lubbock, Midland and Odessa. Drinking suds in wide-open country with other carpenters who took their work and their beer where they found it. But hell, he thought, hadn't you earned the right to knock back a few when you'd spent ten hours swinging a twenty-ounce claw hammer under a blistering sun or in a freezing drizzle?

Breathing deep, Mack sat down at the table, popped the top on the Pepsi, and turned his attention to the listing agreement. He recalled Roxie Komenski saying the terms were standard, but right off, he noticed her fee was seven percent, the high end of the going scale.

"Thought we agreed to six," he mumbled, making a mental note to question the realtor about the elevated fee when he telephoned her.

He also remembered that the realtor had told him she based the listing price on her evaluation of the property. He felt his blood pressure elevate as he recalled her methodology, but he turned through pages until he found the one with the listing price stated.

"Damn," he mumbled, finding the figure much lower than he had hoped. Making another mental note to have the realtor justify the lower price, he inserted the listing agreement back inside the envelope, unsigned.

Wondering how much more he would get for the property if he replaced the roof and made other improvements, Mack made his way down the hall to the bedroom. He tossed the manila envelope on the bed and traded Dockers and a v-neck pullover for jeans and a sweatshirt, debating which chore to tackle first.

His mother had lengthened the list as they sat over lunch at the Hometown Buffet. He hadn't objected as the work would make the place show better. But as he drove up the track to the house, he noticed new saplings had sprung up and some of the brush had suckered. For his own peace of mind, he wanted to thin the grounds to give a clear view of the surroundings. A man had to wrest the land from nature in this neck of the woods and battle to keep it from being reclaimed to his dying day. If he let up a minute, it turned into a jungle. That thought strengthened the pull to haul ass back to the big and wide. The Panhandle offered no such impairment to a man's vision.

Mack sighed. "And after that, I need to get the house ready to flip," he said to the old white dog that still followed him.

Flip. He didn't like the terms Roxie Komenski chose to use when it came to people's property. He rubbed Whitey behind the ears, then laced his worn rawhide work boots, talking to the dog as he did so.

"Maybe if I spruce the old place up a little it'll bring a lot more. How 'bout it, boy? Want to live out your golden years in a patio home?"

As the dog panted his enjoyment with the attention, Mack remembered the lunchtime debate about mules and dogs and souls and Heaven. Then his thoughts went to Sister's revelation about Bill and Jack being buried together, and he wondered again why two mules would die on the same day.

As he made his way to the bedroom door, Mack paused, thinking he needed to hide the envelope containing the realtor's listing. He planned to broach the subject with his mother when the time was right, but he needed to wait a day or two to give her a chance to cool off.

Ruby's health was more a concern for Mack than anything else he'd found out on this trip. She'd always been one to self-manufacture complexities, over-chew matters, and the last year had taken its toll on her. A patio home was the perfect place for her and Sister. They'd both earned the right to their golden years, especially with his father gone and his grandfather in a nursing home. Yes sir, he thought. It's the right choice.

As he walked to the closet to place the packet on the top shelf, he noticed his mother's old photo album. He pulled it down and leafed through it, suddenly remembering a picture that might help in the search for his grandfather's mules. He slowed turning of the pages as his grandfather's life passed before his eyes and stopped to study one photo in particular.

"She *was* a Georgia peach," he mumbled, studying the petite woman dressed in a two-piece suit and holding a bouquet in one hand.

Mack knew little about his grandmother, known by her children as Grace. As he recalled, the reason behind the first-name basis was dictated by the woman herself, who wanted to retain her youthful image and saw a passel of kids calling her Mama as unfitting.

He studied the picture again. The woman was leaning against the arm of a tall proud-looking man whose eyes belied they belonged to Mack's grandfather. The look of a man who made a good catch, Mack thought. He became more curious about the woman's disappearance as he continued to turn pages but he did not find her semblance again. Save for the wedding picture, the woman was non-existent.

"What the hell happened, Pa?" Mack whispered. "None of this is making any sense. How can a woman bear you two children and leave one picture behind?" Remembering the postcard in the living room, a reunion notice, he was struck with another thought.

What if she's not dead after all?

A few pages later, Mack finally found the picture he was looking for. A smiling younger version of his grandfather, sitting on the seat of a buckboard wagon looking between the ears of two long-eared and very serious-eyed mules.

"Bill and Jack," Mack murmured, frowning. He figured each of the mules stood sixteen-hands, maybe taller. "Take one helluva-big hole to bury those two." The mules' simultaneous deaths continued to rub like a burr under a saddle blanket.

Seated next to the man was a small girl in a bonnet. Sister? Mack studied the background in the picture but was unable to identify its location. Slipping the photograph out of the album, he laid it aside and went back to the album.

The next page showed another black-and-white photograph displaying five smiling men in Army uniforms, arms draped around each other's shoulders as a gang of schoolboys would do. Too damned young to be shipped off to Normandy, Mack thought, running his finger down the row until he found his grandfather. He studied the clear-eyed boy with a lop-sided grin and saw a trace of himself in the set of the shoulders and square jaw.

The next picture showed his grandfather with two children. The larger of the two reached his knee and he held an infant in his arms.

"Mama?" Mack said, looking at the baby. He could see nothing more than two eyes and a small puckered mouth inside what looked to be a hand-crocheted baby cap. He looked then at his grandfather's face, studying it hard, and noticed an emptiness in the eyes he had not seen in the previous pictures.

"The Army hung you out to dry, didn't it, Pa." He let out a bitter laugh and mumbled, "Been there, done that, bought the T-shirt."

Feeling a tightness in his neck, Mack turned another page and came face to face with a yellowed newspaper clipping detailing a prison break at the state pen at McAlester. He recognized his own countenance in the face of the man featured in a photograph and closed the book fast.

"C'mon Whitey." Mack replaced the photo album on the top shelf and laid the manila envelope on top of it. "Let's get to those tree limbs."

He walked out the back door to the shed where he found a pruning saw and ladder. "Might as well take a look at the shingles while I'm up there . . ." He flexed his neck muscles to loosen the tightness. "See if I was sold a boatload of marketing hype when I had that forty-year roof put on."

CHAPTER ELEVEN

Christmas flyers had made Nonny run late and worn her patience thin as gauze. The pasty-faced man wearing the Santa Claus suit on the flyer looked as authentic as a tub of margarine.

Margarine, she thought. What a boatload of crap that was.

Nonny could still remember her mother stirring yellow food dye into a white slab that resembled lard, which marketers sold as being more nutritious than butter.

"It's hydrogenated vegetable oil, loaded with trans fats," she explained. Though she'd talked until she was blue in the face about the ills of margarine, her mother preferred it to butter right up to her dying day.

She swore under her breath as she hauled the last empty tray inside the post office, thinking nothing had changed in her forty years on Earth. If anything, it had gotten worse. Her back aching from the weight of the flyers she'd hauled around, she silently damned retail stores and outlets for not allowing Halloween and Thanksgiving to be turned off before switching Christmas on. To her thinking, they could just forget Christmas altogether. Though she enjoyed the study of myths, she was not a believer in them, in particular, the one this season represented. Neither the traditional nor the commercial version.

Nonny was one of the last contractors to finish up. The front lobby almost empty, the sound of laughter from the front lobby caught her attention. It came from a mother and child picking up what looked to be an early Christmas package. She paused to study the little girl, whose eyes were trained on a cardboard box that had just arrived. She wondered how any mother could allow a child to believe in a mythical creature that rewarded goodness with gifts *au gratis*. No strings attached.

In the next instant, an image popped into her mind. The fake Santa Claus on the marketing flyer was handing her the baby Jesus. But as she reached for the baby, it dissolved into a crumpled Big Mac wrapper and the Santa turned into a sneering Ronald McDonald. That dissolved into an image of her discarding the wadded paper into the trashcan. In the next fade, she was standing in front of the trashcan, hearing the crumpled wrapper cry like a baby doll as it fell through the slot.

Her lips numb, Nonny pried the image from her mind. "DTs?" she mumbled. "After all this time, I get the DTs?" She stumbled from the post office, saying, "Pull yourself together, Folsom. You have things to do."

Nonny made sure she always had things to do. This day, she had to pick up outdated produce at the Piggly Wiggly and take it to the Homeless Shelter, which made it questionable that she would get to jelly that afternoon.

"Just have to do it tomorrow," she said under her breath. "Sunday or not."

Her parents would never allow work to be done on Sundays, saying the good book admonished against such things, and she had continued the ritual. Right then, she wondered why and decided it had everything to do with the nature of rituals. Once imprinted, they stuck.

Like margarine, she thought.

She drove the rusty Jeep to the Texaco station on Highway 69, another of her rituals. Filling the tank on Saturday night meant she could drive straight to the post office on Monday, the busiest day of the week. A necessary ritual if she was to finish before dark.

On the way, she recalled how some route carriers found places other than people's mailboxes to deposit junk mail. A carrier in Oklahoma City had stored flyers still in the mailbags in his garage. Postal inspectors found stacks of #3 postal bags piled in a corner and nailed his hide to a jail door. Nonny pulled up to a pump and shut off the engine, talking as she climbed out of the Jeep.

"*El loco dopo*. Anyone stupid enough to leave flyers in their garage, and leave them in official pouches, deserves to get caught."

As she fitted the nozzle into the gas tank, Nonny began to wonder how she would've handled the situation. Return the bags to the post office, she decided. Empty, of course. A lot of people didn't know that postmasters were required to log mailbags, both incoming and outgoing, and had to produce the logs when postal inspectors paid unscheduled visits. To her thinking, that was the mistake *el loco dopo* made. He should've brought back the mailbags and destroyed the flyers. Fire would be her preference. An old oil drum and can of gasoline and *pftttt*, ashes to ashes. Then she recalled that laws now outlawed the burning of trash.

"Crap," she mumbled. "A person can't get away with shit anymore."

Suddenly, she wished for a bygone day when there was less bureaucracy and more freedom, as in territorial days. She recalled how outlaws were considered mythical heroes back then. Jesse James. Cole Younger. Belle Starr. Now there was a woman for you. The famous woman bandit of Outlaw Territory didn't take crap from anyone. She ambushed anyone who stood in her way—even one of her husbands.

Nonny sighed, wondering why she couldn't live someplace like that. Then she had an awakening. "Hell—this *is* Outlaw Territory," she mumbled.

That thought dampening an already dripping mood, she focused on the spinning meter on the gasoline pump. She found the blinking meter not unlike the eyes of students she used to lecture: wide-eyed kids eager to absorb the spiel coming out her mouth. She shook her head, remembering how she once enjoyed being one of the chosen people who spewed humanitarian gospel from a lectern. That line of reasoning led Nonny to consider that some of her last words hadn't been entirely accurate and she felt an ethical need to correct herself.

"This *was* Outlaw Territory," she told the pump. "That myth is dead, too. Dead . . . dead . . . dead—"

"Yoo-hoo, Nonny. What's got you talking to yourself? Did someone die?"

Startled out of her daymare, Nonny looked toward the next pump. Seeing Ruby Barlow filling up her Chevy sedan, she felt her face turn warm.

"No, just daydreaming," she said. "I was wishing this was still Outlaw Territory when there weren't so many rules. I'd like to turn outlaw and burn all these damn Christmas flyers . . ." She waved her words away, preferring not to explain the way her mind worked. "How are things with you?" She watched Ruby shut off her pump, say something to her sister, who sat in the front seat, then walk her direction.

"Well, right now," Ruby said, "I've got an outlaw son running a bit too free for my liking."

"Son? Well, that could only be Mack. He coming back for Christmas this year?"

Ruby looked startled. "Why, he's home right now. But didn't I tell you that already? I was planning on you coming to supper tonight so you two could visit." She paused, frowning. "I'm just positive I told you about Mack being home."

Frowning, Nonny said, "Something troubling you, Ruby? Is Pa all right?"

"What? Oh, we're heading to the home to see him right now. But no, Pa isn't all right. He's still insisting on being buried with those mules—and Mack is planning on looking for them. Sister told him some cockamamie story about Pa burying them animals together and he believed her!"

Nonny put her arm around Ruby's shoulder. "Maybe you're making too much out of this—"

"That's just what Mack said," Ruby snapped, pulling away. "I was hoping for a little understanding from you, Nonny—Lord knows I'm not getting it elsewhere."

As Nonny pulled back, Ruby paused, looking remorseful. "Oh, hon. I didn't mean that. You've seen me through some hard days since you come home—and I haven't even thanked you for those persimmons you left yesterday."

"I had a good time picking them," Nonny said, considering where to go next. "I'll do anything I can to help, Ruby, you know I will. But if Pa won't change his mind, then that affidavit he drew up is as legal as it can be."

"Tell me again what it said." A hopeful look crossed Ruby's face. "Maybe there's a loophole we overlooked. Right now, I need a *big* loophole."

Nonny took a deep breath. "Well, in short, all a person has to do is state his wishes in a sworn affidavit and assign somebody to follow through with it. You can get something like that notarized lots of places. The post office does that. Realtors also notarize things. All kinds of people carry around notary seals."

"Well, I'll swan, that's just what Pa did. I wonder who told him about that dumb law. I swear, who in their right mind would bury one mule, much less two." Ruby hesitated, then held Nonny's eyes. "You think insanity is genetic, Nonny? Pa had a sister put away down to Vinita once."

"I don't think your dad's insane, Ruby." Nonny did not reveal that burying even one mule sounded strange to her. Typically, people had large animals that died hauled to a rendering plant. "Sounds like his memory's improved though, if he told Sister where Bill and Jack are."

"But you see, he *didn't*. Sister came up with that malarkey on her own."

"And you can't remember where they are?"

"Me? Why no, I was just a baby then. But you know how Mack gets when he sets his mind to something."

Nonny *did* know how Mack's mind worked. When he proposed marriage at high-school graduation, she told him she wanted to go to college, to make something of herself before settling down. He had promptly joined the military and disappeared from her life. From what Ruby said from time to time, he had all but disappeared from hers as well.

"Uncle George might know," Nonny said, turning thoughtful. "He and Pa farmed at the same time, sometimes in fields side by side. If anyone would know anything about those mules, he would. Mack might want to run by and talk to him, he'd love the company. Or better yet . . ."

Nonny let her voice trail off, hoping Ruby would not notice.

"Better yet, what?" Ruby asked.

"Well," Nonny said, kicking herself for speaking before she thought things through. "There's a dinner-on-the-grounds tomorrow at Scipio Church. I'm taking Uncle George so he can visit with other old timers. I put a flyer in your mailbag about it just this morning." She paused, searching for words that would give her a way out. "Still, I doubt Uncle George would remember anything. His memory's failing, too."

"A dinner-on-the-grounds. Lord, I haven't been to one of them in a coon's age. My work keeps me tied to the house." Ruby paused, eyes widening. "Why, we'll just all come—Mack, too. If nothing else, we'll have ourselves a good old time, forget about this nonsense for a bit."

Nonny forced a smile. "Guess I'll see you tomorrow then." She reached for the door handle.

"That'd be a good time for you and Mack to catch up on old times, wouldn't it?" Ruby smiled broadly, but the smile faded as quickly as it had appeared. "It's just that . . . Well, I always pictured things turning out different. I wonder to this day what went wrong, what could've caused you two to break up— Oh, there I go, turning sour again."

Nonny put a smile on her face that felt as authentic as margarine.

Ruby paused, looking thoughtful. "Speaking of throwing away useless mail, I'd like it if you'd throw away anything comes addressed to Grace Anderson. Just throw it in the trash with those Christmas flyers."

"But, don't you want to forward it on to her? First-class mail be forwarded."

"You got an address for Hell?" Ruby snapped. "Because as far as I know, that's where she is!" As the words left her mouth, Ruby's face flushed bright red. "Oh, I'm so sorry I said that, Nonny. Just throw anything else to her that comes in the trash. Okay?"

Nonny frowned. "I can't do that, Ruby. I wasn't serious about throwing the flyers away. I'd like to, but I can't break the law."

Ruby sighed. "You always were a good girl. I shouldn't have asked you to bend the rules. Let's just let this whole business go. I'd never break John Law's rules or ask anyone else to." She hesitated, her eyes clouding. "You suppose Mack's broke the law, Nonny? I sometimes wonder if he does his kind of work because he's on the lam from something bad."

A yell from Sister saved Nonny from a need to reply, but she heard her conscience *ping* as she waved to the departing sisters. I can't speak for Mack breaking John Law's rules, she thought, but I've sure as hell broken a few of another kind.

*****

At the back door of the Piggly Wiggly, Nonny loaded a crate of wilted carrots and sack of potatoes on the verge of rot, a half-bushel of limp green beans and bag of sprouting onions, and drove to the Homeless Shelter on Choctaw Street. The old stone building started life as a grocery, migrated to hardware, then to derelict. It now served those in the same situation. The homeless, the drifters, the down and outers.

The rear door opened as she pulled to the back of the building and a scruffy bearded man came toward her, smiling. Chester Barnes. The administrator, coordinator, janitor, and general-all-around flunky that ran the place.

Nonny had met Chester at Norman, where she had taught English and he taught philosophy. His outgoing manner and sense of humor made him popular with his students, but a late-in-life situation that disclosed a side of Chester he'd kept closeted made him unpopular with the administrators of a university in the middle of the Bible Belt. He came out of the incident bearing scars inflicted by a gang of "straight-laced heteros," as he called heterosexuals, a heightened appreciation for tenure, and fewer friends. After retirement, he decided to give back to the community rather than live the remainder of his life vicariously watching TV soaps. He returned to McAlester about the same time as Nonny had.

"I about give up on you," he called out.

"Christmas flyers," she yelled back. She opened the backend so he could retrieve the produce. "Have to cull some of this stuff, but looks like there's enough for a good-size pot of soup."

"Good! I got a pot ready to go, but it's crowded tonight. We'll need another pot later. Cold weather up north's driving people south." The barrel-chested man set the crate of vegetables on the ground, closed the rear hatch, and looked at Nonny expectantly. "Don't suppose I could talk you into helping out. People get busy this time of year, so I'm left shorthanded. You up to ladling soup?"

Nonny snorted. "You know the answer to that one. You want, I can peel and chop this stuff and put it on to cook. But that's all I can handle today."

"Today?" White teeth glinted through gray scruff.

Nonny shot him a look. "Today, tomorrow, and the day after that," she snapped. "I figured by this time you'd know better than to ask." She studied the still-grinning man. "What's up, Chester? Just say what's on your mind, I hate it when you get cute with me."

He folded his hands as if seeking absolution. "I'm thinking that if I keep asking, one of these days you'll come clean with me."

"Clean?"

"You know, tell me why you can't look into the faces of these young drifters."

"Wha—what?"

"Especially, young *women* drifters."

Nonny's back stiffened. "Think you're pretty clever, don't you? I expected more from you, Chester. Do I stick my nose into your *affairs*?"

Chester feigned a wince and kept on smiling. "Difference is, I'm not running away from my affliction of the flesh. When are you gonna face up to your affliction of the mind, or psyche, or soul, or whatever the hell it is? Take it from one who knows, Nonny. You can run but you can't hide."

"You want help or not?" she growled, making a move toward the Jeep.

"Hold up—hold up." Chester Barnes did the palms-together business again. "You're on. You cook and I'll serve."

Nonny followed Chester inside. An improvised kitchen had been converted from the storeroom of the old store and fitted out with donations begged off the Salvation Army. He immediately disappeared through a door to another room, larger and set up with tables and beds. She heard him in conversation with people, the clink of soup bowls being filled, and turned her back on the commotion.

Washing up at the sink, she grabbed an apron off a hook on the wall and set to work with a paring knife, trying to push Chester's less-than-subtle philosophizing out of her mind. She knew he meant well, for the man didn't have a mean bone in his body. He was a caregiver to his core.

She lost track of time, scraping carrots limp as noodles, rubbing skins off onions pushing new sprouts out the end, and scrubbing green beans that looked as though they'd been shat on by a bomb squad of crows. But in the end, she failed to shut down the noise in her mind.

"It's their eyes, Chester," she mumbled, hacking eyes from potatoes as though wielding a hatchet. "I looked and looked for that little girl with eyes like mine until I just couldn't handle it anymore, so . . . " She paused, breathing deep. "I gave up."

CHAPTER TWELVE

Ruby packed the picnic basket with paper plates, plastic eating utensils, and the double batch of brownies she'd stirred up that morning. While she felt optimistic about the day, she had growing concerns on another matter. Her memory.

"I just know I told you about Abe Folsom passing." She looked at Mack, who was studying the picture of his grandfather and his mules that he had pulled from her photo album. "You sure I didn't tell you about Abe?"

She waited expectantly for her son's response, feeling positive that she had told him. But then, she reminded herself, she'd also thought she'd told Nonny that Mack was in town. What was happening? Her eyes had grown a little weaker but her hearing was still good. Was her mind going ahead of her ears? That wasn't the order it was supposed to happen.

"You put nuts in those brownies?" Sister asked. She was pushing deviled egg filling into the whites of boiled eggs with a teaspoon.

Ruby stared at her. "Nuts?"

"I recall now you did say something about Abe." Mack slipped the picture into his shirt pocket. "Think it was in one of your letters."

Ruby let out a sigh of relief on the one matter, then addressed the other. "I'm sorry, Sister, didn't have any nuts. Pound of shelled walnuts is right at five dollars now."

"That's not what surprised me," Mack said.

Ruby looked toward her son. "No?"

Before Mack could answer, Sister spoke up again. "Wasn't wanting you to put nuts *in* them. George Folsom don't have a tooth in his head and won't wear his teeth. Lot of people wear dentures. Figured you'd know that."

Ruby felt like one of the bobble-headed dolls she'd seen on the dashboards of cars. She only had enough attention for one person at a time and debated which one to give it to. Mack won out.

"Oh. You're talking about Nonny moving back home." She dried her hands on her apron and studied her son's face. "What's so surprising about that?"

"How'd that come to pass?"

She rubbed at her forehead. "I could've sworn I wrote you about her picking up the contract on Abe's route . . . or maybe it was when we talked on the phone. Anyway, he had another year to run on it when he died, so she finished out that year and then renewed the contract."

"Just left off teaching school," Mack said, more a comment than a question.

"That's right, going on three years now." As Ruby filled his cup again, she noticed the skepticism on his face. "What's so surprising about that? Sometimes people come back home."

“To deliver mail?” Mack snorted. “Others, maybe.” He pulled the photograph from his pocket, stared at it some more, then said, “How’s she look?”

“Who . . .?” Ruby glanced at the picture in Mack’s hand, studying the two mules. “Oh—you’re talking about Nonny again. She looks good, real good. Held her figure right well. Course, that job helps keep her trim but . . . Well, the girl’s carrying a heavy burden.”

“Burden?” Mack looked up at her. “Abe leave a mortgage? How can that be? He was a member of the Nation, probably got that place free and clear with his Choctaw allotment.”

Ruby rubbed her head some more. “Well now, George gets an Indian allotment so Abe probably did, too.” Why am I having so much trouble keeping things straight these days? she wondered.

“He makes hooch out in those backwoods,” Sister said.

Mack looked at her. “You telling me George still makes his special recipe?”

“Now Sister,” Ruby said, “you don’t know that for a fact—”

“That’s *exactly* what I’m telling you,” Sister said. She looked at Mack and laughed.

When Mack responded in kind, Ruby shook her head. Sometimes she felt as though she were wading in quicksand.

She handed a package of paper napkins to Sister. “Here, fold these. If you’re done with those eggs, might as well make yourself useful.” She turned to Mack again. “That’s not the kind of burden I was talking about. Something—or maybe somebody—hurt that girl after she went away to school. What do you suppose it could be, Mack? I thought on it and thought on it and I can't come up with what it might be."

"None of my business, Mama." Mack scraped his chair away from the table. "Or yours either, for that matter."

"Why Mack Barlow. You always thought the sun rose and set with Nonny."

"I'll get the car ready to go," he said, pushing open the screened door. "Talking to George was a good idea. Meet you outside."

Ruby walked to the kitchen window and watched her son as he pulled her sedan around to the back door.

"Something's bothering Mack," Sister said, not looking up from her napkin folding.

"So you noticed it, too," Ruby murmured, still watching Mack. "I hardly slept last night, wondering where he went yesterday morning . . ."

*****

A grove of redbuds rolled across the hills behind the Scipio Baptist Church, cutting straight lines around patches of newly broken ground, curved lines along creek bottoms. Two meadowlarks called out to each other and then to meadowlarks in other places, who took up the song. Meadowlarks were Ruby's favorite bird for, unlike other birds, they stayed year round. Ruby listened to their music now, feeling thankful that some creatures did not migrate to far places.

Mack set the picnic basket on one of the long tables covered in oilcloth, then left to scout out George Folsom, which did not take long. Ruby unloaded the basket, watching her son from a distance. From the way George acted, she could tell that he expected to see Mack there, and she figured Nonny had told him of Mack's mission to find Bill and Jack.

She also knew that if anyone would remember where Pa buried his mules, George would. She watched anxiously for his reaction, saw him look at the photo Mack pulled from his pocket, and sighed in relief when his head began to shake.

"Maybe my loophole's gonna hold," she murmured.

Ruby put her mind on getting Sister settled. Her mouth was working overtime these days and Ruby felt a need to corral her ramblings. She was glad to find that a table had been set up inside the church for those who found it too cool to sit outdoors.

"Here you go, the perfect spot." She led Sister inside where three of their Anderson cousins, all sisters, were seated. "Out of the cool wind and next to family."

Hurrying back outside, Ruby caught up with Nonny, who was setting out a large macaroni-and-cheese casserole. Nonny had traded her usual blue jeans and chambray shirt for a long dark skirt, a turtleneck, and flat-soled suede boots. Her glistening dark hair and skin and eyes as yellow as precious metal put Ruby in mind of a raven. The color of her sweater was a perfect match for her eyes and Ruby hoped the choice was intentional, meant to help rekindle the flame with Mack.

Her heart fluttered at the thought. Never did she imagine that her son would spend his life alone. A person needed a mate, someone to see them through hard times, and children to see to their care in old age. That was the natural order of things. She had been robbed of the mate, had born only one child—an unmarried child—but perhaps she could fix things. Maybe it wasn't too late for grandchildren. Abraham's wife Sarah had been old, she thought. Real old when she had Isaac.

Ruby set her tray of deviled eggs next to Nonny's casserole. "My, that casserole looks good, and it'll be easy to eat."

"That's what I figured." Nonny placed a serving spoon in the casserole. "No need for knives. Your eggs look delicious, too." She picked up a deviled egg and bit into it. "*Very* good," she said, licking her fingers.

"And I made brownies—no nuts. Some folks can't chew nuts, you know." Ruby paused. "You seen Mack yet? He's over there showing people a picture Pa and his mules, hoping someone will recognize the place. He hasn't changed much, has he? Still looks the same as when you two were dating."

Nonny took her time answering. "Looks like a swinging door took him by surprise. His nose used to be straighter, as I recall. Helluva scar, too. How'd that happen?

"He won't talk about it. He's as bad as Pa when it comes to accounting for things."

"At least he hasn't developed a beer belly like a lot of others, if you get my drift." Nonny indicated a man wedging his body onto a bench at a table.

"Billy Joe has put on weight, hasn't he? And his daddy and grandpa are thin as sticks. Sister thinks it's because they're alcoholics. Don't know why she dislikes them so." She turned to look at Nonny. "But Mack works his weight off, just like you. Neither of you is afraid of a little hard work. Why, you're a perfect match." She smiled encouragingly.

"Doesn't look like anyone can remember anything." Nonny stared intently at the men's table.

Ruby followed Nonny's eyes once more. The picture of her father and his mules was working itself around the table, causing a lot of head scratching.

"That's my ace in the hole," she breathed. "Maybe no one will remember" The more people that looked at the picture, the stronger Ruby's curiosity grew. "Come on," she said. "Let's fix a plate and go listen in."

"Sit with the men?" Nonny gestured toward the table where the women had congregated. "Betty Winslow's saving a place for you over there. I talked with her earlier, she said she'd hold you a spot."

"Not today. I'm a little nervous that someone's gonna remember that place in the picture, though to me it looks like a hundred-and-one other places."

"Can't," Nonny said. "I need to sit inside so I can keep an eye on the older people. But you go ahead, sit with Mack if you want."

Ruby grabbed Nonny's arm to prevent her from walking away. "There's others can see to that today. I refuse to be the only woman sitting at that table with a bunch of men talking mules!"

"But I wasn't planning on staying that long, I have other things to do—"

"Something's going on with Mack, Nonny. Sister even noticed it. *Please*."

Nonny hesitated, frowning. "I think you're worrying for nothing. It's a long shot he'll find those mules. Mack's probably thinking it would content Pa if he just made an attempt to find them."

"I'm not talking about this Bill-and-Jack thing—he's keeping something from me. I hardly slept a wink last night worrying about it." Ruby felt her neck and face grow warm. "I'm getting a bad feeling, *real* bad."

"Ease up, Ruby." Nonny took Ruby's arm. "You had your blood pressure taken lately?"

"My blood pressure's fine, checked it at the Walmart just yesterday. Why won't you believe me when I say something's not right?"

"All right," Nonny said, sighing. "We'll sit with them, but you're doing the talking."

Ruby smiled her thanks. She and Nonny fixed a plate of food and walked toward the table. Like a row of dominoes, the men fell over themselves to make room.

"What's that you were saying, Billy Joe?" Ruby said. They had interrupted an argument triggered by the photo Mack had brought. "I missed part of it."

"We were talking about where these mules might've been buried. I was telling Mack that you can't go and bury a dead animal anywhere. Now, if you *own* the property, that's one thing, but to my knowledge, old man Anderson never owned a lick of anything in his life. Idn't that right, Mack?"

Ruby saw the redness creeping up her son's neck and knew it was time for her to step in. "That's right, Billy Joe. Pa sharecropped all his life."

"Just like my daddy did," Luther Winslow snapped. "Worked hisself into an early grave."

"It's a tough way to serve the Lord," George Folsom added. "For a fact.

As the table grew quiet, Billy Joe put his attention on food and the others followed suit. Ruby picked at her plate, her mind on what Billy Joe had said. She found his words troublesome, filled with implications she had not considered. In time, her worries grew too big to hold.

"Are you saying Pa's a criminal, Billy Joe? If he did bury those animals without permission, is he liable to get arrested?"

"That wasn't the point."

"So there's a point to all of this?" Nonny said.

"Well yes, there is—"

"Everyone here knows your folks own most of the land here about," Mack snapped. "If *that's* the point you're making."

"No, that's not the point neither." Billy Joe's face flushed as he looked around the table. "Look, all I was pointing out is that Mack's grandpa would've had to get permission from the owner of the place he put those animals, maybe the county. You can't bury animals where they might contaminate a water supply."

Mack looked at Nonny. "He's making sense . . . if there is such a law."

"I was thinking the same thing," she said. "I'm sure there's a law against burying a person just anywhere. Could be the same for animals."

"So there might be some kind of record," Mack said, turning thoughtful.

Nonny nodded slowly.

Suddenly, Ruby realized that her son and Nonny were talking to each other, just as in days of old. Her heart filled with gladness at the thought, and she began to wonder if there might not be ray of sunshine behind this cloud her father had put over her. Just as quickly, the thought entered her mind that Nonny had gone over to the other side—actually helping Mack find Pa's mules. As if acknowledging her fear, Nonny became even more encouraging.

"It also occurred to me," Nonny said, holding her fork midair, "that the Turners own most of the land around here. So wouldn't old man Turner be the logical one to talk to?"

"You suggesting I go talk to old man Turner?"

Using the fork like a pointer, Nonny said, "Shortest distance between point A and point B, isn't it?"

Ruby's heart began pounding like a drum. This wasn't going the way she intended. "Now hold on, Mack, you know how you feel about old Mr. Turner— No offense, Billy Joe, your grandpa has been real decent to me, but Mack holds a different sentiment."

"No offense taken, Mrs. Barlow. It's no big secret how our families feel toward one another, leastways the old timers." Billy Joe turned to Mack. "You might wanna listen to your mama, Mack. Not a good idea to be bothering my grandpa."

"Looks like I got no other choice. Might as well run by this afternoon. He still live at the same place?"

Every eye at the table turned to Billy Joe.

"Yeah, we're still in the same place," he said, eyes locked on Mack.

The anxiousness in Ruby's chest made a return. She was thinking hard to come up with another argument when Nonny spoke up again.

"It also set me to thinking that there would be other ways to find where Pa lived from year to year." Her eyes blinked as if synchronized with her thoughts. "Wouldn't be any property tax records, since he never owned any, but there's state and federal income tax records, even census records that might give an idea where he lived." Nonny raised her fork again, punctuating the air as if it were a sentence. "Let's see, the Feds took the census every ten years, and the state might have taken a census in between, probably every other year—"

"Now hold on, Mack," Ruby said again. "That could take a lot more time, even a trip to Oklahoma City. And you need to get back to work."

Nonny shook her head. "The Genealogy Society and Courthouse downtown keep a lot of those records now so people can trace their genealogy. I help people trace their family from time to time."

"Genealogy," Ruby repeated, thinking the word sounded an awful lot like genes.

"Damn," Mack murmured. "This could be easier than I thought. Where is this genealogy place?"

"Downtown, near the Masonic Lodge. You can't miss it. But I'm by there every day and could do some checking if you want."

"Tell you what," Mack said. "Let me start with old man Turner. Depending on what I learn from him, may be no need to go that route. Let's keep it in mind as a backup plan."

As though consensus had been reached, everyone put their attention back on food. Except for Ruby. She sat staring at the others, the anxious feeling she felt earlier taking on uncommon weight and bearing down with tremendous force, as though she were a stone sinking into dark water.

"Ruby, you want to say something else?" Luther Winslow looked her direction. "You look like maybe you got something on your mind."

Luther's question turned the attention of the entire table onto Ruby. She looked at all of them, moving from one face to the next. Each was waiting for her to voice what was troubling her. Thoughts jumbled with feelings—resentment, indignation, shame—and she wanted to shout at them to stay out of her family's business. But she couldn't do that. They were her friends and their wives were her customers. She had to pull herself together.

Job, I have the patience of Job, she thought. Many have told me so.

A calmness came over Ruby then, and she put a smile on her face. Putting everything into the Lord's hands, she opened her mouth and waited to hear what came out.

"Anyone ready for dessert?" she said. "I brought brownies, no nuts."

CHAPTER THIRTEEN

It was late afternoon when the dinner-on-the-grounds at the church ended. Mack dropped his mother and aunt off at the house, then proceeded to the Turner's to talk to Washburn Turner, Sr., Billy Joe's grandfather.

Mack was not a happy man. The encounter with Nonny Folsom had been uncomfortable at first, which he expected it would be. But then, it became comfortable—too comfortable. Years and memories fading like a bad dream. As the day wore on, he found himself toying with the idea of rekindling the relationship. Even now, he was confused as to how that had transpired.

"Just like that—" He snapped his fingers to punctuate his thinking. "Twenty years just disappearing," he snorted. "On TV maybe, but this isn't a soap opera."

Why would he do that? he wondered. Consider changing a lifestyle he had worked so hard to construct? He had come to favor his hit-and-run approach to relationships. It worked well with his job and temperament. He made sure the women he did take the time to acquaint himself with knew the facts from the get-go. Which went something like, a good romp in the hay's one thing, expecting to find me next to you the next morning's another. Now, alone and with time to reason through the abruptness of the change toward Nonny, he could find no reasonable explanation. Recalling how the relationship with her had ended those many years ago, he turned sour.

"Just because a bad dream fades away in a day or two, doesn't mean it never happened."

The thought of having to deal with old man Turner added to Mack's ill temper. He drove through paradisal hills with the alertness of one on enemy patrol. In quick time, he found the asphalt driveway leading to the Turner enclave, three low-slung, rambling brick homes situated in a semi-circle. Pulling up the curving drive, he stopped at the largest of the three, one with a wide portico and hand-carved front door.

Before he could turn off the ignition, Mack saw the settled figure of an aged man open the door. As he walked up the stone steps, he looked through a large picture window and caught sight of a small, pink-haired woman sitting in a large wingback chair. He recognized the sharp facial features and fluffy permed hair instantly. Tootsie Turner. The woman looked the same to him as she had when he had been a boy. Overdressed, over made-up, and cocky as hell.

Locking eyes with the woman, he nodded. In response, she lifted a tumbler of amber liquid that he figured to be Southern Comfort or Wild Turkey. It was a well-known fact that the Turners were not abstainers. He considered that he might be invited in for a drink, which would suit him to a T. He was a beer man personally, but he wasn't opposed to knocking back a few shooters. Alcohol of any persuasion made things go down smoother.

"How you doing, Wash?" he asked when he reached the front door. "Looks like you knew I was coming."

"Billy Joe called me on his mobile phone, gave me a heads-up. The old man spoke from behind a heavy storm door. "Afraid I can't be of any help."

Mack nixed the idea of a whiskey neat and he got down to business. Pulling the picture of his grandfather and his mules from his pocket, he pressed it against the glass. "Maybe this would help."

Washburn Turner waved the picture away. "Memory's not what it used to be."

Though he was looking hard at the man at the door, Mack could see another figure in the shadows. What the hell? he wondered, recognizing the profile of Billy Joe.

"Well maybe the picture would jog your memory," he said, pressing the picture against the glass again.

"Won't help a bit." The old man pushed the hand-carved front door closed, saying, "Don't have time to waste on such nonsense." The click of a deadbolt being thrown served as a final exclamation mark for his words.

Mack stared at his reflection in the storm door a bit, then turned toward his truck. Catching one last glance of Tootsie Turner, still holding a tumbler of liquor, before the heavy drapes closed, he wondered who was pulling the curtain strings. Old Washburn or Billy Joe.

Curiosity getting the better of him, he swung wide at the arc in the curved driveway so he could see the rear of the house. He spotted a black GMC near the back entrance that looked similar to one he had seen at the church, one like Billy Joe drive away in. Pulling down the asphalt track, he stopped at the county road, pondering the situation.

"Someone's trying to snooker me," he muttered, "and I aim to find out why." Without warning, Nonny Folsom popped into his mind. Remembering that his mother said she lived in her dad's old place, he wheeled his Bronco that direction.

Fifteen minutes later, Mack pulled down a dirt track that wound through a tangle of trees and undergrowth so thick he had to turn his headlights on bright to see. By the time he pulled into the clearing where an old farmhouse with peeling paint sat, he could feel a wetness between his shoulder blades and smell the sour odor of sweat in his armpits.

He sat for a moment with the window rolled down before exiting the Bronco, breathing the cool air. As he waited, he reconsidered the wisdom of his decision. It would be better to leave right then, to make the drive back through that dark, matted square of space immediately rather than postpone it. The mind could play tricks on a man, especially if he tried to postpone the inevitable, make a mountain out of a molehill. Right now, that dark place was a molehill—

"Who's out there!"

Mack turned to face a slender woman dressed in jeans and a white tee, long hair pulled back in a ponytail, holding what looked to be a single-barrel scattergun. The time for reconnoitering had passed.

"That you, Mack Barlow?"

"Yeah," he called out. "But it's kind of late. Maybe this wasn't such a good idea." He watched Nonny lower the barrel of the gun. There was no mistaking the hesitation in her movements or her voice, as she waved him to the house.

"I, uh, I just put on a fresh pot of coffee, in case you want a cup. Thought you were going out to the Turner's place. How'd you end up here?"

"Yeah, well, I just left there. Something fishy's going on." He turned as he reached the porch, pointing at the track he had just traversed. "You ever give any thought to having that jungle cleared?"

She stared at him.

"Never mind." He walked into a kitchen steaming from fruit jars sterilizing in a pot on the stove and a pan of melting paraffin. "What the hell you doing?"

"Making jelly." She hesitated as she replaced her gun in the rack over the kitchen door. "Well, re-making jelly, to be more accurate." She pointed to large jars of Welch's grape and strawberry jam sitting on the cabinet top. "Oh hell, to be *completely* accurate, I'm rebottling it. I give it to my route customers on the first Friday of the month. They have quite a sweet tooth, especially the older ones. It means more to them if they think it's homemade."

Mack couldn't tell if the blush on Nonny's face was from the steamy kitchen or her confession. When she waved him toward an old, cane-bottomed chair, he took a seat. Tilting it so he could lean against the wall, he took in the sagging cupboards, uneven oak flooring, out-dated appliances, and woman.

"You won't tell anyone, will you?" she said. "They think I make it from scratch."

He tried to suppress a grin. "That legal? Passing off store-bought jelly as homemade?"

"I never gave it much thought." She filled two mugs with coffee and turned introspective. "I worked at a food co-op in Norman and we repackaged lots of things. Peanut butter, flour and meal, things like that. I figure if I sterilize the jars and seal them with hot paraffin, it's safe to give away."

"*Give* away?" Mack took the cup of coffee Nonny offered. "Can't they buy their own? I mean, they've gotta be on Social Security or the Indian dole."

"Yeah, but a lot of them can't get into town and others . . . Well, they still *try* to make their own and that's where the rub comes in." She took a swallow of coffee. "You see, right after I came back, Uncle George showed me this homemade plum jelly that his neighbor lady gave him—you remember the Clarks?"

Mack nodded. "So?"

"*So,* it was full of ants and Uncle George had eaten half the jar! Mrs. Clark's eyes were so bad, she couldn't see them. So I figured store bought would be safer. Geez, who knows what other vermin these old people might be eating and not even know it. Roaches. Silverfish. Flies." She shivered at the thoughts running through her mind.

He stifled a laugh. "Some places I've been, vermin are considered a good source of protein."

She snickered, then turned serious again. "You think there's a chance of botulism?"

"No. No, I don't."

She nodded confidently. "Me either." She fished a steaming Mason jar from a boiling pot and began ladling jelly inside. "You said something was fishy?"

Nonny's question didn't register immediately as Mack was staring at the woman—dampened hair clinging to her neckline, moist tee shirt clinging to her chest—and feeling his skin burn as though he had run through a patch of nettles. Trying to pull up the sour feeling he'd felt earlier, he considered questioning her about her changed lifestyle, her need to make something of herself—as though marrying him wouldn't. But instead, he got up, took a spatula from a stoneware crock sitting on the counter, and began sliding it along the inside of the filled jelly jars.

Sensing Nonny looking at him, he gave her a sideways glance. “You got air bubbles in the jars. I’m getting rid of the air bubbles.”

“I know what you’re doing. I just didn’t think you’d know such things.”

He shrugged. “It comes back.” He nodded toward the jars of jelly, grinning. “Didn’t take you for such things either.”

“It comes back,” she said, grinning, too. “You said something was fishy?”

“Oh, yeah.” Mack related his visit to the Turner place as he and Nonny worked on the jelly. He finished up with, “That beer gut on the guy in the shadows could only belong to one person.”

“And you’re sure Mr. Turner said Billy Joe had telephoned.”

“‘Called me on his mobile, gave me a heads-up.’ That’s what he said, word for word. Besides, it was clear as the nose on your face that Billy Joe had driven straight there from the church grounds. His truck was parked out back. Hell, I bet the engine block was still warm. Now, why would he hide like that? Wouldn’t you think he’d make his presence known? If everything was on the up and up, I mean.”

Nonny nodded slowly. “That does seem strange, even for one of the Turners.”

“And old man Turner wouldn’t even look at the picture. You got any idea what’s going on here?”

“Not a clue. I’ll get to the Genealogy Society tomorrow and see what I can find.” She paused. “From that picture, I figure Sister was, what . . .? Six or seven years old? How old is she now?"

Mack pulled the picture of his grandfather and mules from his pocket. "Probably closer to nine or ten when this was taken. She's always been on the runty side. I figure she's on either side of seventy by a few years."

"Well, all right then, we'll start checking in that timeframe. We should begin with census records, see if we can pin down where Pa lived."

"Okay. I'll check in with you tomorrow. I need to pick up some things for the house in town anyway. That hardware store still open out there on Choctaw Street?"

"*God*, no. Been closed down a long time. But there's a True-Value on the highway, or you could try the Walmart. It carries a little bit of everything."

Silence settled on the kitchen like a fog, and Mack sensed uneasiness in that stillness. "You want me to leave?" he asked.

"What?"

"You got awful quiet."

"I was just thinking of something your mother said today. She wouldn't want me to say anything, but . . . Oh, crap, have you noticed anything unusual with your mama, Mack? Since you've been here, I mean."

"Well . . ." He stopped working on the jelly. "This thing with Pa has her real upset."

"No, that's not it."

Mack pulled up an image of his mother. The bone-tired look on her face. The way she agitated easily. Suddenly, he recalled the postcard. "A postcard came to the house recently addressed to her mother and she seemed upset about it. Matter of fact, she ripped it to shreds. That it?"

Nonny paused. "No, but it is curious." She looked at Mack. "Why'd she do that?"

He shrugged. "You got me."

"Grace is your grandmother, isn't she?"

"*Was* my grandmother," he said. "She's dead, been dead for a long time."

Nonny's eyes began to blink, as if mulling over something. "That's what I always thought, but Claude Riley, the Indianola route driver, said she just disappeared one day." Shc looked at Mack. "What do you know about your grandmother?"

"Not one damn thing. Why? You think that postcard's important?"

"Probably not. Most of the time it means the school hasn't updated their records and they're using her last known address to try to find her . . ."

Mack waited a half minute, waiting for Nonny to say more. When she didn't, he said, "Mama got a health problem she's not telling me about? Is that what you're shooting at?"

"Not exactly, at least not at the moment." She began work on the jelly again.

"Spill it, Nonny," Mack said, not knowing where to go next. "You know I was never good at guessing games."

"All right . . ." Nonny let out her breath. "Ruby thinks you're hiding something from her, Mack, and she thinks it has something to do with her. Not Pa or this Bill-and-Jack thing—but *her*."

"*Damn*." He laid the spatula on the counter and rubbed his mouth.

"Why, you *are* hiding something, Mack Barlow!"

Mack debated whether to tell the truth or lie and decided to lay it on the line. As if driving nails into a plank, he hammered out his intentions to find a safer place for his mother and aunt to live.

"You're moving them to town," Nonny stated, sounding incredulous.

"It's not safe for them to be this far out anymore," Mack said, hurrying to explain. "Especially given their age and physical condition. You hear about the prison break last Friday? I'm working with a realtor up at Henryetta, putting the place up for sale."

"But what about Ruby's business? She's worked hard to build up her clientele and enjoys what she does. I know these women out here. They won't drive into town to get their hair done. She'll lose touch with her friends."

He considered this. "Not that many left, friends and family's dying off. Besides, it's time she quit. She's not a spring chicken anymore. And Sister's even worse off."

"So, what are you looking at then?"

Nonny's hesitation indicated that she realized he was speaking true. He related the options he had looked at the previous day with Roxie Komenski. "I'm leaning toward the gated community. Safest place by far, with a guardhouse and security patrols. And there's lots of stuff for them to do there."

"Stuff," she repeated, fishing another jar from the kettle. "And you haven't told Ruby yet that you're selling the home place?"

"There's time yet. The realtor is still working out the details. Anyway, I need to get the old place ready to flip. You know, fix it up a little—"

"Or asked her opinion on where *she'd* like to live?"

Mack hesitated, wondering why he hadn't thought to do that. It's because I'm the one that knows what's best for her, he decided. Her behavior today was a clear indication of that. What the hell difference does it make if brownies have nuts in them? Besides which, that route would've taken more time—time he didn't have because he needed to haul ass back to the Panhandle. No, this was the right way to go.

"Did you hear what I said, Mack?"

"Yeah, I heard you. And no, I didn't ask her. She's been so upset over this Bill-and-Jack thing, I didn't think the time was right. But I plan to talk to her real soon."

"That would be a good idea, and the sooner the better. She's worrying herself into a state that *will* affect her health."

"First chance I get." He picked up the spatula and began working the jelly again. "You won't tell her before I do, will you?"

"Uh-uh—not on your life, buddy. Wouldn't touch this one with a ten-foot pole."

Nonny's body language told Mack more than her words did. "You don't think much of the idea, do you?"

"None of my business."

"I'm just trying to do the right thing," he said, feeling a need to break through her coolness.

"I know." Brushing aside a lock of dark hair, she looked at him.

Mack turned away from those hypnotic eyes, which right then looked hard as agates, searching for other things to focus on. He found a broken lock on the kitchen window and a missing deadbolt on the back door, then looked at her again. "You, uh, you give any thought to moving away from here yourself?"

"Not once," she said, screwing a lid down tight on a jar.

The air in the kitchen suddenly felt thick as the jelly they worked on. “That single shot’s not much protection—”

“Not for love nor money.”

“You don’t even have a dog.”

She turned hard eyes to him. “They’ll have to haul my ass out of here in a box. This place is my salvation.”

What the hell? Mack looked at the woman standing next to him as though she were a stranger, someone he had chanced upon out on the Indian Nations Turnpike while traveling to another place in a different time. And he could not help but wonder what had spun Nonny Folsom around a hundred-and-eighty-degrees.

CHAPTER FOURTEEN

The phone rang late on Sunday evening. Even before she reached for the receiver, Ruby picked up a pencil and opened her appointment book to the next week's calendar. Most calls dealt with hair appointments, even those that came at night and on weekends because she made it clear to her customers that she was there to accommodate their needs. In her opinion, it didn't take an MBA to figure out that the customer came first in a service industry. Because she took pride in being a professional businesswoman, she had even come up with a positioning statement for her business card: *When Your Hair Gets U Down, Let Ruby Smarten U Up. Hours: 24/7.*

Recognizing the voice on the phone now, she smiled. She could use some extra money, and this caller promised an extra booking. She listened for a minute, then dropped the pencil onto the counter. Hanging up the phone, she stood stock-still, staring into space.

"Who's calling this time of night?" Sister asked. "It's going on nine o'clock."

"Tootsie Turner." Ruby did not move from the phone.

"She need to change her hair appointment for tomorrow?"

"Tootsie's appointments are on Friday," Ruby mumbled. "She's had a standing appointment for twenty-some years now."

"That's so she'll look good at the Eastern Star meetings on Saturday. Tootsie always did like to put on the dog. She and Grace would spend hours primping in front of the mirror."

Ruby gave Sister a sharp look. "Now, how would you know that? And what's with all this talk about Grace? I never heard you talk so much about her before."

Sister returned the look. "Did you forget which box your brains are in? I'm talking because I *can*, that's why. Pa never allowed us to speak of her before, you know that. But he's not here now, so I'm talking."

Ruby sighed. "I suppose that's right."

"Well, anyways, Grace and Tootsie were best friends."

"My goodness, in all these years, Tootsie never mentioned that." Ruby shook her head slightly. "She never talked about Grace at all."

"Why's she changing to Mondays? Her hair will be a mess by the weekend."

Ruby tried to quell the tension building in her chest. "She's *not* changing to Mondays."

"What'd she want then?"

"To *cancel* her appointment."

"Then why's she calling tonight," Sister said irritably. "Plenty of time before next Friday, it's close to nine o'clock—"

"No Sister— Tootsie's canceling her appointment for good."

"For good . . ." She stared at Ruby. "Why'd she go and do that for? She's had a standing appointment twenty-some years now?"

"I don't know, Sister, I don't know!" Ruby began to wonder what had transpired between Mack and the Turners. To wonder if Mack had insulted them again as he had done after Will died. To wonder if that was the reason Tootsie had canceled her appointments. That's it, she decided, it's Mack, he's the cause. Stomping to the back porch, she fetched the picnic basket and removed the dirty dishes. Squirting dish soap into hot water, she began to scrub them with a vengeance.

"Want I should dry," Sister asked.

"No, sit there and rest. You got to be tired. I know I am."

"How could I be tired? Been sitting on my butt all day."

Ruby breathed deep, reaching for a measure of patience. "You have a good time visiting with the cousins?"

"No, I didn't. Bessie Anderson's deaf as a post. Had to yell to make myself heard. She didn't even know we were looking for Bill and Jack. She remembers them well enough."

"You told Bessie . . ." Ruby's shoulders sagged. The story would be all over the county before morning.

"And Bessie's older sisters was dull as dirt, always have been. I had to do most of the talking. Tired me out altogether."

"Well then, go to bed. I'm gonna wait up for Mack, see what happened out there."

Sister paused. "What happened out where?"

Ruby mentally kicked herself. She had deliberately not told Sister where Mack was going and now she had let the cat out of the bag.

"I misspoke," she said hurriedly. "Mack had some errands to run in town." Lord help, she thought, now I've given over to lying.

"Errands on a Sunday?" Sister said. "Can't buy much on a Sunday, what with them Blue Laws that make you sign a piece of paper swearing what you're buying's a matter of life or death. Like buying a Coca-Cola's gonna save somebody's life. Who do they think they're fooling? Just another way to keeps tabs on us. Blue laws. Tapping our phones. Spies in the sky. If people would keep the Lord's Day, wouldn't need dumb laws."

Ruby reached deeper. "They did away with those laws years ago, Sister. You just forgot."

"They did? Well, doesn't matter. Supposed to keep the Lord's day on Sunday, not fiddle fart around buying Coca-Cola. Shouldn't Mack be home by now? Stores are all closed up."

"He'll be home directly. You go on now, I'll be in soon to check on you."

"Thought we got everything there was to get yesterday at the Walmart. Don't know what he'd be shopping for—"

"For God's sake, Sister—would you shut up!" Seeing the startled look on Sister's face Ruby wished she'd been born mute. "I'm so sorry, Sister, I didn't mean that."

Sister's voice sounded thin. "I was just trying to understand why Mack needed to buy Coca-Cola when we got soda pop in the fridge. Is that too much to ask?"

"No, of course not." Ruby felt a tightness in her throat. "This thing with Tootsie's got me upset, that's all. Why do you think she would cancel out on me that way? She was my oldest and best customer."

Sister scratched at a mole on her arm. "Tootsie always was one to go off half-cocked. Grace, too."

Ruby considered this. "Tootsie does have a temper. I've seen it from time to time."

"What one couldn't think of, the other would."

"But she tipped good, Tootsie did. Real generous. Five dollars for a color-and-cut, ten for perm."

"I'd bc glad she's gone, was me. We'll get by, always have."

Ruby nodded. "We have now, haven't we?"

"You're looking tired, Ruby. You should get to bed yourself."

"I will directly. You go on."

After Sister went to bed, Ruby went back to scrubbing dishes, wishing she could scour her life as clean so easily. Here she was, keeping things from her sister just as her son was keeping things from her. She began to question why she hadn't just told Sister where Mack had gone. It was that call from Tootsie, she decided. It had caught her off guard.

And what was the truth, the *real* truth, behind that call? Why would Tootsie act that way? Was there a secret there, too? Like the one Mack was keeping? What had made him go north at the Y in the road instead of south? All these secrets were bound to be at a price.

Wondering how her life had become a shamble, Ruby decided it was because of one person's fool request. And the upshot was that person was her father, the man who had been the underpinning of her life since her husband had died and her son had moved away. Pa had been the one to set these dominoes falling around her with that fool affidavit, not caring one bit about the consequences such a thing would bring.

Hadn't it begun already? Tootsie Turner's canceled appointment might be the first of many dominoes to fall. And then what? How would she and Sister get by now that Pa's Social Security check had been signed away and Mack's construction job wasn't bringing in as much money?

As Ruby dried her hands and started for the front room to work on mailbags, she thought of Nonny, how she had gone over to the other side—actually volunteering to help find those mules. Remembering the events of the day, she felt her face flush hot as if it were August instead of November. Mack and Nonny had taken the entire matter right out of her hands, leaving her to look like a foolish old woman in front of all those men.

Suddenly, she felt a sinking in her chest, and in the next minute, she was overcome with fatigue. Leaning against the wall to rest, she speculated on what Mack might have said to make the Turners so angry. She wanted to pin his ears to the wall the minute he walked through the front door, demand he apologize to the Turners, one and all . . .

Ruby's mind stumbled as she remembered that she'd done that once before. Mack had stayed out with his high-school friends and she and Sister had driven all over McAlester looking for him. They found them at two o'clock that morning, pushing a car run out of gas down the highway, laughing and talking as if it was the most ordinary thing in the world to do. He had not argued when she called him to the car but had smart-mouthed her as he crawled into the back seat. She had popped him a good one on the ear, she remembered.

Suddenly, Ruby was overcome with remorse, recalling the one and only time she had laid a violent hand on her son, on anyone for that matter. But when all was said and done, he'd apologized. Not just to her but to Sister as well.

"I'll do it again, too," she said. "And after he apologizes to the Turners, I'll march him down to the nursing home to talk some sense into his grandfather about this Bill-and-Jack thing."

Oh Lord, she thought, what if it's too late. What if Wash Turner told him where to find those mules?

Ruby envisioned laying her father out between two long-eared, soulless creatures in an unholy piece of ground and knew, should it come to that, she would have no choice but to comply. For her own father had made her the Assignee in that affidavit and she could not break the law, now could she?

"Loopholes," she mumbled breathlessly, "I need more loopholes."

She hurried to the bedroom where Mack kept his things, feeling an urgent need to look again at the affidavit her father had drawn up. Nonny was smart, she thought, but she might have missed something. Like a revolving door, Ruby's mind went again to the way Nonny had changed her allegiance. Could a person that would do such a thing be trusted, she wondered, even if she did bring them persimmons and paid them well for piecework?

"Why, I doubt she read the blamed thing at all." Entering her son's bedroom, Ruby turned on the light and scanned the dresser top for the affidavit. Not finding it there, she rummaged through dresser drawers, closing them when the document did not surface.

"Where is it? I don't remember Mack taking the blamed thing with him today." Ruby brushed fingertips across her forehead, recalling that the only thing he had in his pocket was the picture of his grandfather with his mules, which got passed around the table like it was a postcard from Disneyland. Remembering the picture, she thought about the photo album and wondered if Mack had left the affidavit inside it by mistake. She opened the closet door, looked at the shelf where the album lay, and saw a manila envelope.

"Why, where'd that come from?"

Knowing the envelope could only be Mack's, Ruby hesitated, for she did not want to jeopardize the trust that had grown between her and her son over the years. Then, reminding herself that she was the Assignee on the affidavit and so had every right to look for it, she reached to the top shelf.

Ruby walked into the living room where she could rest in her rocker and look for loopholes. She studied the return address on the envelope a full minute before the significance sunk in.

"A realty in Henryetta? But Henryetta's north . . ."

Opening the envelope slowly and with trembling fingers, Ruby pulled a legal-looking document from the envelope and began to read.

*****

Sometime later, she did not know how long, Ruby saw headlights through the front window. When Whitey let out a yelp, she knew it was Mack come home. By that time, she had read most of the way through the listing agreement and felt no need to finish it. She got up out of the rocker, picked up the manila envelope, and replaced the agreement inside. Walking back to her son's bedroom, she quickly returned it to the closet shelf where she had found it.

She did not check on Sister as she made her way to her own bedroom. She pulled off her day clothes as she went and pulled on her nightclothes in darkness. She was in bed when she heard Mack and Whitey walk through the front door and made no sound as she listened to the night noises of a man preparing for bed or respond when her son walked to her bedroom door.

"Mama?" Mack whispered.

Ruby slowed her breathing to that of a sleeping person, waiting out the minute that elapsed as her son stood in the doorway and the next as he made his way to his own room. Unaware of time, she stared at the pitch-black ceiling, refusing to allow a single thought inside her head. Then she felt a presence.

Whitey's breathing was as familiar as her own. She was not surprised to find him beside her bed, to feel his moist nose nudging at her arm, for it was his way to do such things, especially when he sensed that she was troubled with thoughts or fretting with worry.

But Ruby found no solace in his presence this night. So she rose from her bed and led the dog to the doorway and closed him out, closed Mack out, closed everyone out. For she was not her father and could not bear the thought of being alone in the infinite darkness with soulless creatures.

CHAPTER FIFTEEN

Smelling coffee, Mack dressed and made his way to the kitchen. He was surprised to find Sister standing at the counter, still in her housecoat with her hair uncombed, buttering toast. "You're up early, Sister."

"Heard you stirring around, figured you'd be hungry. How many pieces you want? Can't do more than one myself. Stomach's shrunk, along with everything else."

"Whatever you got there's fine." Mack took the plate of toast and began to eat. "Where's Mama?"

"Sleeping. I stuck my head in the door earlier. Still out like a light."

He washed toast down with a swallow of coffee and glanced toward his mother's bedroom. "Maybe I should check on her."

"Wouldn't wake her, I was you. Seemed real tired last night."

"She been feeling okay?" Mack recalled the concern Nonny had expressed about his mother's health. "She complained about not feeling good, been to the doctor more than usual?"

"Ruby goes to the doctor less than anybody I know. Complains less than anyone I know, too. Till lately."

"Lately," he repeated. "Oh, you mean this thing with Pa."

"It's loosened her threads good, for the life of me I don't know why." She turned suddenly to face Mack. "She even got riled at me last night—first time she's ever done that."

"Well, I'll just stick my head in the door on my way out, see if she wants me to pick up anything. I need to get to town early."

"Town?" Sister gave him a look. "Can't believe you didn't get all your errands run last night—and you forgot the Coca-Cola."

Mack rubbed his face, wondering if his mother's concerns about Sister might be well grounded. "Maybe I should stick around. Mama might need to see a doctor."

Sister gave a quick wave with her hand. "No need for that. Ruby's tired, not sick. Besides, she's got a haircut later this morning. Hasn't missed an appointment in twenty-some years . . . Oh, I just remembered what tired Ruby out last night."

Mack rinsed his plate and coffee mug at the sink. "What's that?"

"Tootsie Turner called and canceled her Friday appointment for good. She won't be coming back no more."

"Last night? Tootsie called last night?"

"Was almost nine o'clock! Had a standing appointment for twenty-some years. Don't that beat all?"

"Yeah, it does at that . . ."

"Ruby was real upset." Sister stirred cream and sugar into her coffee with a fury. "She probably didn't sleep a wink because of that hussy."

Mack couldn't help but grin. "So Grace wasn't the only tart, huh?"

Sister's eyes went round. "Oh, Tootsie's worse than Grace ever was—totes a gun. Least she did back then. She hails from Texas, you know. Fort Worth, I think. Or maybe it was Dallas. Those Texas gals pack six-shooters in their pocketbooks."

He picked up his jacket. "You need some help with your clothes or anything?"

"Course not," Sister said, puffing up. "Ruby's the one thinks I need help. I just humor her because it makes her feel better."

Mack let out a grunt. "That's what I figured. I'll stick my head in her room on the way out. And in case she's not awake, tell her I won't be home till late, so there's no need to fix a big meal tonight."

"All right then. Don't forget the Coca-Cola this time."

"Yes ma'am."

"And don't sign anything. They did away with those Blue Laws years ago."

Mack laughed as he made his way down the hallway. Then he sobered, internalizing his concern for the safety of his mother and aunt. Opening the bedroom door a crack, he peered inside the darkened room.

"Mama?" he said, talking softly. He listened to the breathing coming from the bed. He wanted his mother to be awake so he could talk to her about the patio home. He had planned to do it the previous night, but she had been sound asleep when he got in.

"Mama?" he said, louder this time. But his mother did not stir. He eased the door closed and stood for a moment, gathering his thoughts. The sooner he could show his mother one of the patio homes, the sooner he could put these kinds of concerns to rest. Deciding to call Roxie Komenski while he was in town to see what progress she'd made with the builder, he went to his bedroom to retrieve the packet of information she'd given him.

She'll want me to sign that Intent to Sell, he thought, taking the packet from the closet. He walked down the hall, thinking of the fast-talking realtor, and was swearing as he opened the front door.

"By God, I'll sign this damn thing when she does right by me," he said, "and not a minute before." The door slammed behind him.

*****

Mack snapped his flannel-lined jacket to his chin and turned up the collar, but the light coat made a thin barrier to the crisp morning air. The leaves were dropping faster now, revealing gnarled trunks sheathed in gray velvet. But still, the denseness of the undergrowth made him uncomfortable. He focused on the caliche-covered road, only giving Big Mac the slightest glance as he passed it by. It looked dismal in the morning light. Like a one-night stand the morning after, he reflected. Harsh and oppressive. How had his father stood working there? he wondered.

He made do, he thought. Hell, isn't that what 99% of us do? Daddy always wanted to farm his own land and when that possibility passed him by, he found the next best thing that would make a living for his young family. He had worked outside the prison's walls, managing the prison farm.

Mack drove straight through town, planning to stop on Highway 69 where he remembered seeing a pay phone. Within ten minutes, he was talking to Roxie Komenski.

"I said I'd give you a call in a couple of days." He stood outside the Seven-Eleven talking over the noise of semis running down the road, people filling gas tanks, and Willie Nelson's Texas twang coming over a loudspeaker. He leaned in close to the phone to hear better. "Well, it's been a couple of days. You talk to that builder yet?" He grimaced, hearing the woman express the need for him to sign the listing agreement.

"No, I don't have time to get it to you today. Besides which, you need to make some corrections on it." Hearing silence on the other end, Mack hurried on. "We agreed to six percent, not seven. And you got the place underpriced—*way* underpriced."

The realtor found her voice and he had to concentrate to keep up.

"Roof doesn't need replacing," he said when she paused. "Those shingles got a lot of life yet. Might wanna ask that guy who climbed on the roof what he was smoking." He listened some more.

"What other things?" He took a pencil from his pocket, pulled up the phone book hanging from a chain, and scribbled notes on the outside cover. Suddenly, he stopped to interrupt the woman. "You wanna slow down? My ears can't listen as fast as you're talking. Did you say the foundation needed fixing because the floors are sagging? How would you know that if you didn't go into the house?"

He listened a bit longer, then interrupted the realtor again.

"So let me get this straight. You're making assumptions based on the age of the house." Mack let the phone book drop on its chain and stuck the pencil back into his pocket. "I fixed that foundation when I bought the place and those floors don't sag, all of which confirms what I just said. You got the place underpriced— No, you listen to me. That'd be a great place for a family with kids and animals. There's a good stand of grass on the back twenty, good mix for ponies. Best in the county. My grandpa makes a profit on it every year. You including that as a selling point?"

The realtor made conciliatory noises.

"Well, I figure it's worth at least twenty, twenty-five thousand more. That's what I mean by underpriced. What did the comps show?"

Mack sucked in air that reeked of gas and diesel as Roxie Komenski shuffled through papers. By the time she stopped, he had begun to question that the woman had bothered to run comparables to see what similar properties were bringing.

"Well, maybe you better take another look," he said. "Here's how I see it. If you'd done it right the first time, it wouldn't be taking more of your time. I don't see that as a reason for me to split that extra percent with you."

She went to fast forward again.

Mack rubbed the back of his neck. "Yeah, you *are* the one dealing with the builder, I'll give you that. Tell you what. You see what he'll do on those changes I wanted and we'll see if we can deal on this percent thing." He felt a strong need to retreat but, tethered by the phone cord, was forced to listen some more.

"No, I don't have time to meet with you today to sign this listing," he snapped. "I'll give you a call in a couple of days."

Slamming the receiver, he backed out of the booth. Walking to his Bronco, he searched out a pocket notebook he kept in the glove compartment and returned to the phone. Pulling up the phone book again, he found his handwriting among that of others who had used it in similar fashion. After transferring his notes to his notebook, he stood a bit longer, staring at the yellow-backed phone book for Pittsburg County, Oklahoma, just like the one his grandfather had scribbled names on.

"Just who the hell are those guys, Pa," he mumbled, deciding to visit his grandfather after he finished at the Ace Hardware.

CHAPTER SIXTEEN

Mack loaded the packages from the Ace Hardware into the rear of the Bronco. Hearing a voice, he paused, gripping the plastic bag that held a deadbolt and window-lock replacement.

You sure you ain't moving too fast on this thing, pard . . .

Mack hesitated, wondering where the voice had come from. It took a minute to realize it was from inside his head. Recalling the warmth he sensed coming from Nonny Folsom the night before, he turned argumentative.

"I wasn't imagining it—it was real."

You sure the warmth wasn't coming from you . . .

Mack wanted to argue some more, but too many failed relationships came to mind.

"Aw hell," he muttered. He made his way back inside the Ace, returned the parts, and pocketed the refund.

He was surprised to find Nonny's rusty Jeep at the nursing home. He waved at the old man standing watch at the front door and waited for the intern to release the lock. He nodded at the men and women that lined the hallway, all looking at him like they were at a parade and he was the lead float, but he did not see Nonny.

He pulled up short when he walked through the door to his grandfather's room. Nonny was seated in a chair next to Henry Carter's bed. She looked just as surprised to see him, which Mack reasoned explained her fumbling the concealment of a bag of candy. At that moment, he knew who Henry's gumdrop conspirator was.

"It's okay," Henry told her. "He won't tell on us. This here's Mack Barlow, Mr. Anderson's grandson."

"We've met," she said.

Mack repeated her words silently, absorbing their coolness and thinking be had done right returning those hardware parts. He took the empty chair next to his grandfather's bed, glad to see him sitting up and looking alert.

"How you feeling, Pa?" The old man was working on finishing a bowl of pudding. "You need help with that?"

"Don't have *both* feet in the grave," Grover Anderson snapped. "I'm capable of feeding myself."

Mack grinned. "Yes sir, I can see that."

"You ain't found 'em yet?"

"Don't know where to look. You remember where you buried them?"

Grover Anderson rubbed thin fingers across the pale skin on his forehead. "I lost that memory . . ."

Mack pulled the photo from his pocket and placed it into his grandfather's hands.

"That's Bill and Jack." He handed the photograph back to Mack.

"Yes sir. You remember where you buried them?" he asked again.

Grover rubbed his forehead some more. "We lost track of them graves. Pained me terrible to leave them lay in foreign soil like that."

"Foreign soil?" Nonny said from across the room.

Noticing Nonny's eyes moving as if she were watching an action scene in a picture show, Mack said, "What's your thinking?"

"Just seems a strange choice of words."

"Well, I figure he meant on someone else's property." He paused. "You don't agree?"

She shrugged. "I'm not disagreeing with you, just trying to do deconstruction."

Deconstruction. Mack tried translating the word in light of what he knew in the building trade. "I'm in construction," he said. "Not salvage."

Nonny ducked her chin. "It's a method I used to teach for analyzing language, looking for hidden meaning behind the words . . ." She waved a hand dismissively. "Forget it. You're probably right, which means you still have to find where he lived back then."

You, Mack repeated silently. The previous day, she had used *We*.

Entering the room to remove the lunch trays, the nurse's aide looked at the two elderly men. "Either of you gentlemen need to use the toilet?"

"Mr. Anderson over there might be due," Henry Carter said. "I went before lunch."

"You folks want to step outside a few minutes?" the aide said, looking at Mack and Nonny.

Mack walked to the door, Nonny close behind. They leaned against the wall on opposite sides of the hallway, arms crossed, and avoided looking at each other. "You, uh, you have any luck at that genealogy place?" he asked to fill the silence.

"Haven't been yet. Just finished my mail run before I came by here."

"I see," he said, looking interested. "Say, when you went by our place, did you see any cars there?"

Nonny turned introspective. "Think one of the Andersons was there, don't know which one. They all drive big Buicks. Why?"

"It's probably nothing, but Mama was still in bed when I left. She had someone coming in for a haircut, so sounds like everything's all right."

Nonny raised her eyebrows. "Still in bed? That doesn't sound like Ruby."

Mack scratched at the stubble on his cheek, wishing he'd taken time to shave. "Maybe I'll just go with you to that genealogy place." The moment he spoke, he realized he'd penned Nonny into a corner and tried to backtrack. "Thought it might save some time, but if you think I'd be a drag . . ."

She hunched her shoulders. "Guess two could cover more ground, and I do have other things to do."

"Yeah, that was my thinking."

"Okay then. I need to take care of some business at the Pigg first. How 'bout I meet you there at two o'clock?"

"That'll work."

The nurse's assistant opened the door and indicated Mack and Nonny could return. Nonny said a quick goodbye to Henry and Grover and left.

Watching her leave, Mack's curiosity got the better of him. "What kind of business Nonny have at the Pigg, Henry?"

"What? Oh, she picks up the leftover produce, takes it down to the shelter. She does a lot of things like that."

Mack let out a grunt and noticed the question in Henry's eyes. "I grew up with Nonny. Never figured her for a do-gooder."

"Oh," the man said again. "Well, sometimes people change. Maybe that fella down there had something to do with it."

Picking at his front teeth with a fingernail, Mack said, "That fella?"

"The do-gooder that runs the shelter. He and Nonny taught school over at Norman."

Uh-huh, Mack thought, figuring he had stumbled onto the explanation for Nonny's cool behavior. Nonny was in a relationship. At first, he found the thought disturbing, but then he warmed to it for it meant he could focus on the reason he had come back home without further distractions. And fewer distractions meant he could get back to the big and wide without further *adieu*. He had plenty to focus on in the next few days without any detours. Checking his watch, he rose to leave.

"Take care, Henry. Don't overdo it on those gumdrops." He turned to his grandfather. "Glad you're feeling better, Pa. I need to catch up with Nonny now. We're gonna look for Bill and Jack."

"Bill and Jack's in Beulah Land."

Mack laughed under his breath. As he turned toward the doorway, the word *genes* popped into his head and he began to think there might be something to it if his aunt and grandfather were any indications. Suddenly he felt a pull on his sleeve.

"What is it, Pa?" He bent close.

"I didn't mean to hurt her like that."

Mack exhaled slowly. "I figured that out, Pa. You must've had one of those nightmares."

"Yeah, I tried to talk to her about things, but she wouldn't have none of it. Sensitive type, Grace."

"Grace?" Mack felt his lips numb.

"I forgave her a long time ago for what she did. Bringing her back proved that, don't you think?"

"Bringing her back . . ." Mack tried to sort through the implications of his grandfather's words. The only reason to bring someone back was if they were dead. He forced himself back to his grandfather's question. "I'm sure it did, Pa."

"I've been thinking that maybe she'd listen to me now. Go get her, tell her I want to explain why I did the things I did."

Mack breathed deep. "Who, Pa? Go get who?"

"Grace."

Pausing, Mack said, "I can't, Pa. Grace isn't here." He watched his grandfather's face flush red.

"I know she's not here! Now, you go out to the house and get her! I need to set things right!"

"Easy Pa." Mack saw a nurse's aide appear in the doorway. He turned to face his grandfather again and spoke slowly. "I'm looking for Bill and Jack, remember?"

The old man's voice broke. "You find them yet?"

"Not yet, Pa, but I will. I swear it to you, I'll find them." He heard a shuffling noise and turned to see a nurse in a stiff white uniform walk in with a medicine tray.

"Move back and I'll give him a shot," she said.

"What kind of shot?"

"He pitches these temper fits now and then. A shot helps him relax, sleep it off."

"Temper fits?" Mack took a stand between the nurse and his grandfather. "No ma'am. He's not to have another one of those shots. Not today—not ever."

The nurse blanched as white as her uniform. "I can't do that. I can't do anything on your say so. You'll need to clear it with the doctor if you don't want him to have any more shots."

He waved a hand at the doorway. "Lead off. I'll cover your flank."

The surprised nurse backed out of the room and headed in the direction of the front desk. True to his word, Mack was right behind her. He made his way down the parade ground in the hallway, his mouth level and his back stiff, set on telling a doctor that had never set foot on foreign soil except for frivolous reasons that some men not as fortunate had earned the right to bear anger.

CHAPTER SEVENTEEN

Surrounded on three sides by the Pittsburg County Court House, the Genealogical and Historical Society sat wedged in a narrow nook on East Carl Albert Parkway. Constructed of dark brick, the narrow building was dwarfed by the Masonic Rite Temple, a neighbor to the north, and paltry in comparison. Bigwigs from an earlier day had used brick and light-colored stone to build the Temple. Hangers-on kept the Masons going now, and their female relatives kept its counterpart, the Eastern Star, alive.

Nonny parked on the upside of the hill where parking was more plentiful. Before proceeding to the Genealogy Society, she paused to look over the town that rolled out at her feet. It was garlanded now in autumn colors that sparkled in the sharp, clean air.

It was an old town by Oklahoma standards, established in the early part of the twentieth century to support the coal-mining business that brought wealth to the mines' owners. But old mine tunnels, the rotten underpinnings crumbling from the weight of dirt in their attics, now caused streets to buckle like an arthritic geriatric left to endure the sins of a wanton youth.

There was little industry left to entice diligent young people to stick around. Non-Indians that remained by choice lived a lower-than-average lifestyle, attributable to a lack of ambition and easy-to-justify welfare assistance. Those with enough blood quantum were entitled to tribal benefits that allowed them to live in relative comfort without breaking a sweat. Those with more ambitions left young.

Nonny had been one of those who couldn't wait to leave, but these days she looked upon the town differently. Ironically, for the very reason she had fought so hard to leave it. It's because old is safe, she thought. What a fraud I am. The gratitude that old people show me isn't deserved, for they're nothing more than a means to an end—a selfish end. Cutting short her philosophical musing, she made her way to the research room.

She felt irritable. Not because she dreaded research, for digging through dusty files and ancient records kept her mind from straying into less-safe territory, but because of the threat Mack Barlow introduced. The careless slouch of his body as he leaned against the wall in her kitchen had brought back too many memories. No, not memories, she thought. Feelings. She couldn't afford those kinds of feelings. Feelings like that were synonymous with chips in a suit of armor.

Pushing open the door to the research room, she was surprised to see Mack deep in conversation with Hesta Bowen, the librarian. "You beat me here," she blurted when the two looked her way. "It's not two o'clock yet."

"I came straight from the nursing home," he said.

"Mack told me what you wanted to look at." Hesta scrunched her nose to push up her eyeglasses.

Hesta had been a classmate of Nonny and Mack's, one of the less-ambitious ones that chose not to leave home. Her hair, tightly permed and left untinted, made her moon-shaped face appear even rounder, and her finger-pleated skirt looked as if it belonged on a vintage clothing rack.

"Thought I'd start him on the Local Records shelf," Hesta said, "figuring you knew your way around the census records better than he would." She indicated rows of computers in the back room.

"Good idea. I'll get started."

"Where do I begin?" Mack looked to Nonny for advice.

Nonny paused, eyes blinking. "Well, Pa's up in his eighties now, so begin when he was about twenty, that's probably the earliest his name would appear in any records. Move forward from there."

"That'd be about right." He nodded, looking thoughtful. "Sister was already born when he joined up."

"What was his full name? I've always known him as Pa."

"Grover Cleveland Anderson. Pretty stuffy name for a down-to-earth man."

"Common back then to name children after presidents. Look for his name in the indexes and write down anything you find." Nonny pointed to a legal pad on the table. "Note the source, too, so you can find it again if you need to. I'll work back there." She nodded toward the computer room.

"Think I can handle that," Mack said. Grabbing an armful of books, he sat down at a table.

"Um . . . you can only take three books at a time," Hesta whispered, standing at his elbow. "You know, in case other patrons want to use them."

Mack looked around the room, then at the librarian. "I'm the only one in here, Hesta. Other than Nonny and she's working back there."

Nonny suppressed a grin. “It’s a rule, Mack. Hesta’s just doing what she’s been told to do.”

“Oh. Well, I’ve had to follow dumb-ass rules, too.” He took three books and let Hesta take the rest.

“Just let me know when you finish with those,” Hesta said. “I’ll give you three more.”

“No problem.” He bent his head low over a book.

Hesta bent her head low over Mack.

Nonny smiled at the attentiveness Hesta was giving Mack, thinking there might be more life under those wire-rimmed glasses than she had given credit. She headed for one of the computers and started with census indexes.

“I can help him should he need help.” Like a shadow, Hesta had appeared at Nonny’s elbow. “It’s my job.”

“Thanks,” Nonny whispered. “That would be helpful.”

And safer, she thought.

*****

Late afternoon shadows were creeping across the table when Nonny exited out of the census record she’d been searching. Decade by decade, she had identified the places the Barlow clan had lived in their sojourn in Pittsburg County, right down to the township they resided in, the post office they got their mail delivered to, and their next-door neighbors.

“They didn’t stray too far,” she murmured.

“Say that again?”

Nonny looked at Mack. “I said your grandpa and his girls didn’t stray too far. And a woman named Grace lived with them for a brief spell.”

“That would be my grandma. We talked about her, remember?”

"I remember." Nonny decided not to mention her conversation with Ruby the day they met up at the gas station. She was still stunned at Ruby's animosity toward her mother and confused as to whether the family matriarch was dead or alive. "You finding much?" She went to see what Mack might have written down.

"Not much. Some funny things though." He hesitated. "Well, more curious than funny, I guess."

"Like what?" She noticed the frown on Mack's face.

"Seems like Pa and his friends would tie one on back in the early days. According to these sheriff's records, they ended up in a jail cell more than once and had to be bailed out."

She shrugged. "You never know what you'll find when you start tracing your family history. We can pick our friends, but not our relatives."

"That's not what's bothering me. It's who he got crocked with that I find curious."

Nonny waited for Mack to offer up his findings.

"Old man Turner. Do you believe that?" he said.

"*Wash* Turner?"

"If I'm reading this right." He handed her a book.

"Son of a gun . . ." She laughed without humor. "Any other surprises surface?"

"No, but I'm just finishing up with this last one."

Taking the book from Mack, she glanced at the spine. "Oh, no need to look at this one. These are old property tax records. He never owned any property."

"Property tax records?" Mack took the book from Nonny and looked at the spine as she had done. "Then what the hell is Pa doing in it?"

"What?" She took the paper that Mack had been writing on and noted the page number. Checking the reference, she mumbled, "Good God . . ."

Mack stared at the entry, too. "What the hell does it mean?"

"It means Pa *did* own a piece of property," she said, leafing through the book. "At least for a short while. There's no other listing for him again in the index."

"Why did he sell it?"

"That information wouldn't be listed here."

"Who bought it from him?"

"Wouldn't be in this record either. Have to look elsewhere for that." She looked at Mack. "You think it's relevant?"

Mack rubbed his mouth. "Hell if I know, but I'm more than a bit curious."

Nonny checked her watch. "That would mean a trip to the county clerk's office, and I think it's closed already." She looked at the entry again. "Most of those records are archived now, unless . . ." She paused. "I think the cutoff date was in the 1950s, so there might still be a paper record." She exhaled loudly. "Could take some digging."

"Then we better stay focused on this Bill-and-Jack business." He indicated the census list Nonny had made. "Pa didn't seem too good today, his mind's wandering. And I got the feeling he's wanting to clear up some things while he still has time." He hesitated. "Plus, I have this other business to take care of."

This other business . . . Nonny recalled Mack's announcement the previous night that he was moving his mother into town.

"I didn't tell her yet," he said, reading her mind. "She was asleep when I got home last night and still in bed when I left this morning. I plan to though, *soon*."

Nonny grunted softly. "Well, back to this Bill-and-Jack thing . . ." She handed him a list she had created. "I'd start with these people—if you can find any of them still alive. I used a yellow highlighter to mark those I know have passed on. Don't know for certain about these others."

"Slim pickings," Mack said, looking over the list. "Maybe that's good, won't take too long. Okay then, I'll get right on it."

Nonny couldn't help but notice the uncomfortable look that crossed Mack's face and the way he shifted his weight from one leg to the other. Something else was on his mind. Translating the non-verbal language, her back stiffened.

Oh, geez, don't ask me out, Mack, she thought. I've got things working in my favor here, don't mess it up . . .

"Thanks for your help," he said. "I'd be glad to pay you something for your time."

"Not necessary," she said, feeling her shoulders relax. "I do this all the time."

"She does," Hesta said from across the room. "Nonny's always helping people with record searches."

"Maybe I can buy you a drink then," Mack said. "I see that bar's still out on 69. Sister's wanting a Coke for some reason. I could pick some up for her at the same time."

Nonny's mind went to fast forward. "Another time maybe. It's time for Hesta to close up and I need to help her shelve these books before I leave."

"Oh, I don't need any help, Nonny. You go on now—"

"It's closing time, Hesta—you *do* need help." Nonny picked up a stack of books and looked at Mack. "Besides,

I've got some things to do before I head home, too. Tonight's just *out*."

Mack nodded. "Maybe before I leave town then."

"Yeah, maybe." She began sorting books according to their call numbers and sighed in relief when she heard the front door close.

"I don't need help." Hesta took the books from Nonny's hand. "I've got nothing to do after work and . . . Well, it's my job."

"I know that Hesta," Nonny mumbled. To give Mack time to get to his car, she picked up his source list where he had left it on the table and looked it over. Then she walked to the shelf and looked at the book on property tax records again. "The courthouse," she said, turning to Hesta. "When exactly is the record's room open?"

"Between ten and twelve, and then the whole building closes down for the dinner hour. It opens up again from two to four." Hesta raised plucked eyebrows. "You planning on checking out that old record?"

"Maybe." Nonny's mind was still on the property the Grover Anderson had owned and why he had given it up. In that part of the country, land ownership was as much a part of a man proving himself as going off to war was.

"What happened, Pa?" she murmured. "Did you turn into an old drunk and have to give up the only thing you could call your own? Or was it the other way around?"

"Ought not speak ill of the man, him sick and all," Hesta said. "I would never have taken Mr. Anderson to be a drinking man either, he was such a teetotaler when we were growing up—and a good churchgoer, too. But the good book says 'Judge not lest ye be judged.'"

Nonny's response was bitter. "I was planning to check out the property record, Hesta, not the drunk charges."

Seeing the look on Hesta's face, Nonny immediately regretted her harshness. Though her irritability was back, there was no need to make others pay. She left the librarian shelving books and made her way toward the door leading to front steps.

Like Mack, she found that Pa being a hard drinker was not as surprising as finding he was a drinking buddy with Wash Turner. She wondered again if there was a connection between Pa selling the land and his drinking problem. The Turners were notorious for searching out pieces of land that could be bought cheap. They turned the worst pieces for a fast profit, holding onto the better pieces just for show. That thought led Nonny to think about the irony of it all, that the man who loved the land like it was a brother ended up with nothing.

Hesta turned off the lights before Nonny reached the door, forcing her to stumble the rest of the way down in darkness. Climbing back up the hill, she looked out over a town just as dark and air grown bitter. The Masonic Temple shone in the moonlight like an ancient temple, and like a prophet from on high, Hesta's judgment admonition echoed again in her mind.

"I was commiserating, Hesta, *not* judging," she whispered.

Nonny closed her mind to Grover Cleveland Anderson's need to drink. It was dangerous to delve into reasons that would lead a person to the brink of the abyss.

CHAPTER EIGHTEEN

Mack took it as a good sign that the mailbox was empty, figuring his mother had felt good enough to walk to the county road to get it. He parked close to the back door and carried a six-pack of Coke and another of Budweiser into the house. The smoke and smell emanating from the kitchen were not good signs.

"Hey Sister. Looks like you're the chef again. Mama still feeling poorly?" He walked to the refrigerator with the two six packs and studied the crowded interior. "Oh, and I picked up the Coke you wanted."

"*I* wanted?"

"Yeah, I'll take out some of these other things to make room."

As Mack made space for the drinks, he examined the expiration dates of the various jars and tossed several in the trash. He held a partially filled jelly jar up to the light, studying the contents, and replaced it in the refrigerator. It had passed muster. No ants.

"You were the one wanted the Coca-Cola, not me. Ruby said last night that was why you ran late getting home."

"She did?" He paused. "You sure about that, Sister?"

"Of course, I'm sure. She said you was running errands in town and then we got to talking about Blue Laws and Coca-Cola and . . ." Sister hesitated. "Well, maybe I got confused about the Coca-Cola. Can't drink the stuff myself, keeps me awake."

"That right? Well, next time I'll get the decaf kind." Mack slid a couple of cans of Coke into the refrigerator for safe measure, then popped the top on a Bud. Looking over his aunt's shoulder, he saw an egg frying, the edges ruffled brown lace.

"Want a sandwich?" she said. "I'm having one."

"I could eat a couple if we have enough eggs."

"We got plenty. Ruby's in a blue funk, been dragging around all day like her best friend died. Did one haircut this morning, canceled the rest."

He frowned. "You go get the mailbag then?"

"I did, but there wasn't anything in it worth the trouble."

Mack took the plate Sister offered him and set it on the table, then walked to the pantry to find something to fill out the meal. Honing in on several bottles of blackberry brandy, he pulled up short. He read the label on one of the bottles and noted it was forty-percent alcohol. Replacing it, he found a bag of potato chips held shut with a clothespin and carried it to the table.

"Can you eat chips?" he asked. "They're pretty salty."

"Got no problem with salt. Doctor says I'm healthy as a horse." Sister slid her plate forward so Mack could pour some chips onto it.

"What's got Mama in a blue funk?" He ate a handful of chips as Sister thought about his question.

"Can't rightly say. It take you all day to buy Coca-Cola and beer?"

"No ma'am. I met up with Nonny to look at records at the Historical Society. We were looking for something to help us find Bill and Jack." He pulled a paper from his shirt pocket and laid it on the table. "Nonny made a list showing where Pa lived over the years. You remember which one of these places you lived on when he had those mules?"

"Well now, let me see. I wasn't very old back then." Sister straightened her glasses, studied the writing for several minutes, then shook her head. "Why are these names marked out with yellow Crayola?"

"To show they're dead. At least Nonny *thinks* they're dead."

She nodded. "As a doornail. You might telephone these others. They were grown men back then, might could place the house we stayed at. We never owned our own, you know. Always lived in someone else's."

Mack shook more potato chips on his plate, held the bag towards her aunt.

"Can't hold another one," she said, waving the bag away. "You wouldn't remember, of course, but we were no more than squatters back then. It was real good to finally settle down someplace."

Mack paused, digesting her comment. "House is showing its age, Sister, and it's a long way from town." The years had bequeathed Sister a seamstress's hump, pale skin threaded with blue veins, and sagging skin, which did not go unnoticed. "I've been thinking maybe you and Mama would like to live in a new house closer in. What do you think of that idea?"

"New house? Nothing wrong with this one, least to Ruby and me. Pa neither. He thought it was the next best thing to Beulah Land."

Mack's mind traversed back in time as he finished off his sandwiches. "That sounds like something Dad would've said. After the war, he wanted a place of his own, too. He called this part of the country Heaven on earth."

"I remember that. I think Ruby's been thinking about your daddy and that's what put her in a blue funk."

Mack remembered those blue funks. His mother used to grieve each year on that day in July when the prison riot happened. But over the years, she'd come to terms with his death, at least outwardly. But now, thinking about the time of year and how it was long past the time the riot had broken out, he began to question the connection Sister was making.

"I should've talked to her more about that," Sister went on. "It helps a body to talk about their losses, so they can let it be."

Let it be . . . Mack sat up straighter. "You ever talk to Pa about the war, Sister? Or about Grace?"

"Pa never allowed us to talk about such things," Sister grumbled. "Anyway, wasn't much time for talking. Being the oldest, I took care of Ruby. Pa had to work, you see, and that's when I took up sewing. Then after your daddy died, Ruby took up the hair business and I went on sewing and . . . Well, life went on." She looked at him. "But you'd know that. You was here by then."

Mack nodded. "What about Grace? Why'd she leave?"

She shrugged. "Pa never said. There's a picture of her in that photo album, you want to see what she looks like. Ruby favored her more than I did. I took more after Aunt Ida—in looks, not lunacy. Ida was crazy as a bedbug. Pa took her out of that place in Vinita, you know. She's buried there in the Hugh Low graveyard."

Mack recalled his mother's concern about Ida's condition and her fear that the gene had been passed on in the family. To him, Sister sounded saner than anyone else he'd talked with since he'd arrived.

"You, uh, you know how Grace died?" Mack could not get his grandfather's words out of his head. Where did he bring Grace back from?

"For a fact, I don't," she said, sighing. "Pa never was one to talk, but I know he grieved for her. I think that's partly what turned him inward."

Mack considered Sister's comment. Men turned inward when they did things they couldn't face openly. He had witnessed more than one good man pull inside himself. Again, his thinking went to Grace, wondering how she'd died. He forced his thoughts back to the present.

"Pa said something today about bringing Grace back. She buried at Hugh Low, too?" Mack held his breath, not certain he wanted his question answered. He grew apprehensive as Sister rubbed her forehead in the same manner as his grandfather had earlier that day.

"Didn't we talk about this a couple of days ago?" she said, speaking slowly. "When we was all there at the Hometown Buffet."

Mack picked up on the uncertainty in her voice. "We did, Sister. You said Grace was in Beulah Land."

"Thank the Lord," she said, sighing again. "The way people been carrying on here lately, I was worried my mind was slipping." She began clearing the table. "You through with these chips? I'll put them back in the pantry if you're through with them."

"Yeah, I'm done." Laughing quietly, Mack set aside more questions. "I'll call these men now. Leave these dishes, I'll take care of them." He picked up the phone book.

"I got nothing better to do." She filled the sink with hot water. "I worked all day on that piecework of Nonny's. Looks like I'll have it done by Christmas now. Even finished ours. Want to see it? Made it out of the prettiest piece of material that Nonny brought by and took special pains with the embroidery stitches. Best work I've done in a long time. I laid it on Ruby's dresser so she would see it first thing she gets up. But I can fetch it, you want."

Damn . . . Mack wished he'd told his aunt about the move to town before she had put so much work in on a new mailbag they'd never get to use.

"Maybe later," he said. "I need to call these people." Pulling a chair next to the counter. he made the few calls he needed to make in well under a half hour. He sat down at the table when done, rubbing his face.

"Didn't sound too promising." Sister wiped the table with a dishrag.

"Wasn't at that." Mack stared at the list Nonny had made and his check marks along the page indicating he had exhausted all the possibilities. Then he picked up the phone book and flipped through the pages, wondering if there was anyone else he could call. He ended up staring at the list of names his grandfather had scribbled on the front cover.

"Why do you think Mama was thinking about Dad today?" he asked, reading over the list again. "Dad died in July, not November."

"Well now, let me think . . . *Oh*, I saw her looking for the photo album in the closet, that's why."

Mack's spine turned stiff as a plank. "Mama was in my room— You sure she was looking in the closet?"

"Course, I'm sure. I can see into that room from the rocking chair. She was rummaging around in the closet and the only thing in there any more's that photo album. She looks at his picture now and then, the one in that newspaper article, so I figure that's why she took a blue funk."

"That was today?"

"While I was sewing on Nonny's mailbags. She gets the blue funk from Pa. He'd get blue when he looked at that photo album, too." She settled into a chair across from Mack. "Lunacy must run on the Anderson side."

Mack picked up the phone book and stared again at the list of names his grandfather had made. "So Pa also looked at that album . . ." He rose from his chair suddenly and made a move toward the doorway.

"Where you going?" Sister asked. "I just got set down."

"I'm sorry, Sister." He turned to look at her. "But I need that album."

"You want to look at your daddy's picture, too?"

"Not exactly. I think I'm getting close to solving something here, something Pa's been trying to tell us."

"Well that's good, I'm real glad for that." She scooted her chair away from the table and walked to the pantry. "It's my bedtime now and you don't mind, I won't look at those pictures with you."

"No, you've been real helpful."

Mack did not leave the kitchen, however, for the next scene was one he had not witnessed before. For that matter, it was one he never thought he would witness. He watched wordlessly as Sister took a bottle of brandy from the pantry, noted how carefully she measured three fingers into a juice glass and continued to watch as she returned the bottle to the pantry. When she took his arm and indicated he was to escort her to her bedroom, he could think of no reason to refuse.

"You don't ever have to worry, Sister," he said when they reached her bedroom. "You'll have a place of your own from now on.

"Wasn't worried I wouldn't," she said.

The last thing Mack saw was the glass lifting to her lips. A voice inside his head translated that image into words.

You fell asleep on your watch, pard. Should've checked up on these gals more often.

CHAPTER NINETEEN

Ruby opened her eyes to a light that washed the space around her with whiteness. She and Will were driving in their old Buick with the windows down, the sun warming her face, and she held Mack in her arms. Will drove confidently, fields of cotton whizzing past like snowflakes in a storm. She was about to tell Will how happy she was that they could take a holiday when the whiteness began to take on the look of plaster. She closed her eyes, trying to recapture the moment, but it was gone. As a sinking filled her chest, she opened her eyes once more.

Someone had opened the window shade. She looked around the room and saw the door was open, then looked to the dresser where she saw a brightly colored mailbag. Reaching for the bag, she studied the gold and purple pattern in the fabric, the name BARLOW centered perfectly and embroidered with fine stitches done in gold thread, and felt her spirits lift again.

"Why Sister, where'd you get this thread?" she murmured. "This is royal, downright royal." Ruby began to sink again, thinking that she would not be seeing the bag the coming year because Nonny would not be delivering their mail to this address. Their mail would be going to a strange place. She reached out and replaced the mailbag on the dresser, planning on covering her head with the quilt, but a photograph lying on top of the phone book stayed her hand.

"I figured out the list."

Hearing the voice, she turned to face the door. Mack slouched against the doorframe, arms folded across his chest and eyes staring at her, and she wondered how he had gotten there without her hearing him.

"I figured out the list of names Pa made on the phone book," he said, walking into the room.

"You did?"

"Yes ma'am."

Mack picked up the phone book and photograph, then took a seat on the edge of the bed. When he pulled the pillows upright behind her, Ruby had no choice but to scoot into a sitting position. She took the eyeglasses that he handed her and fitted them on her face.

"Sister can take the credit," he said. "She said both you and Pa would go into a blue funk after looking at the photo album."

She frowned. "Sister said I took a blue funk?"

"She saw you in my bedroom yesterday, in the closet."

Instantly, Ruby became alert. She did not realize that Sister had been watching her search the bedroom. But the photo album had not her objective. The manila envelope from the Henryetta realty was what she looked for. She hoped to find something that might shed light on why her son would sell their home right out from under them, hoped to find something that would give her a reason to forgive him. But the envelope had disappeared. She did not tell Mack the real reason for her being in his room, however. She withheld the truth as he had with her. Instead, she looked to where Mack held an old, yellowed photograph next to the list on the phone book.

"Take a look, Mama. There's four names on the phone book and, count 'em, five men here in this picture. Pa would be the fifth. If I was a betting man, I'd wager ten against one, these guys are the same ones on the phone book."

Ruby stared first at the list and mentally counted off the number, then at the photograph and mentally counted off the men. "What does it mean," she said, looking at him. "I don't understand."

"I thought about this most of the night . . ."

Ruby watched her son rub his face, noticed lines around his eyes that indicated he had not slept, and tried to focus on what he was saying.

"I think Pa's confusing events in the past. Nonny picked up on it yesterday at the nursing home."

"Nonny was at the nursing home yesterday?"

"To see Henry Carter. She happened to be there when I went by to check on Pa. Nonny takes Henry gumdrops to take the edge off . . ." He waved his hand in the air as if brushing away a pesky fly, then resumed talking. "Anyway, Pa said something about having to bury them in foreign ground. I thought he was talking about Bill and Jack being buried on someone else's property, but Nonny thought that was curious wording. She said something about needing to de-construct the meaning behind the words, and . . ."

Ruby covered her face with her hands.

"What are you thinking, Mama?"

She looked at him. "I'm thinking that you're going too fast. I'm just not getting it."

"These men never made it home, that's what I'm saying. I think Pa was the only one that made it back alive." Mack tapped the photograph as he talked and the sound resonated like a drum. "Did Pa ever talk to you about his war years? I think the bodies of these men were never recovered."

"Lord have mercy." Ruby sat up straighter. "Pa never talked about anything like that. He wouldn't allow us to ask questions either."

"That's what Sister said."

"I'm still not getting it." Ruby shook her head, looking dazed. "What do these men—God rest their souls—what do they have to do with anything?"

Mack started pacing. "I haven't figured all of it out, but I think Pa's confusing Bill and Jack with his war buddies. He wants to be buried with them—with his buddies."

"Lord have mercy," she said again. "Why would he want to do that?" She stared at the young faces in the old photograph. "Why them, and not us?"

"It's . . . hard to explain."

Ruby heard the thickness in Mack's voice and watched as he turned away. Sweet Jesus, she thought, he's walked in Pa's shoes . . . At that moment, Ruby understood more about her son than she had ever known before and more about her own father having come to understand her son. Suddenly, the word genes crept into her mind and she pushed the covers aside so she could breathe.

Feeling the need to hold Mack close, Ruby got up from the bed. Seeing his face hardened like plaster, just as her father's used to do, she stopped abruptly. She pulled on her bathrobe instead and listened as he went on with his explanation.

"What's important is those memories are what's causing his nightmares. The war, he's reliving the war."

She nodded slowly. "I've heard of that. But those fits only started recently so I never made a connection . . ." She paused, seeing hesitation in his eyes.

"They didn't just start, Mama. That's why Grace left."

Ruby felt her lips go numb and her legs grow weak. Then she felt Mack's arms around her waist and the next thing she knew, she was back in the bed. "Are you saying . . ."

"Just like he did with you that night. I bet he woke up thinking he was in a battle and—"

"You don't have to say anymore." She clutched at the bed covers. "Can he get help? I mean, surely the Army will help him. He's a veteran, they'll give him medicine."

"Pa doesn't need the Army—or any more medicine. He needs to talk to Grace, to explain to her why he did what he did." He hesitated. "And she needs to listen this time."

The noise that came out of Ruby's mouth was closer to a cackle than a laugh. She thought briefly about her Aunt Ida, locked away in Vinita, then pulled herself together. "Grace isn't here, Mack—she run out on us years ago."

There was a pause in Mack's eyes. "But you're here," he whispered.

Still dazed, Ruby watched as Mack started pacing and talking again.

"Sister made the connection. Well, she didn't really, but she set me thinking about the way you resemble Grace." He walked to the bed suddenly, pulled something from his shirt pocket, and put it into her hand. "Here, take a look, Mama. Look at Grace."

Ruby looked at the black-and-white photograph that Mack handed to her. It was one she had looked at seldom over the years for she held such resentment for the woman in it—for *any* woman that would abandon her man and children. Then, for the first time, she noticed the similarities. In the shape of her face to her mother's. The way her hair grew into a widow's peak just as her mother's had. The slightness of her mother's build, so like her own.

"Good God, you're not suggesting . . ."

He paused a beat. "That's exactly what I'm suggesting."

"I can't."

"You have no choice, Mama. Pa needs it, he's earned the right to be heard."

"Lord have mercy." Ruby heard a buzzing in her ears and wondered if she was suffering a stroke, then she noticed Mack was looking toward the door.

"Did you hear what I said?" Sister stood in the doorway, looking fixedly at Ruby. "Or have you gone deaf again?"

"No . . . I mean, I'm not going deaf. What was it you said, Sister?"

"I said, how do you like our new mailbag? That's what I said."

Ruby picked up the mailbag again. "It's royal, Sister, Downright royal."

"Aw, hell." Mack rubbed his hand across his mouth.

"You don't like it," Sister said, staring at him.

"No, it's pretty, real pretty. You did a fine job, Sister."

"I did, didn't I? You're done with it, I'll take it back now. I want to show it to cousin Bessie next time she comes."

Mack took the mailbag from Ruby and handed it to Sister.

Ruby watched as Sister left the room and as Mack walked to the bed again. Why are they moving so slow? she wondered.

"There's something else I need to talk to you about, Mama. Get up, we've got a busy day ahead of us."

This can't be happening . . . This isn't real . . .

For the second time since dawn, Ruby waked from a dream. She said nothing as Mack pulled the robe from her shoulders, and remained silent as he took a dress from the closet and pulled it over her head. She did not object that it was wrong for the season. Or that her hair had not been done in three days. Or that her grown son was looking at his own mother, half naked. Nor did she complain when he led her from the room as a father would lead a child. Why should she?

I'll wake up, she told herself. I'll wake up soon enough . . .

*****

The crisp November air cleared Ruby's head. She stared at the slick advertisement showing the gated community in McAlester and tried to focus on what Mack was saying. But her mind wandered—from her father and the mysterious fits that had come on him, to her mother and her disappearance, to Bill and Jack and four dead men, to this colored piece of paper.

"It's too much," she said. It's just too much."

"I can swing it," Mack said. "If I can get enough out of the old place, I can just about swing it."

"I'm not talking about *this*." Ruby held up the marketing brochure. "I mean this thing with Pa. What am I supposed to say? Hi Grover, it's Grace, I'm back from the dead and thought I'd drop in to see you for a bit. By the way, why did you black my eye and knock me senseless all those years ago? I mean, they'd put me in Vinita for sure, I did something like that." She felt her face flush as Mack started to laugh. "This isn't funny, Mack Barlow!"

"I know it's not." Mack snorted a last time, then sobered "Just lay it on the line, Mama. There's no time for double-talk that would just confuse him more. Tell him you're Grace and you want him to tell you about the war." He pulled a photo from his pocket. "And take this photo, see if these men are the ones on the phone book."

"It's deceitful," Ruby said, tucking the picture into her purse. "And you think the nurses are going to let me waltz in looking like this? Why, they're liable to put me away, wearing this hat and coat. I can't believe Sister hung onto this stuff all these years." She bent her nose to the coat's lapel. "I smell like mothballs—and I never wear this much makeup." She turned to Mack as he started to laugh again and repeated, "It's not funny, Mack!"

"I know."

"And my customers, I had three appointments today."

"Not a problem. Sister's calling them."

Ruby folded her arms across her stomach, then pulled the coat together in an attempt to button it. "I'm fatter than Sister. Her clothes never did fit me. I feel ridiculous. And I'm gonna lose every one of my customers because of this nonsense. First Tootsie Turner and now—"

"All that's not important. Anyhow, it's time you gave up being a kitchen beautician."

"Kitchen beautician . . ." Ruby felt as though she'd been slapped. "Are you ashamed of how I make a living?"

Mack sighed. "That's not what I'm saying. It's just time you stopped working so hard."

"It kept food on the table and clothes on our backs for many a year!"

"Would you just take a look at that brochure, Mama? At the fun things to do there?"

"I can't think about this right now." She slid the colored brochures back inside the manila envelope and pitched it to the back seat. "And I can't believe you kept this from me."

"Yeah, well, I'm sorry about that, but sooner or later, we have to talk. I've got a deal in the works."

"I can't, not right now. Besides which, we're here."

Mack parked near the entrance of the nursing home and Ruby walked with him to the front door. "Oh Lord," she whispered as Mack rang the buzzer, "I can't do this."

"Yes ma'am, you can."

Again, Ruby was not given a choice. Mack guided her down the hall as though she were a missile that could not slow down or it would be blown from the sky. She focused her eyes on the floor so she would not have to look at the people sitting on either side and did not breathe until she reached her father's room.

"Hold on a minute," Mack said, "I'll clear the way." A minute later, he rolled Henry Carter out of the room in a wheelchair. "I'll take Henry to the rec room. Don't worry, I'll make sure you have privacy for as long as you need it."

Don't worry . . .? Ruby watched as Mack and Henry Carter disappeared down the hall, sure that a million seconds passed as she stood there. I cannot do this, she thought. It's not right—it's insane! She turned to leave, wondering why she had allowed herself to get into such a predicament.

You're doing it because your father is dying and needs to find peace before he passes over . . .

Hearing the voice, Ruby's feet rooted to the floor. She looked to see if Mack had returned, if he had read her thoughts and was talking to her. He hadn't.

"God help, she thought, now I'm hearing things. Fearful the voice would return to chastise her again, Ruby uprooted her feet. She walked into the room and sat next to her father, and with sincerity in her heart if not on her person, she began to speak.

"It's me, Grover. It's Grace. You never told me about the war, and I'd like to hear about it."

She listened for two hours.

CHAPTER TWENTY

"Can I go back to my room now, Ruby?"

"Yes, Mr. Carter." Ruby had made her way to the table in the corner of the recreation room where her son and her father's roommate sat. "I'm sorry to keep you out here all this time." She took off the old felt hat and long tailored coat that belonged to Sister and laid them on an empty chair. "I never expected to be this long."

"Didn't mind a bit. Me and Mack have been playing chess. Can't find too many people play chess anymore." He waved goodbye as a nurse's aide wheeled him away.

Mack pulled a chair out for her. "How'd it go, Mama?"

"He's sleeping now, but I couldn't stop him from talking, Mack. He saw so much."

"I know."

"And was made to do some awful things."

"I know. Those names on the list?"

"They're the ones in the picture, just like you thought."

"How'd it end?"

"He asked me to forgive him and I said I did. That was all right, wasn't it?"

"Perfect, Mama. Just the right thing to say."

"It wasn't a lie, at least not coming from me. Of course, I can't speak to what Grace might've said. I can't believe she wouldn't listen to him."

"It was the perfect thing to say." Mack went to the coffee machine and carried back two cups. "This stuff's been perking all day. They've got that powdered stuff, if you want it white. No milk. I checked already."

"This is fine." She studied her son's face, the distant look in his eye. "What are you thinking?"

"I'm just trying to figure out what to do next, where to go from here."

"Maybe I can help with that."

Startled, Ruby thought at first that she was hearing things again. She was relieved to see Nonny Folsom standing behind them. She'd had enough of bodiless voices for one day.

"I called the house and Sister told me you were here," Nonny said quickly, face flushed. "I've been at the courthouse all afternoon."

"You find something else?" Mack pulled a chair up so Nonny could join them.

"Yes, more about Pa's piece of land." She handed two pieces of paper to Mack and laid a thick stack on the table.

"Pa's piece of land?" Ruby looked at Mack.

"Damn . . ." He tapped his forehead with the heel of his hand. "Did I mention that we found out at that Historical place yesterday that Pa once owned a piece of land?"

"No, you did not!"

"Well, I meant to, other things got in the way."

"What happened to it?"

"We don't know."

"We do now." Nonny pointed to one of the papers Mack held.

As Mack became engrossed in reading the paper, Ruby turned to Nonny. "Tell me what it says, Nonny."

"Old Mr. Turner bought the land, Ruby. Not long after Pa got out of the service."

"She's right," Mack said, looking up from the paper.

"What? All these years, Tootsie Turner never said a word about that. Why would she keep something like that from me?"

"I knew something was fishy," he said. "Those Turners hovered over us like mother hens, then wouldn't give me the time of day when I asked about Bill and Jack. I'd bet a dollar to a donut, those mules are buried on Pa's land."

"And that's not all." Nonny pointed to the other piece of paper that Mack held. "We shouldn't be looking for Bill and Jack."

"Thank the Lord," Ruby said, laying a hand on her chest. "You found a *loophole*."

"No, Ruby. I mean we should be looking for Grace instead of those mules."

Ruby heard a buzzing in her ears. "I'm not following you, Nonny."

"I'll be damned," Mack mumbled, not giving Nonny time to respond.

"What is it?" Ruby asked.

"A death certificate for Grace Anderson."

"My mother's death certificate?" Ruby took the paper from Mack's hand but found she still could not focus her eyes. "What's it say? I can't see a thing."

"It says she's buried in Beulah Land," he said.

Ruby fell back in her chair. "You mean, Pa's piece of land is called . . .?"

Mack laughed. "Yeah. He called it Beulah Land."

"Lord have mercy. Sister tried to tell us, and . . ." Ruby laid a hand on her chest, an attempt to slow her racing heart. "Oh my God! Grace is buried right *here*?"

"Pa said something yesterday about bringing her back. Looks like he did just that." Mack turned to Nonny. "You find the location?"

"No, it's the proverbial needle in a haystack. The Turner's own half the county. See?" Nonny pointed to the thick stack of paper on the table.

"What about the legal description?" Mack asked.

"I just found that bill of sale there and no legal description was attached. I don't know how we'll ever find it, so much has been archived and so many old records have been lost or destroyed." Nonny tapped the stack of paper. "I printed off what I could find of the Turner's land transactions in that timeframe, but it's overwhelming. Pa's piece might've been sold many times over . . . or the Turners might still own it."

"But the Turners know where it is," Mack said, his eyes narrowing. "And for some reason, they don't want us to find out."

"Why would that be?" Ruby murmured. "Why would they do such a thing?" She watched Nonny rise from the table and float to the coffee pot, then back again. Why are people moving in slow motion, she wondered. It's because this isn't real, she thought, none of this is real.

"What is it, Nonny?" Mack said. "Is there something else we should know?"

"No. I just don't know where to go next." Nonny rubbed her eyes. "I've exhausted every means available, which leaves us with the Turners themselves."

Mack blew out his breath. "If the Turners wouldn't tell us before, they sure as hell aren't gonna tell us now. And I made Pa a promise. He wants to be buried with his war buddies."

"War buddies?" Nonny said.

Ruby listened numbly as Mack related to Nonny what he had figured out with Pa and his Army buddies. His voice was low and his words spoken as if in confidence, and she began to feel left out again, just as she had at the church picnic. Feeling a tightness in her chest, she battled it down, thinking, *I will take no more of this helplessness*! Suddenly, the tightness moved from her chest to her jawbone, and she realized she was gritting her teeth. It was then that she turned to the conversation again.

"Good God, I bet you're right," Nonny was whispering to Mack. "Maybe if you told that to the Turners, they'd tell you where Pa's land is—what *used* to be Pa's land."

"You know the answer to that one," Mack said. "No way in hell they're gonna tell us, and there's gotta be a reason they're not."

"Like what?" Nonny asked.

"I don't know."

"Well, even if they did tell," Nonny said, "there's still has to be a law against burying someone on private property." She sighed deeply. "That's another obstacle to circumvent, burying Pa on privately-owned land. It's hopeless. What do we do now, Mack?"

Ruby watched Mack rub his mouth and Nonny massage the back of her neck. As she absorbed their silence, she found a strange pleasure in someone else's sense of helplessness.

Then she noticed the anguish in her son's eyes and lived again the hours spent with her father. She began to wonder how Pa had born such torment all these years, then realized he had not. It's why he's in this place, she thought, letting her eyes roam around the nursing home. And I'm the one that's put him here. She became overwhelmed with a sense of guilt then, wondering how she—a child of her father—could have done such a thing. Turn her back on him in his hour of need. Betray his trust. Why, he had even made her the Assignee on that legal affidavit.

Ruby had learned the affidavit by rote and recited it now silently, but for some reason, she could not get past one word: Assignee. Suddenly, the power in that one word smacked her between the eyes, and the darkness in her mind and numbness in her body healed simultaneously.

"I'll tell you what we're gonna do," Ruby said with conviction in her voice. "We're going to find those mules."

"What?" Mack looked her way.

Nonny shook her head. "I'm confused, Ruby. What do you mean?"

"I mean, we start looking for those two mules ourselves—piece by piece, acre by acre, until we find them. To hell with the Turners. Pa made me the Assignee on that affidavit and if he wants to be buried with those mules, *by God*, that's what we're gonna do."

"Well hell, I'm game," Mack said, grinning. "Let's hear your plan, Mama. Anything's better than sitting on our butts."

Nonny smiled, too. "I'm up for anything. And you have to be happy about finding Grace after all this time—"

"*Grace*— I'm not doing this because I want to find Grace!" Ruby picked up the stack of papers Nonny had laid on the table, eyeballed the thickness, and divided it into thirds. She handed Mack and Nonny each a portion.

"I don't understand," Nonny said, taking her portion. "Why don't you want to find Grace?"

"Because she deserted her children, that's why!"

Mack took a packet of papers, then paused. "Hold up, I think we forgot about the fly in the ointment. Even if we find them, we may not be able to bury Pa where he wants. The law might prohibit—"

"We cross that bridge when we get there," Ruby snapped. "First we find those mules."

Ruby bent over her stack of papers and feigned looking at it, for she still could not focus her eyes. But she noticed in her peripheral vision than Nonny and Mack were following her lead, looking at the papers and talking between themselves as they had come to do. Let them figure it out, she thought. That's what they're good at.

She detached from her surroundings then, and that detachment spread to her thinking. Though her future was uncertain, she found satisfaction in having a path to follow, to be in control. She thought then how strange it was that, though she had lost the war with her father, she felt no resentment toward him. The knowledge she had gained this day only reinforced a truth—that her resentment of Grace was well grounded and deserved. How could that woman—

any woman—turn her back on those that so desperately needed her?

And Tootsie Turner is no better, she thought. As Ruby thought about Tootsie's deceit, a taste bitter as gall filled her mouth. She couldn't remember the number of times she'd gone to the Walmart to buy Fawn-Beige hair coloring—which she had reserved for Tootsie alone—and how the woman had made her dye her eyebrows the same Fawn Beige so she would look natural.

Natural? There was no one more fake in the world than Tootsie Turner.

The next thing she knew, she was envisioning the woman leaving a five-dollar tip on the table without even a backward glance, as if saying "Thank you" to a kitchen beautician was beneath her.

Now I know why you were so generous with those tips all these years, Tootsie Turner, she thought.

Ruby Barlow went deep into herself then. As she sat there sipping on bitter coffee that had been perking in a dirty pot most of the day, she became aware of an uncharacteristic sensation. For the first time in her life, she thirsted for revenge.

CHAPTER TWENTY-ONE

Nonny stood at the sorting case, her mind racing as fast as her hands. Before parting company with Mack and Ruby Barlow the previous evening, she had convinced them that she could save time by grouping the Turner property transactions according to location. She had a folder in her Jeep now, containing three packets of information, but she had waked off and on through the night with another thought nagging at her. She was eager now to be through with casing the mail so she could check it out. She glanced at her watch again.

Nine o'clock. The place should be opening about now . . .

"You taking medicine?"

"What?" Nonny turned to face Claude Riley at the next case.

"You've looked at your watch every minute on the minute for the last half hour."

"Need to make a stop before I head out of town. The place doesn't open until nine." She paused, studying the man. "You've been here a long time, Claude. What do you know about Grover Anderson's wife?"

He rubbed an earlobe. "Mostly hearsay. I'm only a couple years older than Ruby, but when a couple split the blanket back then, it raised a few eyebrows. These days, splitting up is more common than not."

"Split the blanket? The Andersons separated?"

"Best I can recall." His brow wrinkled as he gave the question more thought. "No, I'm sure they did 'cause she just up and took off one day. Left those two girls with their daddy. That caused quite a stir, you can imagine. A mother leaving her children behind like that."

"Well . . ." Nonny paused. "Maybe she had a good reason."

"Ain't saying she didn't. But back then, the mother always took the children when she left her man. Not natural for a woman to just walk out on her babies."

"Not natural . . ." Nonny backtracked, trying to regain her original thread. "Well anyway, I learned yesterday that Grace Anderson's dead and I'm interested in how she died. So you never heard anything about that?"

"She *is* dead?" He rubbed his earlobe some more. "No. One day she was here and the next day, gone. She's dead, I figure it must've happened after she left. What's got you so curious about her? Got anything to do with old man Anderson's funny behavior?"

She paused. "What do you mean?"

"Nightmares. Least that's what my mama calls 'em. She's out at the home, too. But you'd know that 'cause you took her fresh plums last summer."

Nonny nodded, thinking about his comment. "I heard about those nightmares. Guess he gets pretty loud."

"Gone the other way now. Least that's what Mama said when I went by this morning. Sleeping all the time. Couldn't get him awake enough to eat his supper last night or breakfast this morning."

"Oh? Well, maybe he's just making up for all that lost sleep." She picked up her loaded trays before Claude could respond. As she walked outside, she realized she had not answered Claude's question about her reason for searching out Grace Anderson. But she did not return to give him an explanation for she did not know the answer to that question herself.

Nonny coaxed the cold-hearted Jeep to life and proceeded through the gray morning light to the Chapman Funeral Home. The former two-story residence had a wrap-around porch that gave it a homey feel, but the backyard had been turned into a sheet of black asphalt. She walked up the back steps and rang the doorbell.

"Too early to check a few records, Bertie?" Nonny had checked the funeral records kept at the Genealogy Society and come up empty handed. That meant, she would have to dig deeper.

Alberta Tumlinson returned the smile. "Who've you lost now, Nonny?"

Nonny followed the short dark-skinned woman to the basement, talking as she went. "Mr. Anderson's wife, Grace. I'm hoping you handled the funeral."

"Grace Anderson?" The woman's look was skeptical. "Name doesn't ring a bell and I been here a long time. But let's take a look." She pulled several old file boxes from a cabinet. "I got a funeral to get ready for, so just let me know when you're done."

Nonny faced the boxes of old records, then sat down to do what she had become good at. Searching for the lost. An hour later, she left the funeral home carrying a copy of a receipt. It showed that Grover Cleveland Anderson had purchased a coffin and marble headstone for the sum total of $995, an amount that Alberta said bought a top-of-the-line casket and grave marker in its day. But there were no burial records.

"At least Pa thought a lot of her." She studied the simple wording that Pa had paid to have etched into the stone: *Grace, God Grant Forgiveness to Thee and Me*. As her eyes returned to the word *forgiveness*, a reprimanding voice sounded inside her head.

What the hell do you think you're doing?

*****

Nonny had trouble focusing. Her hands worked mechanically, inserting and removing mailbags from mailboxes, but her mind was powered by a will of its own. Throughout the morning, she questioned her impulse to search out information about Grace Anderson, especially in light of Ruby's sentiments. What had started as simple interest was now bordering on an obsession, and that thought made her mouth go dry. Obsessions of any kind were not a good thing. She worked hard on tweaking her thinking, attempting to put a reasonable focus on the matter. But by the time she reached the Barlow place, she was talking aloud.

"It's only normal for a child to want to know a mother she never knew . . . Ruby's just overwhelmed right now . . . she'll come around, I'm *sure* she'll come around."

It was mid-afternoon when she parked outside the Barlow's house. She reached for the folder of information she had worked up, which now contained the receipt for Grace's headstone, and looked around for Mack's Bronco. It was nowhere in sight. She was going to have to face the changed Ruby alone.

Nonny was both puzzled and dismayed at Ruby's behavior at the nursing home. The woman's change in attitude on finding Bill and Jack flew in the face of her previous stance. Her bitterness toward Grace was even more bewildering. The latter behavior disturbed Nonny the most for it smacked of a loss of faith. From the cradle to the grave, people raised in that part of the country were taught to believe in indefinables, such as love, charity, forgiveness. What had happened to Ruby?

I'd want to find out everything I could about my mother, she thought, no matter what she'd done.

In spite of that sentiment, Nonny removed the receipt for the headstone from the folder, carrying only the property transactions and the Barlow's mailbag to the front door.

"Hey, Whitey," she said to the old dog that greeted her on the porch. She knocked hard, loud enough that someone would hear in case a hairdryer was running. She smiled at the stooped little woman who opened the door, glad her first encounter was with Sister.

"What you got there, Sister?"

"What do you think of it?" Sister handed Nonny an embroidered mailbag.

"Why Sister, this is the prettiest one you've done yet. Where did you get this thread? I didn't bring it, did I?"

"Found it at the Walmart. Feel it—pure silk, not that blended stuff you find these days. Only skein like it so I grabbed it right quick. Don't know why someone hadn't snapped it up. Just meant to be, I guess. Meant for my hands alone."

"I've never seen such fine handwork."

"You don't mind that I used the good stuff on ours, do you? I don't have enough of it left for another bag, so ours will be one of a kind."

"Not that we'll get to use it," Ruby snapped. She stood in the hallway leading to the kitchen, drying her hands on a dishtowel.

Nonny deduced Ruby's meaning immediately. Mack had told her about selling the house. In a sense, she was relieved that Mack had come clean about his plans. She wondered if the news could account for Ruby's change of behavior—and appearance. The woman's hair looked as though it hadn't been brushed since she's gotten out of bed, and she hadn't bothered with makeup at all. One thing was clear. The tone of Ruby's voice indicated she was still bitter, making Nonny glad she had left the receipt from the funeral home in the Jeep.

"Why wouldn't we get to use it?" Sister looked at the remainder of the silk thread. "I could use it to embroider something small."

Nonny caught her breath, realizing that Sister did not know about the move. Ruby saved her from needing to respond.

"That today's mail?"

"Yes," Nonny said, "but it's just more sale flyers. I have the other information pulled together on the properties, though."

"Already?" Ruby glanced at the folder Nonny held. "How's it look?"

"Not too bad." Nonny opened the folder to reveal three paper-clipped packets. "It made sense that you would take the area closest to home—"

"*Home*?"

Ruby's tone gave Nonny pause. "How 'bout we have a cup of coffee while we sort through these, Ruby. I'm sure Sister needs to get back to her sewing. Right, Sister?"

"I paid for that gold thread with my own money," Sister grumbled. "Reckon I can use it on anything I want." She picked up a crimper tool off the side table and handed it to Nonny. "Here, might as well crimp snaps on these mailbags while you're jawing. Pressing on the thing makes my arthritis kick up."

Nonny took the stack of mailbags that Sister handed her, a package of snaps, and the crimper tool. Leading Ruby to the kitchen, she deposited her armload of goods on the table. "Okay," she said, pouring two mugs of coffee. "Get it off your chest."

"Can't talk about it." Ruby took a seat at the table.

"Can't talk about what?" Picking up a mailbag, Nonny secured a snap on the flap and waited for Ruby to speak.

"About what Mack's planning on doing, that's what I can't talk about."

Nonny took a deep breath and picked up another bag. The crimper made a loud *click* as she pressed a snap in place. "Have you tried talking him out of it?"

"Out of it . . ." Ruby stared at Nonny. "You *know*?"

Nonny felt her face flush. "Well, yes. That night Mack went over to the Turners and they wouldn't talk to him, he came by my place."

"Why didn't *you* didn't try to talk him out of it?" Ruby's face flushed. "First Tootsie and now you—all my friends are deserting me."

"You think I've deserted you?" Nonny stared at the distraught woman. "Why would you think that, Ruby?"

"Because of those mules! At the church, you were supposed to help talk Mack out of looking for them. Instead, you're helping him find them."

Daylight dawned for Nonny. "No, it wasn't like that. I just got carried away. When it comes to research, I do that."

"And now you're siding with him on this move thing."

"Oh, Ruby. I'm not. It's just none of my business." Nonny laid the crimper on the table. "He's got your best interest at heart, you have to believe that." She paused. "Besides, what makes you think he'd listen to me anyway?"

Floundering for words, Ruby said, "You could've *tried*."

"Ruby, Mack and I aren't close anymore." Nonny sipped her coffee as she gathered her thoughts. "I take it you don't like the place he picked out for you."

"Haven't looked at it, just pictures he brought. He's planning on taking me to see it soon as he can turn loose. He's spending most of his time fixing up *this* place so he can sell it. That's where he is right now, picking up paint for the front room— I painted that room not three years ago. Picked the color out myself . . ." She choked up.

Nonny struggled with words, a fact she ordinarily would have found humorous. But there was nothing funny about this situation. "So Mack owns the house outright, you don't have part ownership?"

"Why, no. Will and me had no money saved when he passed. Mack was real good to buy this place for us to live in. I just always considered it my own. Picked out the paint colors, the furniture, ran my beauty shop business the way I liked— He called me a *kitchen beautician*. How could he say that?"

Nonny looked at the hairdryer in the corner. The bookshelf holding beauty products. The stack of clean white towels next to the sink. "You think he meant something bad by the remark?"

"I think he's ashamed of me, that's what I think. What's wrong with fixing hair, I'd like to know? It's honest work—besides, I *like* to fix hair."

"And there's nothing that says you can't continue and make more money while you're at it. Let's face it, Ruby, fewer and fewer people live out here. I bet you'd have a larger clientele in that gated community Mack talked about."

"It just wouldn't be the same. Town people are different."

Nonny sat for a bit, watching Ruby struggle to regain her composure and wondering how to console her. "You might like it better. Think about it, a new house closer to shopping, and—"

"Would you move into town?"

Nonny sighed. "It's different for me."

"How's it different? With your job, it would make more sense for you than me . . ." She paused. "Oh, I see. Because you're younger, that's what you mean."

"Age has nothing to do with it. It's just that I need my solitude."

"Solitude? Why do you need solitude? It's not normal for a woman to want to be alone unless. . . ." Ruby hesitated, her face flushing. "Unless maybe you're, uh, you know." She made a wiggle-waggle movement with a flattened hand."

Nonny stared at Ruby. "What are you talking about?"

"It doesn't affect my feeling for you one way or the other if you are a . . ." Again, Ruby made the wiggle-waggle movement. "Beside, no need for that these days. Even women hosts on those TV shows are marrying other women."

"Are you saying . . ." Suddenly, Nonny did find the situation laughable. "I'm not a lesbian Ruby, if that's what you're implying. Not that I don't have friends who *are* . . ." She gave her hand a wiggle waggle to finish out her sentence. Then she grew serious. "How the hell did we get off on *me* anyhow?"

Ruby thought a minute. "We were talking about why it's okay for me to give up my house and not you."

"The *house* doesn't have anything to do with it, Ruby. A house is just a house." Nonny lifted her hands in a helpless gesture. "Look, maybe we better stick to the business at hand."

Opening the folder, she pulled out three packets of information, each with copies of plat maps attached that she copied from postal maps. Taking the three packets Ruby had divided home the night before, she sorted them by area to make the search go faster. She quickly explained how she had divided the packets to accommodate Ruby's work, her postal route, and Mack's ability to look at more remote properties.

Abruptly, Ruby let out a groan.

"What is it?" Nonny said. "Are you sick?"

"No . . . Well, yes, but not the kind of sick you're talking about. How in the world are we going find the burying place of two long-dead mules? What was I thinking?"

"But you wanted to look for them."

"I know, I know, but any sign of the graves would be long gone. Land might've gotten overgrown or everything plowed under. Lots of folks turn cattle into their fields now. Cows could've trampled everything into the ground."

But marble's indestructible, Nonny thought. Wondering if it was time to retrieve the receipt for Grace's gravestone, she chose her next words carefully.

"What if I looked to see if Pa bought Grace a grave marker of some kind. People typically mark graves . . ."

Ruby rose from her chair and dumped the rest of her coffee down the drain. "I told you how I feel about that—"

"What are you carrying on about, Ruby?" Sister stood in the doorway.

"I am not carrying on—"

"I guess you are! People in the next county could hear you."

"*Bill and Jack*," Ruby snapped, picking up her folder of property listings and waving them at Sister. "We know where to look now but that there may not be any trace of them left to find. So I can't fulfill my duties as Pa's Assignee."

"Maybe it's not as hopeless as it seems," Nonny interjected. "Remember, Grace was buried with Bill and Jack. And if Pa put up a marker for her—"

"He wouldn't have done such a thing, not for a woman that deserted her children!"

Ignoring Nonny, Sister took the papers from Ruby's hands and studied the map. "Was me, I'd look for Bill and Jack's grave marker."

Ruby glared at her sister. "There you go again, talking nonsense. Do you actually think Pa would buy a grave marker for mules?"

"Didn't say he bought one." Sister settled into one of the empty chairs and picked up the bags Nonny had finished crimping. "This all you got done? For pity sake, I can work faster than that." Irritably, she began to fumble with the crimper.

"What do you mean, Sister?" Nonny took the crimper from the little woman's hands. "Don't worry with this. I'll take the rest home with me. What did you mean, look for the marker Pa put up?"

"I mean he made a marker for them. Made it out of their doubletree."

"Doubletree . . ." Nonny envisioned the pivoted wooden bar with metal fittings Grover Anderson would have used to hitch up his team. "You mean, Pa used the mules' own harness to mark their graves?"

"You couldn't remember that," Ruby snapped. "You weren't old enough . . ." Ruby hesitated, turning to Nonny. "Could she remember that?"

Nonny called up classes she had taken in educational psychology. "Well, she might. A child's memory begins about the age of four."

Sister gave Ruby a smug look. "I was older than that."

"Well, I wasn't," Ruby snapped. "I don't remember a thing."

"I'm going back to my embroidery." Sister pushed away from the table. "Mack's gonna paint when he gets back and I got a few more bags to finish up."

Ruby let out a sigh as Sister left the room. "Well good, now we got something to look for." She poured another cup of coffee, picked up the crimper and bag of snaps, and mumbled as she worked. "I wasn't even out of diapers, how would I remember something like that?"

Nonny felt an ache in her chest as she watched the woman who had no memories. She wanted to tell Ruby about the receipt for the headstone that Pa had bought for Grace, to show her the wording on it, but she knew to do so would be a mistake. For the woman not only had no memories, she didn't want any. At least, not of her mother.

Nonny began to question all the time she had put into such a wasted effort, then numbed, realizing the truth of the matter. She had not searched out the information about Grace for Ruby's sake. She had done it for herself. *She* was the one who needed to know that the woman had existed, had been born, lived and died.

A child's memory begins at the age of four . . .

Nonny listened to the words that slipped uninvited into her mind and felt a sudden need to leave, to get away from Ruby Barlow and the house she grieved for. Without a word, she picked up her folder of properties, picked up the stack of mailbags on the table, and jerked the crimper and snaps out of Ruby's hands.

"It's just a *house*," she told the startled Ruby. "You're supposed to grieve for people—not houses."

Nonny left Ruby sitting at the kitchen table without as much as a goodbye. She finished her work at the post office perfunctorily, then drove through evening shadows to a house set in a dark and isolated wood and worked at crimping snaps on mailbags far into the night. In solitude.

CHAPTER TWENTY-TWO

Mack recalled hearing the wind shift in the night and sensing it was a front moving in from the Gulf. Now, standing under the willow tree in the front yard, he could taste salt and feel moisture in the air. He was glad he'd finished the outside work on the house the day before. The windows were caulked, a fresh coat of Hunter Green paint covered the sills and the front porch, undergrowth and trees were trimmed.

As he walked to his Bronco, he paused to admire his handiwork. The old Craftsman had weathered the elements nicely, and the five acres fenced off as a yard looked more like a park than a wood. Beyond the yard, the twenty-acre pasture was trimmed short as a man's beard. Each year, his grandfather had it baled it and used the receipts to pay the taxes. Working hard to achieve just the right mix of alfalfa to grass, he'd produced a bale that brought top dollar from horse people: timothy grass mixed with just enough sweet alfalfa to be nutritious but not so rich that a horse would founder and ruin its feet. The pasture was the old man's pride and joy.

Surveying the place, Mack was put more in mind of an English estate than a backcountry farmstead. He told himself that feeder calves would probably bring in more money than hay, then quickly dismissed the idea. Even a couple of head would ravage such a small piece of land, leading to overgrazing and weed growth. Abruptly, something fluttered behind his eyelids, like a yellow sticky note stuck on a refrigerator door, and he recalibrated his thinking.

Place will belong to someone else before long, he thought. New owners will be making those decisions.

He went back to surveying the results of his labor. No two ways about it, things were coming together. A quick paint job inside and he would be finished. It was time to give Roxie Komenski another call to see if they could come to terms—*and* see what she had been able to negotiate with the builder.

This morning. I'll call her right after Mama and Sister look at that duplex.

Hearing a noise, he turned and saw his mother and aunt making their way toward his Bronco. He'd made an attempt to convert the SUV to a vehicle meant for people instead of a bachelor's trappings, but it still carried the scent of stale beer cans, Vienna sausages, and Fritos.

Settling Sister into the back seat and his mother up front, he was passing the state pen outside McAlester a half hour later and reprimanding himself for not taking a different route. One that wouldn't bring up bad memories. He glanced his mother's way, but she stared out the window, seemingly unperturbed. But then, he reflected, she hadn't said a word since they left the home place. He was being given the silent treatment. He looked into the rearview mirror where he could see the face of his aunt, thinking that even the Bill-and-Jack thing was falling into place.

"That was good news, Sister. About the doubletree, I mean.

"Hadn't thought about that in years. Funny how things come back."

He nodded. "Save a whole lot of time, you could remember where that was. I wonder if Pa stuck the pieces in the ground or constructed a cross for Bill and Jack."

"A *cross*—" Ruby came to life. "Pa wouldn't have done such a thing." She hesitated, looking toward her sister. "Would he have done such a thing?"

"Can't remember, we moved around too much. Besides, one place looked pretty much like the other."

Mack recognized an opportunity waiting to be taken. "Speaking of places, I think you'll like the one you see today. Brand-spanking new."

"That's what you said," Sister replied. "Don't know why you want to do this for us, but it's right nice of you."

"Safety. You're too far from doctors and hospitals. And don't forget that prison break."

"Oh, not that many anymore. What do you figure, Ruby? Maybe a dozen in as many years?"

"Can count the breaks we've had in the last ten years on one hand."

Mack decided silence was the best response. Putting his foot to the pedal, the gated community soon came into view. He stopped at the security hut, took the pass he was issued, and drove toward the open house he'd arranged for his mother and aunt to look at.

"Take a look around," he said as he drove. "There's a fence all the way around the place and patrols run day and night. No need to keep a shotgun anymore."

Ruby gave him a sharp look then turned back to the window. Unable to decipher that look, Mack parked in front of the show home and led the way to the front porch where a guide waited. She introduced herself as Mary Jane.

"So we'd have a neighbor on one side?" Sister asked her, indicating the adjacent unit.

"That's right," Mary Jane said. "Let's start with the entrance. Note the overhang that will keep you dry as you unlock the front door."

Mack figured the slender young woman guide was still in high school and this was a part-time job for her. The rote manner she used to describe the place indicated she was still learning her lines.

"There are two patio homes per unit. They are joined with a double-wide . . ." Mary Jane paused, her eyes blinking as though reading an invisible user's guide. "No, double-*thick* walls. That ensures privacy, but you have someone right close if you need assistance. Now, let me show you the living room." She held one arm out stiffly, as a movie usher would do.

"Hope the neighbors are nice people," Sister said, stepping through the front door.

"Probably nosy," Ruby said.

Mary Jane took over again. "No, there's double-wide—I mean, double-*wall* construction between the units, so it shouldn't be noisy at all."

Ruby raised an eyebrow. "I didn't say *noisy*—"

"Mama," Mack whispered. "The girl's just doing her job."

"Looks like our furniture would set in here all right," Sister said. "Wouldn't go real well with the color of this rug though. What color you call this?"

"Sierra Gold," Mary Jane said. "You can choose this or Sage Green. There's a sample of it at the office."

Mack recognized another opportunity waiting to be taken. "How 'bout you two pick out a new davenport? A sleeper sofa that would go with the carpet you want. Maybe put it right there across from the front window so you could look outside."

Ruby walked to the front window. "Look at what? Other duplexes like this one?"

Come on, Mama, Mack thought. Chill out. Walking up to his mother, he laid a hand on her shoulder and felt more than just *her* coolness. He made a mental note to make sure the builder caulked the windows on the unit he bought.

Mary Jane chose that moment to become technical. "They're called patio homes, not duplexes. Want to see the patio?" She walked into the kitchen and took up a stance at the sliding glass door.

Ruby raised both eyebrows. Mack looked around quickly, searching for another opportunity. "What do you think about this color, Sister?" He pointed to the walls in the living room.

"*Real* white," she said. "Clean looking though."

"It's called Dover White," Mary Jane called from the kitchen. "All units are the same so any color furniture will work." She hooked an arm toward them. "Well, come on. It's time to look at the kitchen." As directed, Mack, Ruby, and Sister filed into the kitchen.

"I see the new appliances you talked about, Mack . . ." A confused look crossed Sister's face. "But, where'd they put the stove?"

Pointing to a glass cooktop, Mary Jane resumed her spiel. "A glass cooktop provides easy clean-up and is astha—estha— It's pretty to look at."

"A glass stove?" Sister ran her hand across the cooktop. "Well, I'll swan. I've seen those on the TV."

As Ruby walked to the patio door, Mack walked up next to her. "See the treed areas out back? Just like the woods at the home place."

Mary Jane spoke up again. "The woods are called—"

"Green spaces," Mack said, giving the girl a look. "I know."

"More duplexes," Ruby said. "That's all I see. More duplexes."

Mary Jane said, "They're called patio homes—"

"We know!" Mack gave the girl another look, then turned back to his mother. "It's not as built up out back. That's where I intend to buy."

Ruby turned her attention to the kitchen. "Well, looks like this room would be big enough for everything to fit—*if* we get rid of my big old table and chairs. Maybe I could trade it for one of those little chrome dinettes. My hairdryer could set in that corner." She looked outside again, studying the slab of concrete under the awning. "And we could put a doghouse out there."

"Cats and dogs under twenty pounds are allowed." Mary Jane's eyes flipped through the instruction manual in her head again. "You must keep your pet in the house at all times except to walk. And then you must have them on a leash and, uh . . . well, you have to carry a plastic bag to pick up their . . . uh, their . . ."

"Doo-doo?" Mack said, observing the girl's red face.

"Yeah, doo-doo."

"Wha—what? But Whitey weighs more than twenty pounds." Ruby looked at the blushing girl. "You mean, we couldn't bring our dog with us?"

"That realtor didn't mention that." Mack turned to Mary Jane. "What the hell's the reason for that rule?"

"It's called a restriction, not a rule. And it's 'cause big dogs cause problems. They dig holes and make big . . . doo-doo. The Association voted to keep them out to keep dues from going up." She smiled. "So, see? It's to save you money."

Mack recycled the girl's explanation, looking for some semblance of logic in the cause-and-effect chain of events she'd hammered out. Ruby honed in on something else.

"Association dues?" She looked at Mack.

"They mow and trim the yard in the summer. Winters, they shovel the driveways and put down salt on the sidewalks."

Ruby sniffed. "Never had to pay for that before. Always had a friend that would plow us out if need be, or haul off brush in exchange for a haircut. How much that cost, those Association dues?'

"I'll take care of the dues, Mama. Don't worry your head about it."

"Or you can have birds, like canaries and parakeets," Mary Jane said, picking up her spiel again. "Or fish. Lot of people have a bowl of fish."

Ruby and Sister looked at each other.

Mack rolled his head side to side, cracking the vertebrae in his neck. "I'll talk to the manager, see what I can work out with Whitey. Nothing else, I bet Nonny would take him. She could use a dog."

"Never in my born days did I think I'd have to give Whitey away," Ruby whispered.

Though Sister said nothing, Mack noticed she was swallowing hard. He turned to the tour guide. “Show them the two bedrooms and bathroom.”

“Only two bedrooms? For certain we won’t be bringing Pa with us,” Ruby said.

“We might could,” Sister said, eyeing the larger of the two bedrooms. “We could take the big room and give him the little one.”

“Pa’s not well enough to leave the home,” Mack said, intervening. “I wouldn’t count on him *ever* leaving.”

“Well, let’s go then,” Ruby said.

Mack took her arm. “Would you just look around some more, Mama.”

“What’s left to see?” Ruby stood in the middle of the living room and looked toward the kitchen and then out the front window.

“The clubhouse, you haven’t seen the clubhouse,” Mary Jane said.

Another opportunity, Mack thought. “Lead the way,” he told her. A few minutes later, they followed the high-school girl to the entrance of the chalet-looking building.

“There’s lots of activities.” Mary Jane walked them to a large room where groups of people sat at tables.

“So when do we move?” Sister said, looking at Mack. “You decided that yet?”

Finally, he thought, one of them was on board. “A few things to make happen yet,” he said, “but I have a realtor working on listing the home place right now.”

“Oh my Lord!” Ruby clutched her chest with one hand and pointed inside the recreation room with the other.

"What is it?" Mack stared in the direction she pointed, saw women playing cards at two tables and a game played with brightly colored dominoes at the others. "Don't worry, Mama. They'll teach you how to play."

"It's not that. Look at their hair. They're all . . . *Fawn Beige*!"

"Oh yes," Mary Jane said, smiling broadly. "That's the last thing on the list. There's a beauty shop right across the street that caters to the residents here. And you get a senior-citizen discount!"

"Well, thank Heaven for small blessings," Sister muttered.

*****

"I need to run an errand," Mack said. "Go on in, I'll catch up with you." He left his mother and aunt at the front door of the Walmart and drove to a nearby store on Carl Albert Parkway that had an outside pay phone. Dialing the Henryetta realtor's office, he found Roxie Komenski at her desk.

"Hey, I just showed my mother and aunt the gated community. Yeah, it went pretty well. They're still trying to adjust to the idea, but my aunt's on board and I'm sure Mama will come around. What have you found out with the builder?" Cold raindrops began to fall, spattering his face.

"Well, that's good news. Glad to hear he's willing to go heavier construction. Say, I want a unit out back there. Mama would like it better if she could see something other than duplexes through the window."

Roxie Komenski's voice rattled like a machine gun.

"What do you mean, a slight glitch?" Mack's forehead wrinkled as he listened. "Well yeah, I can understand the builder needing to do the same kind of construction on both units. Basically, it's one building divided in half, so the price should go up accordingly. What's the problem?" The next part of the conversation didn't smooth out the wrinkles. "Why wouldn't someone want to pay a little more to have a better-built place? That doesn't make sense."

Mack zipped his coat as the sky opened up in earnest. "I hadn't given any thought to buying both units. Ten thousand dollars extra construction costs for the two sounds a bit out of line, but if I get enough for the home place, I guess I can swing it. Could rent out the other side, I suppose. I know of someone who might be interested—"

Mack's mouth dropped open. "The hell you say." He took a minute to absorb the realtor's latest revelation. "You didn't tell me there was no renting allowed." He scooped the water off his face as the realtor did more talking. "You're kidding. So you're saying I would be responsible for finding a buyer for the other side since I'm the one causing the changes to happen." He paused. "Wait up. Why won't you handle it, get two commissions instead of one?"

Mack's face mirrored his frustration. "I guess I didn't understand that. So you're not getting any commission on the duplex, just on the country place when you sell it?"

How the hell can she afford a Cadillac? he thought.

"Yeah, I see now why you wanted seven percent. By the way, have you given any more thought to the asking price?"

He listened some more. "Uh-huh," he mumbled a minute later. "So you think that's all the market would allow." He paused to listen again, looking interested. "A good lead on a buyer. That does sound promising."

He leaned closer to the phone as the wind picked up. "No, I haven't mailed the listing agreement yet. Tell you what. You up the selling price ten thousand to cover the additional cost of construction and we got a deal. I'll go back out to that gated community and sign the contract on the duplex today. You follow through with that lead and I'll sign the contract when I hear back from you— What'd you say?" Mack let out a short laugh. "Yeah, I get your drift."

Hanging up the phone, Mack turned his face to a sky the color of gunmetal and replayed Roxie Komenski's parting words: "Balls in your court, Barlow. I'll follow up on that lead when I get that signed contract."

She's got you by the nuts, pard . . .

"I know, I know," he mumbled to the anonymous voice in his head. Jogging to the Bronco, he pulled the manila envelope from under the front seat, signed the listing agreement, and stuffed it into a prepaid envelope that Roxie Komenski had had the goodness to provide. Spotting a blue postal box sitting on the corner, he made a dash for it and dropped the envelope through the slot. Glancing toward the front door of the Walmart, opening and closing as if under the control of some higher power, he debated retrieving his mother and aunt or leaving them inside.

Hell, he thought. I can be there and back in the time it would take to load 'em up. He slogged back to his SUV one last time. Driving to the gated community to sign the contract on two patio homes, he felt like a rodeo bronc that had been rode hard and put up wet.

CHAPTER TWENTY-THREE

Ruby adjusted the hood on her parka and stared at the clutter in the living room. Mack had pushed the davenport, chairs, and tables together and covered them with a blue poly tarp so he could paint the walls and ceiling. He'd also decided to give the kitchen a fresh coat, to get rid of the smell of permanent wave lotion, so another blue tarp covered things in there. He'd worked late and, not one to sit on her hands, Ruby had picked up a brush. She'd been up most of the night and her head hurt.

"I like this color better than that Denver White at the duplex." Sister was dressed in long pants, zippered coat, and a stocking cap. Except for a face lined with wrinkles and eyes distorted from triple bifocals, she could have been mistaken for a girl.

"*Dover* White," Ruby said. "It was called Dover White."

"Oh. What color you say this is?"

Ruby read the label on one of the paint cans. "Warm Butter. I swear, who comes up with these names?" She set the can down and looked at the walls. "But it is warmer than that other color. Reminds me of the rinse I put on Betty Winslow's hair. Honey Gold. She wanted to go redhead but I talked her out of it." She wagged her head. "Some people work overtime looking for ways to make themselves the laughing stock of the county."

"You get too worked up over things. Betty wanted to go red, you should've let her."

Ruby frowned at her. "You think I should let my friends make fools of themselves? Besides, I'd get the blame for it. They'd say, Ruby talked me into this fool color, it was all her idea. You know they would." She sighed as she slipped on driving gloves. "You sure you want to go? That rain cooled things down considerable."

"I'll stay in the car if I get too cold. All I know is I want to get out of this smelly house. Besides, I'm tired of working on those mailbags. My fingers are so raw, I had to dope them up with bag balm last night."

"I'll air out the place while we're gone." Ruby cracked a window. "Mack said he'd put the rooms back together when he got up. He knows I have two haircuts later in the day."

Sister studied the map Nonny Folsom had brought. "Looks like we can circle around to the left or right, end up back here. Which way you want to go?"

"You decide." Opening the door, Ruby found the old white dog waiting on the porch, anticipation in his eyes. "Oh, all right," she said. Retrieving an afghan from the davenport, she spread it over the back seat of the car. Settling Whitey in the backseat and Sister in the passenger, she started out.

"Go left," Sister said at the country road. "Mack said he got three places looked at while you was fixing supper last night. I figure we can do three this morning, we work at it."

Ruby turned left and looked out over trees the color of gray suede and a cold blue sky. "You really like the place we looked at yesterday? Or were you just saying that because Mack was standing there?"

"He's a good boy," Sister said. "Most kids these days move off and never give their folks a second thought."

"That's what I thought," Ruby snapped. "You were lying through your teeth."

"No such thing! You hear him come right out and ask me if I liked the place? I just didn't volunteer my feelings. That's not telling a lie."

"It's not being honest."

"So? Did you tell Betty Winslow she'd look like the fool if she colored her hair red?"

"Well, no." Ruby laughed, then sobered. "What are we gonna do with ourselves if we move there . . ."

"Slow down," Sister said, directing Ruby to pull off the road. "This here's the place. I'll get the gate. We can drive around this one. It's nice and flat."

Sister tugged on the piece of jagged wire bent into a circle and strung over the gatepost until she worked it loose. Throwing the gate aside, she climbed back in the car.

"Didn't see any signs of cattle, so I left the gate down. This pasture's been overgrazed real bad. Shouldn't be hard to spot that doubletree, it's here."

Ruby picked up where she left off. "I can't do hair there at that place, you know."

"We still got the mailbags, can do those anywhere. You can sew up the sides and put on the snaps, and I'll embroider them—*if* Nonny still wants us to do the bags, that is. I never saw her as upset as she was night before last. Didn't even say goodbye when she left. What'd you two get into it over anyhow?" She glanced at Ruby. "And slow down, that doubletree might be laying flat on the ground."

Ruby felt her face turn warm as she thought about Nonny's visit. "Well, basically she told me I was being ungrateful. Seems everybody's trying to put me in my place these days. I swear, I had the money I'd just buy the home place off Mack and tell him to butt out of my life."

Sister pointed toward something in the grass. "There, does that look like a doubletree? Stop so I can get a look." Over Ruby's protest, Sister stepped out of the car, followed by Whitey.

Ruby watched the old dog snuff around a log, her sister poke with a stick in a clump of grass, then head back toward the car. Sister let the dog into the back seat, filling the car with the smell of wet dog hair, and took her seat again.

"An old wagon axle," Sister said, "but we're on the right track. That doubletree would have metal rings attached to it, metal caps on the end, too. How much you figure it would it take to buy the place?"

"What?" Ruby gave Sister a look. "I wasn't serious, Sister, just doing some wishful thinking."

"Well, maybe between the two of us, we could swing it."

Reaching the back fence line, Ruby circled the car around. "Nothing here, at least I didn't see anything that looked like a doubletree." She stared out the window, making no move to retrace their path. "I told Nonny I thought she was a lesbian."

"You did *what*?" Sister's eyes were round saucers. "Well, hell's bells, I would've left mad, too. What got into you?"

"I don't know. It's just that she's so pretty and smart, but she lives alone and never married."

Sister rubbed her glasses on her coat lapel to clear away the fog. "Is that what you think about me?"

"You? Lord have mercy, *no.* Women in our day that couldn't marry, stayed maidens. Women these days don't stay maidens—"

"*Couldn't* marry." Sister glared at Ruby. "You saying I wasn't pretty enough to catch someone? Or too dumb? You saying that's why I never married?"

Ruby rubbed her aching head. "I don't know what I meant. Things are just, I don't know . . . out of control. I can't seem to make sense of anything."

"I didn't marry 'cause I let myself get spoilt."

"Wha—what?"

"Remember Sonny Stovall? Happened before he went off to work the oil fields down in Texas. Damned fool got himself blown to smithereens."

Ruby's face reddened. "Why are you telling me this after all these years?"

"'Cause I can, that's why," Sister snapped. "Couldn't talk about such things back then for the shame. That's what kept a lot of women single, you know it was. And now . . . well, I'm old and Pa's not here to clamp the lid on things. And I have to say, it feels good to talk."

The force of Ruby's sigh caved her chest. "Well, women don't look on things the same these days. Nonny wouldn't have let getting *spoilt* stop her from getting married."

"I'm sure you're right on that score. I figure Mack took care of that business while they were in high school."

Getting more information than she wanted, Ruby said, "Let's just let this thing go, Sister. I'm sorry I ever mentioned Nonny."

"Hmm . . ." Sister grew pensive. "She might not have let getting spoilt stop her from marrying, but that doesn't mean something else she's ashamed of didn't."

Ruby sat quiet, considering the implication. "Are you saying Nonny did something she's ashamed of? Why that girl's got a heart of gold. She'd give you the shirt right off her back."

"I'm just speculating, nothing more than you did when you called her a lesbian."

"Yeah well, that's what I was doing. *Speculating*."

Sister raised her eyebrows. "Well, I'm speculating we're not gonna get through this list, we don't move faster."

Still, Ruby did not step on the gas. "Does this make sense, Sister? What we're doing, I mean?"

Sister threw her hands in the air. "Would you make up your mind! First, you *don't* want to find those mules. Then you *do*. Now you're back to *don't*."

"No, not that. I still mean to find those mules. I mean if Grace is buried with Bill and Jack, don't you think Pa would've visited her grave now and then, even if it was on someone else's property? I just can't believe she was here all this time and we didn't know it."

Sister blinked slowly. "Always was good to let us know what he was about, wasn't he? He'd say, 'Going to the feed store in McAlester, be back in an hour.' Or, 'Gotta plow that forty over on the north fork of the Canadian, take most of the day.'" She paused. "Now I think on it, he'd disappear from time to time, never say a word about where he was going."

"Was never gone long, was he?" Ruby eased the car back down the track. The car bounced over the rough ground like a hoochie dancer bumping and grinding her hips. "So what do you think?" she said.

"I think you hit a sore spot with Nonny, that's why she got mad. If it wasn't the lesbian crack, it was something else. What else did you say to her?"

"I wasn't talking about Nonny. I was asking what you thought about Pa visiting Grace's grave." Sister's response, however, caused Ruby to backtrack on her conversation with Nonny. "I think she got mad because of something I said about the house."

"The *house*?"

"She said I ought to be grieving for people, not a house."

Sister turned thoughtful. "That girl's grieving for someone."

"What?"

"That's the sore spot you hit."

As they neared the gate, Sister picked up a former thread. "Pa wouldn't be gone for more than a half hour those times he was gone. If he was visiting Grace's grave, he wasn't traveling too far . . ." Her words trailing off, she pointed toward the county road. "Thought I left the gate open."

"You did. Who would've closed it— Oh, no. Someone's waiting for us."

"That Billy Joe Turner?"

"My Lord, it is. We can't tell him why we're here. What am I gonna do?"

"Only one thing to do," Sister said. "Lie."

Ruby sputtered, "I can't lie!"

"Then just tell him Whitey got out and we went looking for him."

"Sister, Whitey's in the back seat!"

"I know that! Tell him we found him and we're bringing him home. You don't slow down, you're gonna run him down."

Ruby hit the brake so hard, the new tires on the Chevrolet bounced like rubber balls.

Billy Joe Turner walked up to the driver's side door. "Ruby Barlow, that you?" He looked inside the car and said, "Hey, Sister."

"Why'd you close the gate, Billy Joe?"

"What you doing trespassing on our land? Leave gates open, cattle get out."

"Didn't see any cattle," Sister said, "or I would've closed the gate behind me. Don't treat me like I'm the dullest knife in the drawer, Billy Joe Turner. I picked up plenty of cow pies in my day." She pointed to the dry cow plop in the field. "Those are a good thirty days old, maybe older."

He took a step back. "I wasn't insinuating anything like that, Sister."

"Then I'll thank you to open that gate."

He unhooked the gate, then stopped. "What'd you say you were doing?"

Ruby hesitated seconds, at best. "You see Whitey there in the back seat? Or have your eyes gone bad?"

"Yes ma'am. I mean, I see him."

"We'll take him back home now, you'd be so kind as to open that gate."

Billy Joe hesitated briefly, then pulled the gate open.

"I'm glad your eyesight's not failing," Ruby said as she pulled past. Turning right onto the county road, she turned to Sister. "How was that? I didn't really lie, did I? I just didn't tell the truth."

"No, you didn't," Sister said, talking slow. "But Billy Joe' probably wondering about now why you headed the opposite direction of home."

Ruby looked into her rearview mirror. "That would account for why he's standing in the middle of the road, staring at us." Suddenly, she began to laugh and when Sister joined in, she stepped on the gas, not even trying to account for the joyful feeling in the car. Sometimes it was best to accept goodness without question.

"Why do you figure Billy Joe's checking on the properties?" Sister asked a minute later. "That's his daddy's job since he left off working at the pen."

Ruby looked into the rearview mirror again. Billy Joe Turner looked like a bowling ball stuck in the middle of the road. "Well, old Mr. Turner got old. He's ever bit as old as Pa. And Junior Turner's ever bit as old as me. He quit his job at the pen to manage things. Maybe it's time for Billy Joe to take on the family business."

Sister snorted. "You don't *really* think that's why Junior Turner stopped working at the pen."

Ruby gave Sister a glance. "You think otherwise?"

"Hold up. Next piece of property's on the left. Let's close the gate behind us this time so we don't have any surprises waiting when we leave."

Ruby pulled left into another dirt track, pulling through quickly so Sister could close the gate behind them.

"Those downed leaves should hide our tracks," Sister said, settling into her seat again. "Thick as a carpet. Kinda looks like that rug at the duplex, don't it. What was that color again?"

"Sierra Gold. Leaves are a lot prettier than it was. Cheap carpet, too. Wouldn't hold up long."

"I figure Billy Joe's daddy left the pen because of that suspension."

"What?" Ruby jammed the brake.

"Don't stop here," Sister said. "Pull into those sugar pines or you-know-who will be after us again."

Ruby pulled inside a grove of pine trees that shielded them from the road. "What suspension?" she asked, staring at Sister.

"It's right there in that newspaper article."

Ruby tried to concentrate. "I don't remember reading anything about that. Why didn't I see that?"

"Because you were grieving. People that's grieving wear blinders, don't see anything but what they want to."

"Mack tried to tell me something was fishy, that Junior knew more than he was telling, and I wouldn't listen."

"Well, don't kick yourself too hard. The paper didn't mention Junior's name, and right then you couldn't add two plus two. Understandably, of course." Sister reached for the door handle. "Kill the engine, let's walk this one."

Ruby did as Sister instructed and followed Sister and Whitey into the thinly wooded pasture. "What do you mean blinders? Sounds like you're saying grieving is selfish, like you would know anything about it."

"What?" Sister spun on her heel. "Just because I never had a husband or child to lose, you think I don't know about grieving? You *are* selfish, Ruby Barlow."

"Now, I didn't mean that, Sister. I've seen how you've grieved for Grace, and I know you don't understand why I don't. But I just didn't know her like you did and it's hard to grieve for someone you never knew."

"I'm not talking about *Grace*. There's other kinds of grieving, you know."

Sister took off again and Ruby hurried to catch up. She pulled up short again as Sister came to a stop.

"Oh my Lord," Sister murmured.

"What is it?

"I just figured it out. Nonny's grieving for herself."

"Herself?" Ruby hurried along, trying to catch up.

Sister stopped when she reached the back of the field and pointed toward the left. "We'll cover more ground if I go one way and you go the other. Meet me back at the car." She took off on her own, the white dog behind her.

"But, you could get lost," Ruby called out, hurrying after her. "I'd feel better if we stayed together. We could lose our way."

"Get lost? Oh for goodness sake, take Whitey with you so you don't get *lost*." Before Ruby could object, Sister sent the old dog back and went on her way. Poking with a stick into clumps of grass, she disappeared into the gray morning light like a specter in a fog.

Ruby called out, "So Nonny's grieving for what she never had, is that what you're saying?" Her voice fell flat, as though it had run into an invisible barrier. Turning around, she followed after Whitey as he snuffed around holes and under logs. As she did so, she came to a realization that stopped her in her tracks.

"Pearl Anderson," she whispered. "You weren't just talking about Nonny. You were talking about yourself." She paused, then said, "Lord help, how could I have been so selfish."

CHAPTER TWENTY-FOUR

It was early evening when Ruby pulled the photo album from the top shelf of the closet and walked down the hallway to the kitchen. Following her last haircut appointments, she had put the wet towels on to wash and dry, setting the room to humming and smelling of perfumed fabric softener. Save for that, and the sound of the television from the living room where Sister watched the evening news, the room was quiet.

Ruby did not make a habit of watching the news, finding terrorism and violence depressing. But she knew this evening she could no longer avoid what discomfited her. She took a seat at the kitchen table and opened the album to the page holding twenty-five-year-old newspaper articles from the *Daily McAlester Democrat.* She avoided focusing on the picture of her dead husband, for the first time reading the articles slowly and with deliberation. She paused to read one paragraph aloud.

"The warden apparently does not know who called in the release from the prison and I don't plan on letting him find out because the person would probably lose his job, a representative from the radio station said."

"That's right," Ruby murmured, pausing. "The radio station got wind of the escape before we were notified and wouldn't reveal its source." She continued her reading.

"Members of the family tried to call through the prison switchboard but could receive no verification. One family member went to the main OSP gate but was not allowed admittance to see the warden . . ."

"Was that Mack who did that?" She paused to think. "No, more likely that was Pa." She turned again to the article.

"That evening, the prison chaplain was sent to see Barlow's widow . . ."

Ruby felt her throat closing and try as she might, could not swallow. She filled a glass with water from the kitchen faucet and sipped on it until she could swallow once again.

"But where does it talk about a suspension?" Returning to the table, Ruby read the follow-up article.

"The city council established a notification system with the prison in the event of an escape. As it stands now the prison notifies the city immediately if they suspect an escape and then they verify the report when a count is completed. Police report that the penitentiary notified them at 12:30 p.m., which was just after the escapee was found to be missing at the prison. The guard on duty has been placed on disciplinary suspension pending investigation."

Ruby studied the words. "I don't understand," she said, rubbing her forehead. "They knew the man escaped early in the afternoon, and they called the radio station and police before we were notified? Why would they do that?"

"Because someone was negligent, that's why," Sister said, entering the room. "But you'd never get those bureaucrats at the pen to admit it."

Ruby had been so engrossed that she did not hear the sound of the TV being shut off or Sister's approach. "But it doesn't mention a name."

"I already told you that. But don't you think it's funny that Tootsie's boy Junior decided to quit his job right after that investigation? You want some cocoa? That walking around this morning's got me a little stiff."

"You sit down, I'll make us both a cup. You should've stayed in the car. Did you catch the weather report?"

"Stayed in the car? Why today's the best time I had in a month of Sundays. I already have tomorrow's route mapped out. This weather's supposed to hold another week, then a front's coming in from the Gulf. Could bring freezing rain. We don't have a minute to waste."

Ruby set the teapot on to boil and rummaged in the pantry for the box of cocoa mix.

Sister laid the plat map on the table and asked, "Where's Mack tonight? He didn't go back out to look for Bill and Jack, did he? Could break a leg in the dark."

"No, he had to follow up on something on this house deal. I'm scheduled to give cousin Bessie a perm tomorrow. It'll take all morning, and I have a color and cut at one-thirty."

"I suppose Bessie's bringing her own perm, like she always does."

"You know that's my policy. She saves a little money buying those boxed perms on sale."

"Bessie could buy out the Walmart if she wanted to. She's got more money that she knows what to do with." When Ruby did not reply, Sister picked up another thread. "You heard from Nonny? What kind of luck's she having?"

"Yes—*no*. She left a note with the mail saying she hadn't found anything, but she didn't call."

"It's because you made her mad."

Ruby sighed. "I'll apologize next time I see her. So you figure Junior Turner was the one called the radio station?" She looked puzzled. "Why would he do that? It doesn't make sense."

Sister pushed the photo album aside. "No, it doesn't. It makes more sense that he was the one called the police. Then he probably called his mother to let her know he was all right, figuring the word would reach her about somebody at the pen getting killed." She paused, eyes blinking. "Tootsie probably called the radio station. That's just the kind of flamboyant thing she would do."

Ruby drummed her fingers as she waited for the water to a boil. "Does sound like her, doesn't it? And of course, the pen would record who made the call to the Police, maybe even track *all* the phone calls that were made. That means they would've found out Junior Turner called Tootsie and put two-and-two together, which would take hours—and delay the Warden talking to Pa."

"Water's boiling," Sister said.

Ruby stirred water into the cocoa mix and carried it the table. "So all because of Tootsie Turner, we weren't notified of Will's death until after the rest of the world knew about it."

"Water under the bridge, Ruby. Doesn't do any good to dwell on such things."

"I know, I know . . . But I have to say, it's a good feeling when things start to fall into place. Well, not *good*, but you know what I mean." She sighed. "That would account for Tootsie suddenly deciding to come to me to get her hair fixed—*and* those big tips. Lord, I'd just like to . . . to hurt her—hurt all them Turners!"

"That kind of thinking will just bring hurt to yourself." Sister blew her cocoa to cool it. "At least the woman's got a modicum of conscience."

"Modicum of conscience?"

"I just heard that on the news program. The reporter was talking about this terrorist who didn't have a modicum of conscience. It means he felt no regret for what he'd done. Tootsie must have a little bit of one or she wouldn't be feeling guilty."

Ruby snorted. "Must not feel too guilty, else she wouldn't have canceled out her Friday appointment."

Sister tapped her spoon on the side of her cup, filling the kitchen with a *tink-tink-tink* sound. "Might not have been her doing."

Ruby considered this. "You might be right. Even if she was the cause of us not being told about Will right away, it still doesn't explain why old man Turner won't tell Mack where Bill and Jack are buried . . . *or* explain why Tootsie never talked about her friendship with Grace in all these years."

"No, it doesn't." Sister's fingers tapped a slow, staccato beat on the oak table. "That'll take a little more figuring out."

Ruby nodded slowly. "You're thinking there's some kind of connection between the two things."

"Aren't you?"

The dryer finished its cycle and shut down, but Ruby did not fold the towels. The breeze rattled the limbs in the tree over the roof, but Sister paid the noise no mind. The sisters ceased their conversation altogether. All was quiet in the old Craftsman-style house under the sweet gum tree. Serenely quiet, save for the sound of two sets of fingers drumming out a staccato rhythm on the top of an old wooden table in a dimly lit kitchen.

CHAPTER TWENTY-FIVE

Mack pulled off the county road and drove up a half-mile track to a one-story house with a pyramidal roof and weathered boarding. His plan was to feel George Folsom out about buying the duplex next to his mother and aunt. He couldn't think of a better neighbor and was sure his mother's animosity would lessen with someone next door that she knew. As icing on the cake, Nonny would visit often, helping to keep an eye on things. The perfect plan.

Climbing from his Bronco, he called out, "Uncle George—"A row of rusted-out farm equipment lined the fencerow around a dilapidated barn, long past usable. The remains of an outhouse sat back of the house, grown over with thick, dead vines. Mack lifted his nose to the air and could have sworn the honey-suckle was still in bloom. The sound of a door opening drew his attention to a figure at the front window, waving him onto the porch.

George Folsom ushered him into a house laid out in a square plan with four rooms, typical of the 1920s and '30s when such houses were built. The old man disappeared into the kitchen as Mack took a seat on an old divan covered with a wash-worn quilt. As he waited, he picked up the scent of

Bull Durham tobacco, something greasy cooked up recently, and dust.

He was not surprised to see George return with two water glasses and a quart jar of golden-colored liquid. But he was surprised when the thought entered his mind that the color of the homemade brew was the exact same color as Nonny's eyes. He pushed that thought from his mind, reminding himself of the purpose for the visit, and nodded as the old man held a glass his way. An invitation to sample the wares.

"Might want to take it slow," George said. "Got a good bite on this jug."

Mack took a swallow and felt his chest turn warm from his gullet to his stomach. "I'd say you did," he croaked.

Chuckling, George said, "Not having any luck with finding old Bill and Jack, huh?"

"Not yet," Mack said. "How'd you know?"

"I figured that's why you come by, wanted to see if I could remember anything else. I can't. I tried to place where Grover might've put those mules, but it's just not coming. And I gotta say, that surprises me."

"Why's that?"

The old man sipped his glass and stared at the oil heater he'd lit earlier, which now glowed orange. "Me and Grover was always tight. Not like blood kin, I'm saying, but we kept up with what the other was doing. He never said a word about those mules being gone till I asked him one day where they was."

"Pa never was a talker."

George sipped some more, continuing to stare at the stove. "Time of year, that's what I figure. We didn't see much of each other after growing season was done. Must've lost those mules after we stopped working the fields."

"What'd he say when you asked him?"

"Nothin', that's what he said. Just turned his back to me and walked away. Took to himself after that. Course, like you said, he never was one to run off at the mouth. And then . . . Well, that was about the time that woman of his took off. Grover had his hands full, trying to raise up two children on his own."

"And you never asked him again about those mules?"

The old man eyed Mack. "He wanted me to know, he would've told me. Nonny ain't had no luck finding 'em neither."

Mack took a sip, letting it mellow on his tongue before allowing it to trickle down his throat. "So you talked to Nonny today?"

A nod. "Funny thing though, she thinks someone was watching her. She said she covered her tracks pretty well, picking some late persimmons as she walked around to hide what she was up to."

Mack felt a jolt hit his stomach that did not come from the Mason jar. "Who was it? She recognize who it was?"

"A dark truck's all she could tell. It hung back though, so she couldn't get a good look."

"She call the sheriff?"

"Naw. She figured it was old Turner, that middle one that takes care of the grazing land."

"That'd be Junior."

"He's got on to her before about trespassing. She watches when the wild plums and persimmons come on, you know."

Mack nodded. "Seems kind of funny he didn't just drive up and confront her if he's done it in the past."

"She thought so, too." The old man scratched his chin. "Didn't know what to make of it."

"You think he's up to no good? I mean, with Nonny."

George snorted loudly. "Don't have to worry about Nonny. That girl don't take nothin' off nobody. Besides, *that* Turner's not a worry. The old man was meaner than a rattlesnake, but that son of his always kowtowed to everyone. I figure that's why he left the prison. No backbone."

My sentiments exactly, Mack thought.

"Better suited to taking care of cows, I figure," George said. "Cows are stupid creatures. Sheep, too. Or so I heard. Was never around sheep much myself."

"Doesn't sound like much of a threat to Nonny then. Wouldn't want her to get into trouble on our account."

The old man laughed softly, his eyes taking on a glow as warm as the drink in his hand. "Can't tell you how glad I am to have that girl back home. Any chance we could get *you* to move back permanent? Know Ruby and Sister would like that, 'specially now that Grover's failing."

Mack downed the rest of his glass, waited for the burn to subside, and cleared his throat. "Well now, that's the reason I come by, Uncle George." Jumping to the point of his visit, he told about his plans to move his mother and aunt into a duplex at the gated community. He intended to feel George out about the other unit next door, but he did not get that far.

"I cannot believe you'd do that to them," the old man said.

Mack sat still, studying the change that had come over the man.

"It'd kill me, Nonny tried to move me into one of them places." George turned his eyes away, fixing his gaze on the stove as though Mack was not fit to look upon.

Mack listened to the uncomfortable silence for a minute more, then set his empty glass on the table next to the divan. He had worn out his welcome.

"Well then, I won't keep you any longer." He paused at the door. "Sister and Mama haven't said a word about not wanting to move into town, Uncle George. Just wanted you to know that."

The old man refilled his glass. "Your grandpap never said a word about not wanting to give up them mules neither."

Mack stood on the porch looking over dark hills, thinking he had been a fool to think George Folsom would be a likely candidate for the other duplex unit. "Stubbornness runs in that family," he muttered.

Climbing into his Bronco, he drove back to the county road. Shifting into neutral, he sat for a while, listening to the engine idle and debating which way to turn.

"You got no choice, Barlow. Anybody knows of someone who might be willing to buy that other unit, it would be Nonny." He turned to the right and stepped on the gas, then wheeled the Bronco into a tight turn the opposite direction, toward home.

"No, I'll sleep on it. I am not in the mood to eat more crow tonight."

CHAPTER TWENTY-SIX

Mack slept later than he planned and hurried to the kitchen for a cup of coffee before he started to search again for the mules. He found his mother twisting the hair of an old woman onto curlers. A pair of glasses lay on the table, thick as the bottom of a coke bottle. From the opaqueness of the woman's eyes, he figured she was all-but-blind.

"You remember Bessie Anderson," Ruby said, speaking abnormally loud. "She and her sisters live at Peaceable. They'd be your cousin, second time removed. Or would it be third? Well, doesn't matter. Family's family."

Mack nodded toward the woman, taking note of his mother's coolness.

"You off to look for them mules?" Bessie cradled a mug of milky coffee in her hands and sipped it now and then.

"Yes ma'am." Mack spoke loudly so the woman could hear him.

"They was a fine-looking pair of mules, matched set of black and tans. Grover thought the world of them."

"Yes ma'am."

Mack finished his coffee and gave his mother's stiffened shoulders a quick hug. "I'll be gone most of the day." He debated mentioning Nonny's experience with the mysterious watcher the day before, but decided he might be jumping the gun. "You and Sister don't take any chances," he said instead. "I'll probably finish up with my list today. You want, I can finish yours, too."

"We'll be fine," Ruby said, her tone businesslike. "Whitey goes with us."

"Did you say Whitey?" Bessie said. "Why, that old hound can barely get around."

"You wouldn't know it these days," Ruby said. "He's acting like a pup."

Mack left his mother dabbing permanent-wave lotion on Bessie's hair. Slipping into his jacket at the front door, he stared openmouthed at new blue Buick sitting inches from his Bronco.

"Now there's an accident waiting to happen," Sister said, looking through the front window. "You believe they renewed her driver's license last month?"

"Bessie did get a might close, didn't she?"

Sister clucked her tongue. "She buys a new car whenever it's time to renew her license. Doesn't want the DMV to see what a bad driver she is—her sisters, too. Got more money than sense. Their Pa did oil drilling down in Texas, made it big."

"All their cars bent up that bad? I'm surprised they haven't been hurt or reported."

"Why, she fell down walking up the front steps to the Driver's Bureau! Had to call the paramedics to band-aid her arm, but she refused to go to the hospital. Said she was there to get her license and she wasn't leaving till they gave it to her."

"And she passed the driving part?"

Sister nodded. "Course, they don't make you parallel-park anymore. You just have to pull up sideways to the space, turn your wheels a little, and say, I can't make it. That's all I did last time I took the test. I figure it's because you can pull in straight these days, like over to the Walmart. Easy parking or not, Bessie's too old to be driving."

"How old would that be?" Mack sidled up next to his aunt. "She's ever bit as old as you, isn't she?"

Sister bristled. "You saying I'm old? People these days are living longer than ever before. Sixty's the new fifty—and seventy's the new sixty."

"How old you feel today?" Mack grinned at the feisty woman. "Don't look a day over thirty."

"Oh, go on." Sister grinned, looking pleased. "You want some company looking for Bill and Jack? Drives me nuts trying to talk to Bessie. She's deaf as a post."

Mack shrugged. "I have some other things to check into, but Mama's planning on going back out later. She'll want you to keep her company. Be careful walking around those pastures and woods."

"Pastures are grazed down, can see real well."

"Yeah, I noticed that. For cattle people, those Turners don't show much sense when it comes to the land."

"That's why they need so much of it."

Mack chuckled. Sometimes Sister's insight amazed him. "I'll check on Pa while I'm in town. You and Mama don't need to drive in."

Mack worked several minutes to get his car out of the driveway where Bessie Anderson had wedged him against the old willow tree. He laughed again as he pulled past a new Buick that now resembled a crushed beer can.

No two ways about it, he thought. It's in the genes.

*****

Mack spent the morning checking the remaining plots of land that Nonny Folsom had marked on his map. He kept an eye on his rearview mirror for a dark pickup and felt glad the trees had dropped most of their leaves so he could see distantly. As a precaution, he scanned the areas to be searched before setting out, looking for anything that might look out of place. A practice he'd gotten good at years ago.

At one point, he caught himself thinking that the closeness of the undergrowth was not as bad as he had found it when he first mustered out. But then a sharp *snap* in the brush brought him to a squatting crouch and reaching for a weapon that was not there. He ran a zigzag pattern from the woods, eyes over his shoulder searching for movement, palms so sweaty he had to wipe them dry on his pant leg.

Back at the car, Mack noticed the tremble in his hands. What the hell's got into me? he thought, thinking he'd seen meaner bush in Colombia and Bolivia. Though logical thinking filled his mind, his body was slow to respond. Pulse throbbing like a drum, an image of wide empty spaces popped into his mind. He needed to shed this country, he thought. Get back to safe ground.

Not tarrying, Mack ticked off the rest of his list, continuing to move warily, an eye to his rear. But he did not find the doubletree or a black pickup. It was the latter he found the most puzzling.

Why was Nonny seen as a threat and he wasn't, he wondered, and decided it had to be because of where she was looking. Deciding to take another look at her map, he added her name to his to-do list, which was growing longer by the minute.

Swinging past the nursing home, he found his grandfather sleeping soundly. After confirming with the nurse that she had discontinued the use of meds, he went back to looking for a buyer for the spare duplex.

He bought a *McAlester News-Capital & Democrat* out of a curbside newspaper box and stopped at Popeye's for chicken strips, French fries, and coleslaw. As he ate, he scanned want ads for buyers looking for horse property, but no prospects surfaced. Pitching the newspaper into a waste barrel, he decided to return home using the route Nonny would travel. If he ran into her, he could take a look at her map and ask her about possible buyers for the other duplex unit. Two birds with one stone.

But as he drove down Choctaw Street, he was drawn to an old rock building that once served as a grocery store. He sat outside for a while, staring at the buckling sidewalks lined with umbrella trees and a sagging roof that needed bracing. Then, kicking himself mentally for succumbing to curiosity, he walked to the door where an unprofessionally painted sign read SHELTER.

The interior of the building had been gutted since the days he frequented the place. Counters and shelving had been replaced with folding tables and, along the back, two rows of cots had been set up, separated with a makeshift partition. One side was marked WOMEN and the other, MEN.

"Coffee's always on."

Mack turned to the voice and was surprised to see an older man smiling at him. He was soft looking, both around the middle and in his eyes, and had a flat nose that spoke to having been broken at some point. A scar at his hairline resembled the bottom curve of a wine bottle.

"Got a pot of soup cooking, be ready soon," the man said. "Some dunkers next to the coffee pot. Couple days old, but still good." He paused, studying Mack. "Just passing through town? Haven't seen you in here before."

"No sir, I'm visiting family. Name's Mack Barlow." He stuck out his hand.

"I go by Chester. I run this place."

"It used to be a hardware store. Before that, a grocery. My folks used to shop here when I was a boy."

"Right, right. Well, here's how it came down, Mack. Town condemned the building, I circulated a petition to start up a homeless shelter, and the town went for it. Seems they could get more as a tax write-off than sell it outright."

"You live here then?" Mack nodded toward the cots at the back of the room.

"Not here, up on the hill there." Chester jerked a thumb over his shoulder. "Above the canal in my folk's old place. I moved back from Norman after I retired. Taught philosophy there."

"Philosophy—in Oklahoma?" Mack laughed.

"I get that response a lot. You know, it's not like I'm the only philosopher Oklahoma ever produced."

Mack grinned. "Some would consider Will Rogers a philosopher."

Through the beard, Chester's teeth made a showing. "Only a native son would remember that nugget. If you want to look around, go ahead." He waved an arm around the building. "Not much to see. Like I said, coffee's on."

"Thanks, but I didn't really come to look at the place." Mack got a questioning look. "I'm, uh, I'm a friend of Nonny Folsom."

Chester's grin widened, along with his eyes. "No kidding? Well, that's good, *real* good. She could do with a *friend*."

Mack read the implication in the words. "Not that kind of friend," he said, wondering if the man ever stopped grinning. "I mean, maybe once, but we said our *adieus* a long time back."

"*Oh*, I see. So you thought Nonny and I were . . . *friends*."

"No, nothing like that," Mack said, feeling a sudden need to retreat.

"Sure it is. You thought we had a thing going, came to check me out."

Mack took a step backward. "No, it's just that this . . ." He waved his arm in an arc. "This *do-good* stuff is out of character for Nonny, at least the one I knew twenty years ago. Back then, all she wanted was to make something of herself."

"Do-good stuff." Chester nodded thoughtfully. "For a fact, it is out of character for the old Nonny. She turned out to be a fine teacher, a real loss to the profession." He paused. "But I'm inclined to think their loss means a bigger win for mankind—if I could just get her to face off, that is."

Mack shook his head. "You lost me."

"I mean she chose the wrong battle to begin with. Those spoiled brats filling up classrooms aren't the ones who will inherit this earth. It's the kids that walk through *these* doors got the guts to go head-to-head with the bad guys. Most of them are battle savvy before they reach puberty." Another pause. "That's why I'm here."

Still lost, Mack said, "It is?"

"Yeah, I was one of those brats. Went to college on a full-ride scholarship. Got a doctorate degree and holed up in that philosophy building all my life—my entire life. Then I got old. I asked myself the day I retired what it had all been for. Speculating about the meaning of words—*words*. Debating what long-dead men said hundreds of years ago. Who the hell cares? I never fought a battle in my life, not a real one."

Mack studied the scar on the man's head again. "Well, from what I seen of some of the guys that who inhabit these soup kitchens, you just might find one."

"Oh, I hope so, Mack. One with a righteous purpose." The smile disappeared suddenly. "You the reason Nonny's turned so sour?"

"Sour?"

"Dark. Moody. Like the old days. I've been worried she was close to falling off the wagon."

"Wagon." Mack stared at the man. "You mean, as in . . ."

"You didn't know she was a recovering alcoholic?"

"We, uh, we haven't seen each other in a lot of years." Mack's head began to spin, as though his parachute hadn't opened and he was free falling. "But no, I didn't know that."

"She's been dry for three years now, ever since she came back home."

"So that's why she came back," Mack murmured, things starting to fall into place.

"That, and the fact she got fired."

"*Fired*." Mack began a slow retreat toward the door. "Why are you telling me all this? It's none of my business."

"Because you want to know." Chester grinned again. "I can see it in your eyes. I've known Nonny for a lot of years, ever since she started teaching, and pride myself on being a pretty fair judge of man—as in mankind." His mouth took a downturn. "Even so, I didn't see it coming. Whatever it was that drove her to the edge, I mean. One day, she just dropped over. Couldn't face her students anymore. Laid up in her apartment drunk as a skunk. Then a female student filed a complaint about strange behavior, and she got fired."

"Strange behavior." Mack digested the words slowly. "Are you saying . . ."

The grin appeared again. "She's not. Trust me, I would know."

The old saying, It takes one to know one, crossed through Mack's mind. Though he wanted to leave, he held his ground because the man had hit one nail square on the head. He *did* feel a strong need to know what had changed Nonny.

"To finish this saga," Chester said, "Nonny's dad died and I told her his passing was her redemption, to take it and run—and, she did. I retired not long after, so we both moved back home. She's been doing all right until just recently. You the reason?"

"Can't imagine I would be. At least, not directly."

Chester raised his eyebrows and waited.

"See, she's been helping me out with some family business." Mack lifted his palms. "But I don't see how that could be connected. I'm at a loss."

Chester nodded. "Well, hopefully she'll get whatever's on her chest off it before she backslides." He turned, sniffing the air. "I need to stir a pot in the back room. It was good to meet you. Stop by again."

Mack shook the extended hand out of habit. When Chester didn't loosen his grip, Mack had no choice but look him in the eye.

"You give any thought to laying down your sword and shield, Mack?"

Mack heard the words but did not linger on them for he was hammering on another nail. The softness of the man's hand in his own and the possibility of what the lingering handshake was telegraphing.

"I don't know what you're talking about, dude, but you might want to turn loose of my hand."

Chester let go of the hand, but not the thought. "All I was saying is I see a lot of people who've done battle walk through these doors." He motioned toward the kitchen again. "*Must* stir that pot."

Mack watched the man disappear through a door leading to the back of the building, then left through the front. He digested Chester's words as he drove, rechewing the revelations about Nonny, her need to fill her time with things like jelly and persimmons and dusty books, the possibility that he could be the cause of her backslide.

No two ways about it, he thought. For everyone's best interest, he needed to close this business down and get the hell out of Dodge.

CHAPTER TWENTY-SEVEN

Mack met up with Nonny about two o'clock, by chance, not plan. At his own front door, talking to his very excited mother.

"What's going on, Mama," he said, stepping from his Bronco.

"Sister's taken off. I thought she was napping like she does in the afternoon, so I didn't miss her until right now."

"Do you know how long she's been gone?" Nonny asked.

"No, I don't. She might've left when Bessie did. Maybe that's why I didn't hear her drive off."

"*Drive* off?" Mack said.

"She took the car and Whitey."

"Bet you she's looking for those mules," Nonny said.

Mack motioned his mother and Nonny to his Bronco. "Let's go find her."

"She has to be close." Nonny helped Ruby into the front seat and climbed into the back. "None of those places I marked are too far from here."

"You know which ones you already checked, Mama, so you have to guide me." Mack slowed to a rolling stop at the county road. "Which way do we go?"

"Right, go right. We went left yesterday."

"That makes sense," Nonny said. "Several of the plots on that road were lined up. It would make sense, she'd go that way."

"That dark pickup follow you again today?" Mack looked at Nonny through the rearview mirror.

"How'd you know about that?" She frowned slightly. "But yes, it did. Early on, but I didn't see it later in the day." She paused. "So you saw George?"

"Dark pickup?" Ruby said. "Billy Joe Turner drives a black pickup and he stopped us on the road yesterday."

"He what—? Why didn't you tell me about that, Mama?"

"I don't know, just didn't seem important. Is it important? I mean, he was just warning us not to trespass—Look, up there. That's my car."

Mack pulled up behind his mother's gray sedan and spotted a little woman in muddy clothes and boots standing in front of a gate. The old white dog was next to her, mud caked to his belly. His mother and Nonny beat him to Sister's side.

Sister looked confused as the trio surrounded her. "Lord help, what's wrong? Is it Pa?"

Ruby threw her hands in the air. "*You're* what's wrong! Why'd you take off like that? What's got into you, Pearl Anderson."

"I'm tired of sitting on my butt, that's what's wrong with me!"

"You fall down, Sister?" Nonny checked the little woman over. "You're muddy to your knees."

Mack gave his aunt the once-over, too. "You trying to prove a point because I teased you about your age, Sister?"

Sister clapped her hands over her ears. "Would you all just *hush*. You're getting me all confused."

"Give her some space," Mack said. "You gave us a scare, Sister, that's all. Now promise me you won't go looking for those mules again by yourself."

"No need to. I found 'em."

"What?" Ruby said. "You found Bill and Jack?"

"Not exactly, but I'd bet a dollar to a donut, they're in there." Sister pointed beyond the gate to the pastureland beyond.

"So you *haven't* found them!" Ruby wagged her head. "Sister, you've got to stop this nonsense."

"Nonsense! See that padlock on the gate? I checked three other places before I got here and none of the gates were locked. And none of those we looked at yesterday were either."

Mack studied the gate, made of heavy-duty rolled steel attached to metal posts set in concrete. "And I didn't find any padlocks on those I checked either."

"Nor me," Nonny said.

"You ever see so many posted signs?" Sister pointed to the fence line. "And look at that field. Hasn't been a brush hog on it in years. Thickets taking over, grass taller than Whitey. This is the only place that hasn't been overgrazed."

Mack scanned the brushy acreage. "You're making sense, Sister."

"And it's close enough Pa could have visited it real quick. He could walk it in ten, twenty minutes, he was to cut across the hill from our house."

"Like we were talking about last night," Ruby murmured.

"And listen." Sister held her finger to her mouth, then pointed to Whitey, whose ears were cocked forward.

Mack looked in the direction the old dog was looking. "What is that? Wind chimes?"

"Not wind chimes," Sister said. "That's the sound of a doubletree clanking against trace chains. We've been looking on the ground and Pa hung it in a tree. *Looky there*." The little woman pointed to a clump of trees not too distant where a hinged object swayed between two hickories.

"You *did* find them." Ruby gave her sister a quick hug. "Come on, let's have a look. We can squeeze through the wire right down there."

As Ruby made her way through the stiff grass along the barrow ditch, Nonny grabbed her arm. "Wait, Ruby. There's something else you need to know before we go in there."

Mack noticed the troubled look on Nonny's face. "What is it? You find something else?"

"I tried to tell you a couple of nights ago," Nonny said, talking to Ruby. "But you have such hard feelings against your mother and I just couldn't understand how you could feel that way. You know, be so judgmental. So . . . unforgiving."

"What are you saying," Ruby said.

"It's Grace. She's out there, too."

"We know that," Mack said. "You're the one brought the paper saying she was buried in Beulah Land."

"Yeah," Sister said. "And we're looking at Beulah Land right now."

"But you don't know that Pa bought her a grave marker and had it inscribed."

"Inscribed? What's it say on it," Mack said.

"It says, 'Grace, God Grant Forgiveness to Thee and Me.'"

"Forgiveness?" Sister said. "Forgiveness for what?"

"Oh, my Lord." Ruby looked at Nonny. "And you didn't tell me?"

"I tried, Ruby. I wanted to."

"That's why they let that grass grow up so tall." Sister resumed her tramp down the fencerow. "But why wouldn't the Turners want us to know Grace had a tombstone out there?"

Mack looked up and down the road to make sure the coast was clear, then pulled the strands apart so Sister could climb through the fence. "You've earned the right to be the first one to step onto Beulah Land, Sister."

After his mother and Nonny crawled through the fence, he stepped over it and he walked up next to Nonny. "So, you saw that pickup this morning?"

"Yes, *early* this morning. Could've been Billy Joe, I suppose. He works the afternoon shift at the pen."

"What about Junior? He's supposed to be managing the properties. Why haven't we seen him?"

"He's down with the gout," Ruby called over her shoulder. "I heard that just last week, can't remember who it was mentioned it. One of the ladies getting a perm, I think."

"Thank Heaven for small blessings," Sister said, following Whitey who had taken the lead. "Maybe the enemy won't see us."

Minutes later, the entourage congregated beneath a pair of hickory trees where the remnants of an old doubletree was strung between chains. The bark on the trees had grown around the chains so they became part of the trunk, securing the hinged wood bars between them. The oak bars were white with age but still solidly attached to the two metal rings that linked them. The entire contraption made a harsh musical sound when it rattled in the wind.

Mack stood between his mother and aunt, staring at it. "Now that took some effort," he murmured. "Bet those mules are buried right where we stand, laid out like they were still hitched to that doubletree."

"I'm surprised it's still of a piece," Sister said. "Wouldn't be, cattle was let run."

Mack nodded. "Cattle would've used it to rub the flies off. And cattlemen would've put it to use for just that purpose, hung bags of fly repellant from it. What surprises me is the Turners didn't."

"Must be because of Grace." Sister looked around. "It's a right pretty piece, idn't it? I can see why he called it Beulah Land. I bet he planned to put a house right there." She pointed to a spot beyond where the two mules were buried. "And plant a crop on that back piece."

"That would make sense." Mack surveyed the plot of land, thinking a drilling of alfalfa seed would enrich the grass tenfold.

"Well, here she is." Nonny pulled clumps of grass away from a headstone.

Mack joined her. "Stone's a mess. What is that stuff?"

"Lichens." She rubbed her hand over the lettering. "You want, I can do a rubbing so you can read what's on it."

Sister joined them. "Why not just wash it down good with bleach?"

Nonny shook her head. "Bleach would ruin the marble, but there's other ways to clean it that wouldn't. I can read up on how it's done, you want."

"Idn't that something." Sister stared at the stone. "All these years and this is the first time I visited my mother's grave."

Mack turned toward his own mother, who was still standing beneath the two hickories. "Mama, don't you want a look?"

"I just don't know what to think," she called across the distance. "I can't believe she's been here all along . . . and with a tombstone."

"And all alone," Nonny murmured, running her hands along the marble inscription.

Mack eyed Nonny, recalling her mother had passed away when they had been in high school. "Does she make you miss your own mother, Nonny? Is that what you're thinking?"

"Mama? No, why would you think that?" She rose quickly and stepped away from the stone. "It's just so isolated out here, that's all."

"Ruby, get over here and take a look," Sister called out. "You're being foolish."

"In a minute," Ruby replied. "I need a minute."

Mack walked to where his mother stood and took her by the shoulders. "What is it, Mama? Most people would want to pay their respects to their mother. I'm just not getting it."

"Now isn't that surprising!" Ruby made her way to the tombstone, leaving Mack standing.

Suddenly, the wind jangled the contraption hanging in the tree, startling him. Studying the oak bars that made up the doubletree, he felt in his pocket for his knife. Taking hold of one of the pieces, he dug around until two objects fell into his hand. Bullet fragments.

What the hell happened here? He studied the ground, looking for shell casings. Finding nothing, he rejoined toward the others, listening to their conversation as he approached.

"Must've cost Pa a pretty penny," Sister said. "That's a fine-looking stone."

"Almost a thousand dollars," Nonny said. "For the stone and the casket."

"A thousand dollars—" Ruby turned to her sister. "Where in the world would Pa get that kind of money?"

As his mother and aunt debated the cost, Nonny walked up beside Mack. "What'd you find in that doubletree?"

"Some, uh, some old nails."

"Don't bullshit me, Mack Barlow. What'd you find?"

Reluctantly, he opened his hand. "What's that look like to you?" Two lumps of metal rested in his palm.

"What is that?" Sister joined them and picked one of the small pieces of metal. "Piece of carriage bolt?"

"It's not a bolt." Nonny picked up the other piece. "That's a bullet, what's left of one. Geez, what do you figure the caliber to be?"

Ruby joined them and examined the piece Sister handed her. "Target practice more than likely. Or kids hunting."

"Pretty large caliber for target practice," Mack said. "And the only thing people would be shooting out here would be squirrels or rabbits, using a .22. Anything else would've blown a small animal to pieces. Anyhow, from the looks of these slugs, they've have been in that oak a long time."

Mack heard Whitey's low growl and looked toward the road where a passing car had slowed. "C'mon," he said, "let's get back to the house. Don't want to alert the enemy we been here."

*****

Nonny took charge of Sister, helping her through the tall grass, and Ruby followed behind the pair. Mack stayed behind to hide their passing and straightened the fence wire after everyone had crawled back through. Ruby drove Sister back to the home place while Mack followed close behind, Nonny beside him and Whitey in the backseat.

"What do you figure?" He looked toward Nonny, who sat quiet. "You deconstructed this mess yet?"

Nonny's response was caustic. "What do you think?"

He sat silent, long enough for Nonny to look his way.

"What *do* you think, Mack?"

Mack hesitated. "I think I've troubled you enough with this business, Nonny. We couldn't have done it without you, but I can't ask you to do anything more."

"Oh no you don't, buddy," she snorted. "Not after I come this far. Now, what do you think?"

Knowing the battle was lost, Mack put his mind on winning the war. "Those records, did we check everything there was to check? Find everything there was to find?"

"At the Genealogy Society and courthouse? I can't think of anything we might've missed."

"What about those arrest records? Would there be any more like that? Maybe a police or a missing person's report?"

She grew thoughtful. "Not there. Still, anything of significance should've been listed in that book you looked at. What else would there be?"

"Well now, that's the question, isn't it." He paused, rubbing fingers across his mouth. "Anything that might smack of being odd, out of the ordinary?"

She sat quiet a minute. "Well, around here anything unusual would have made headlines . . ." She paused, blinking rapidly. "And the *newspaper* keeps microfiche archives. Go on."

"What do you think a plot of land the size of that one back there would go for fifty, sixty years ago? Maybe a couple hundred dollars?"

"At most— *Oh*, you're thinking Pa sold off Beulah Land for the money to buy the casket and stone."

"Right. And why do you figure anyone as tight as old Washburn would give Pa that kind of money for a piece of land worth two hundred bucks?"

Nonny smirked. "You're getting pretty good at this deconstruction business, Mack Barlow. I'll check newspaper records."

Recalling Chester Barnes' concern again, Mack did some quick reconnoitering. "No—you've done enough. You need to get back to . . ." Mack waved a hand in the air. "To whatever it was you were doing before I dumped this mess in your lap."

Nonny frowned. "Such as?"

"Your job. And jelly. Helping Chester out. Taking Henry Carter gumdrops—"

"Chester?" Nonny jerked upright. "First you go see Uncle George, then you go to the shelter? You checking up on me, Mack?"

"No . . . Well, not with Uncle George anyway." He blew out his breath. "Aw hell, I've run into a situation with this duplex deal, the one I'm buying for Mama and Sister. The only way the builder will make the changes I want is if I can sell both sides. I'm looking for someone to buy the other half of it."

"And you thought Uncle George might be a good candidate?"

"He's not a spring chicken anymore, can barely get around."

"What did he tell you?"

"I figure you know that already." Mack pulled to a stop behind his mother's car. "That's the honest-to-God truth, Nonny. Uncle George isn't getting any younger. Believe it or not, I'm just trying to do the right thing here."

Nonny laughed, humorlessly. "Yeah well, I used to think I had all the answers, too. And Chester?"

"Curiosity, pure and simple. Just wanted to see what kind of a guy turned your crank these days. He's a nice guy, for a . . . you know."

She smiled. "Yeah, he is. And?"

He hesitated. "And he's worried about you. Says something's put you into a blue funk the last couple of days and he's afraid you might . . ." He rubbed his mouth. "Aw hell, he's afraid you might fall off the wagon."

She stopped smiling. "What else did he tell you?"

Mack looked out his side window, saw his mother and aunt walking up the steps to the house, then faced Nonny again. “He said alcoholism led to your getting fired from your teaching job.”

She remained silent.

“Look, I didn’t go there to pry.” Mack studied Nonny’s face, which had turned to stone. “Chester volunteered the information.”

“It was actually the other way around,” Nonny said, talking slow.

“What?”

“The classroom led to the drinking.” She got out of the Bronco. “I’ll run by the newspaper office on my way back to the post office,” she said. “And I’ll think on who might be a likely candidate for the other side of that duplex.”

Watching Nonny drive off, Mack scratched Whitey’s ears. “Damn,” he muttered. “All I’ve done since I got here is kick over one can of worms after another.”

“*Mack*, did you hear me?

He turned toward the house. “What is it, Mama?”

“I said I called your grandpa to tell him we found Bill and Jack and the nurse said they can’t wake him up. They think he’s gone into a coma.”

Hurriedly, Mack opened the car doors for his mother and aunt.

“I thought you went by to check on him today, Mack.” Sister settled in the backseat.

“I did. He was sleeping.”

“And you didn’t try to wake him up?”

“Didn’t see any reason to. I thought they might’ve started the shots again, to make him sleep through those spells. So I checked in at the nurse’s station, then left.”

"Had they?" Ruby said, hope in her voice. "Give him another shot, I mean?"

"No. That's why I figured he was asleep."

"Oh, Lord," Ruby mumbled. "He just has to know we found them mules. I'd never forgive myself if he died not knowing."

"Or dies before we can get our hands on Beulah Land," Sister said.

"What?" Ruby turned to her sister.

Mack followed suit, looking through the rearview mirror to where his aunt sat. "What do you mean, get our hands on Beulah Land?"

"How else are we gonna bury Pa next to Bill and Jack if we don't get our hands on Beulah Land?"

Hell, Mack thought. Sister's right again. We still have *that* fly in the ointment.

CHAPTER TWENTY-EIGHT

Nonny munched on a wilted carrot from the cardboard box on the passenger seat. As the grumbling in her stomach now reminded her, she had skipped lunch to visit the newspaper office. She had barely made a dent in the microfiche archives before the record room closed the previous night, necessitating another visit today. What she found produced more questions than answers.

In the time it took to drive from the Piggly Wiggly to the Shelter on Choctaw Street, she had consumed two more carrots and a parsnip. Age had not softened the bitterness of the raw parsnip, and she still felt its bite on her tongue as she pushed open the back door to the Shelter.

Chester turned toward the noise her entrance made, his smile fading as she slammed the box on the rickety table in the center of the room.

"I never took you for a gossip," she snapped.

"Gossip? *Oh* . . ." Chester let the word hang in the air. "Gossips tend to exaggerate the truth, spread malicious lies. Are you saying what I told that friend of yours wasn't true?"

"Don't pull that cute stuff on me, Chester. What's this crap about me being in a blue funk?"

"Blue funk? *Oh . . .*" Chester let the word hang again. "I would never have described your recent depression in those terms, but I like it. Mack's description works better than any I could've come up with." He paused, grinning. "Would you prefer *dejection*? No? How about something more scientific, like *melancholia*—"

"Shut up, Chester." Nonny unloaded the box of vegetables into the kitchen sink, heaving those beyond salvage into a waste can with less-than-average accuracy.

Chester watched as vegetables piled up on the floor, then faced her. "So he talked to you about it. That's good." He set a pot on the stove and poured a large can of chicken broth into it. "Sounds like a man that doesn't beat around the bush."

She scowled. "He hovered like a mother hen, and you know how I hate that."

He chuckled. "Whatever works, that's my motto. I'll have to file that one away for future reference. Forget subtlety, go for hovering—"

"Shut up, Chester!" Nonny gouged bruises out of potatoes, then diced them into a beat-up colander. "He always did hover, even when we were kids." She shook her head as if to dislodge something stuck there, then began working on carrots.

"Is that when you started practicing avoidance? Let's see, so that would be twenty, thirty years now?"

"What?" Nonny brushed the hair from her eyes.

"Old habits are the hardest to change." He rolled his sleeves and began rinsing the pared vegetables. "Is that when Mack started running away, too?"

The statement brought Nonny to a standstill. "He didn't run away. He joined the Marines."

"Marines, huh." Chester looked thoughtful. "That could explain the tattoos."

"What tattoos?" She frowned. "I haven't seen any tattoos."

"I'm not talking about those done in tattoo parlors," he said, talking as he worked. "I'm talking about internal ones. Pricks that accumulate under the skin, not unlike cuts from paring knives, or scrapes from wading through brambles. Interlacing and overlapping until an indelible pattern emerges, permanently separating the person from others. It shows in the eyes."

Nonny took a minute to wade through Chester's academic parlance, then said, "Eyes? What'd you see in Mack's eyes?"

"Caution, like that of a hunter . . . or maybe, the hunted. And he never moved back here after you two split up?" He paused to look at her. "Interesting."

"Are you saying it's my fault Mack never moved back here?" She gave her head a vigorous shake. "I *won't* take the blame for that. He left before I did." She waved a hand through the air, indicating the space around them. "There just wasn't anything to move back to. He's in the construction business and, in case you haven't noticed, this is about the deadest place on the planet." She took a long breath, then turned her attention to parsnips.

Several minutes passed before Chester spoke again. "Weather's turning cold up north."

"What?" She looked at him, her brow puckered.

"Homeless have started their migration south. Half dozen young people came through here just last night. Even a couple of young women. I'd say about twenty years old or so."

Nonny cleared her throat. “So how’d we get from blue funks to the weather?”

“Weather? I thought we were talking about people running away from themselves, from what they can’t stand to face up to.”

“I’m not running—”

“Good. About time. Then you won’t mind serving this soup to those youngsters when they come back tonight. They’d be just about the age of your students—had you stayed at the university. You know, the young women you took to hovering over like a mother hen at the end there?”

Nonny dropped her paring knife in the sink and walked to the back door. Slamming it behind her, she stomped to her cold vehicle. Chester’s smugness still stinging, she drove a meandering path, wondering where to go and what to do. She’d planned to spend the afternoon at the shelter, but Chester had ruined that plan.

Her carefully orchestrated day had gone to hell from beginning to end. Earlier in the day, she’d stopped at the Barlow’s, planning to leave the information she had found at the library with Mack, but she had found no one home. Given Ruby’s state of mind, she’d decided against leaving it in their mailbox, and so carried it back to town. Now, glancing at the folder on the passenger seat, she pulled over at a payphone to call Mack. Surely he was home by then.

A chilling wind hit her full face as she stepped to the ground. Temperatures had dropped quickly and moisture hazed the air. Headlights were rimmed with fluorescent haloes and barren trees looked like knobby-limbed skeletons. She fumbled coins from her purse and dropped them into the slot.

Listening to the rings on the other end of the line, she thought again of her anger with Chester. She hadn’t planned to get into it with him, but she had, and so here she was standing at an open phone booth freezing her ass off. She found herself wishing she could turn back the clock, take a different path than the one that had brought her into the Barlow's problems in the first place. But that grace period had passed. She exhaled a breath that smelled of parsnip, filled her lungs with air smelling of the Gulf coast front that had moved in, and tried to focus. Now that Grace had been found, maybe things would go back to normal.

Normal. That thought produced a bitter laugh. Getting no response at the Barlow place, she headed for the nursing home. The day's still young, she thought, and old people love to shoot the breeze.

*****

Finding Mack's Bronco in the parking lot, Nonny sensed something amiss. She hurried down the hallway and opened the door to Pa's room. She saw the IV bottle hanging above the bed, then Mack sitting beside the bed. The circles under his eyes indicated he'd been there all night.

"Come on in," he said. "He can't hear you."

"What is it?"

"Coma."

"What happened? He was doing fine."

"Mama's blaming herself—or me. Well, maybe it is my fault." He rubbed his eyes. "You remember that day I had her pretend to be Grace, talk to Pa about the war?"

"But I thought that went well."

"So did I. But after he got things off his chest, seems he decided it was time to lay down and die."

"Good God, what next." Nonny looked around the empty room. "Where's Ruby? Sister?"

"Lunchroom. The nurse's aide fixed then a bowl of soup, insisting they eat something."

"Mr. Carter?"

"They moved him to another room because . . ." He nodded at his grandfather.

"What about you? You could probably use some food, too."

"Not hungry." He glanced at the folder in her hand. "That what you found at the newspaper office?"

"Oh . . . yes." Handing him the folder, she stood at the end of the bed, looking down on the old man who had shriveled to a rack of bones and wondering at the ultimate act of freedom his forgiveness had wrought. "I didn't find a police or missing person report, just that little article with a Tulsa byline."

"What do you make of it?" he asked, skimming the article quickly.

"I don't know." She pulled up the empty chair next to him. "Grace died in an accident. Wouldn't have figured that one. You?"

"Hell, no. And here I was thinking Pa had a hand in it. Kind of anticlimactic, isn't it?"

Nonny turned to stare at Mack, wondering how he could think his grandfather had a hand in Grace's disappearance . . . her death.

"Article says she was trying to flag down a Greyhound bus, got sideswiped," she said. "No luggage, just a hundred-dollar bill in her pocket. Now *that's* strange."

Mack skimmed the article again. "Plenty of witnesses on the bus. They all said the same thing. The woman just appeared out of nowhere, not the driver's fault."

"What do you figure happened?"

Staring into space, he said, "I figure she was running away. Pa probably had one of his spells, scared her so bad she ran. That's what I think."

"Pa was suffering from post-traumatic stress even back then?"

He shrugged. "I think that's why he wanted Grace to forgive him. He, uh, he also hit Mama. That's when we put him in here."

Nonny drew in a breath. "What about the tombstone?"

He frowned. "I'm not following you."

"There's more to it than that. Why would Pa want forgiveness for himself *and* her? And why did she leave the children behind?" She swallowed. "That's not . . . normal."

Mack reached into his shirt pocket and pulled out the two slugs he had dug from the double tree. "Someone shot those mules."

Nonny made a grunting sound. "Now that's a stretch, Mack. How in the world did you come to that conclusion?"

"Because I know killing." Mack turned away, his eyes set on some distant place. "Someone was shooting wild, out of control." He shook his head as if to clear it. "I figure Grace shot them, that's why they died at the same time."

Nonny absorbed this. "I thought Grace was a little bit of a woman."

"She was, and from what I understand, none too brave. But the gun these slugs came from would've equalized size and given someone a lot of courage." He shook the slugs in his hand, producing the hollow *clink* of metal rattling against metal.

"I don't know, Mack," she said, sounding skeptical. "Who in their right mind would kill two mules?"

"Someone who *wasn't* in her right mind. She was running away, that's for sure, and I think it was from something more than Pa's nightmares." He looked again at the remains of the two bullets. "She shot those mules."

"What on earth would drive her to *do* that?" Nonny massaged a throb in her temples.

"I've been sitting here for hours trying to figure that one out." Mack looked at the newspaper clipping again. "I better go show this to Mama."

"Shouldn't you wait a bit? She has to be exhausted."

"Don't want her thinking I'm keeping something else from her. She's running on a short fuse these days."

"I'll do it." Nonny took the clipping from Mack's hand. "You sit with Pa, in case he comes to."

"You think he will?"

Deciding against uttering false promises, she responded with a shrug.

*****

Hurrying to the recreation room, Nonny spotted Ruby and Sister sitting at a corner table. They were wearing the same clothes she had seen them in the day before and their faces were wrung with fatigue. She felt glad when they seemed pleased to see her. Accepting the offer of coffee from the nurse's aide, she laid the clipping in the middle of the table.

Ruby eyed the paper suspiciously. "What now?

"Nothing pleasant," Nonny said.

"Just tell us what it is," Sister said. "My eyes are so gritty, I couldn't read anything, my life depended on it."

Nonny read the clipping and watched the fatigue in their faces deepen.

"Well, I'll swan," Sister murmured finally.

Ruby let out a bitter-sounding laugh. "I swear, sounds like something in one of those daytime soap operas."

"You worried we'll be the laughing stock of the county if this gets out?" Sister tapped the article on the table. "That why you're laughing?"

"No, Sister," Ruby said. "I'm laughing because I'm too tired to think."

"Well, at least we know where Pa brought Grace back from," Nonny said. "And why."

"Pa's in a coma," Ruby said.

"I know. I stopped by the room first. Mack told me you were here."

"You figured anything out?" Sister looked at Nonny. "You think of any way to get him buried there in Beulah Land? Any *legal* way?"

"I haven't given it any more thought, Sister. But if Grace was buried there, it sounds as though the deed to that piece of land wouldn't prohibit Pa being buried there."

"You saying the deed to the piece of land would say that?" Ruby said. "It would say a person could or couldn't be buried there?"

"Not exactly." Nonny raised her hands, sighing. "It would spell out prohibitions, like easements and water rights and any other restrictions. Billy Joe talked about it at the church that Sunday. Remember?"

"That's right, he did."

"Besides, with Grace there, a precedent's been set. So, a case could be made for burying Pa there. Of course, that route could take time, and I'm not sure how much time he has left."

"I asked the doctor about that," Sister said.

"You did?" Ruby said, looking at her sister. "What'd he say?"

"Said it depended on the person. Could go tomorrow, could last a month or more. Said it was up to the family to take him off life support should he not come out of it on his own."

Ruby sat up straight. "We'll do no such thing!"

Nonny reached for her hand. "We're not there yet, Ruby."

Ruby's eyes grew liquid. "I got so much I need to say to him, things I should've said." She looked at Nonny. "I'm so sorry I called you a lesbian. I'm just not thinking straight these days."

"Not a problem, Ruby. It was a reasonable assumption."

"I told her you wasn't," Sister said. "I let myself get spoilt, too. That's why I never married."

"Spoiled?" Nonny gave Sister a look. "You don't mean . . .?"

"I told Sister that women these days didn't worry about such things," Ruby interjected. "Shoot, on the TV, girls are losing their virginity by the time they're twelve years old. These days, men don't think anything about it if a woman's not a virgin when they marry."

Nonny rubbed her face, thinking she was being told things that she had no need to know. Then she began to worry that people would learn more about her than they needed to know—than she *wanted* them to know. She recalled Mack's admonition about her needing to detach herself from the Barlow situation and considered they were finally in agreement on something.

"Can we have this newspaper clipping?" Sister said. "When I get my glasses cleaned, I'd like to read it."

"Sure thing." Nonny rose from her chair, glad for the opportunity to disengage from the Barlows.

"Where you going?" Ruby asked.

"I need to run the trays back to the post office. What say I check in with you later?"

Nonny was already moving in the direction of the door when both the sisters said their farewells. Wondering how her own life had become so public and when it had taken on the flavor of a TV soap opera, she wished for a way to backtrack. A chance to take a different path than the one she had chosen. Pushing through the front door of the nursing home, she decided it was time to move on down the road. She halted suddenly, realizing there was no place for her to go.

When Uncle George came to mind, she thought about how much she would miss the old man. How he was alone and the last of his line. How he made moonshine just to fill the time. The next thing Nonny knew, she was thinking about a still in the piney woods back of his barn.

"Just one," she mumbled as she made her way across the icy parking lot. "I could stop with just one." Nonny climbed into the cold Jeep but did not turn the key in the ignition. She sat there, staring through a windshield edging with frost. "That's what you said that day you took the first one" she mumbled. "The day you decided to look for *her*."

As though repetition would turn a cliché into a truism, Nonny reached for the ignition and reiterated her previous thought. "I could stop with one, just one to take the edge off . I know I could . . ."

CHAPTER TWENTY-NINE

Ruby sat across the kitchen table from Sister, staring at the newspaper clipping that told of her mother's death. "I can't believe we never heard of this."

"Speaks to the respect people had for Pa, doesn't it."

"How you figure that?" Ruby asked, frowning.

"People tend to enjoy rubbing salt into the wounds of those they don't like. No one ever said a word about this, least none I heard. Says a lot about the man, to my thinking."

Why, that makes sense, Ruby thought. Why didn't I see it that way? "Well, one thing for sure," she said. "No way we're taking him off life support. He lived life his way, he'll leave it the same way."

Sister nodded, then indicated the article again. "Says here, Grace was struck by that bus up close to Tulsa. You figure she was going back to Georgia?" Sister scratched the mole on her arm absentmindedly. "How you suppose she got up there, middle of the night?"

"Middle of the night?" Ruby reread the clipping. "Oh, I see what you mean. That's why that bus driver didn't see her. You think Pa drove her up there?"

"Can you see Pa giving *anyone* a hundred-dollar bill and leaving them on the side of the highway like that?"

Ruby ran her hands through her hair. "You're right," she mumbled. "You're right. Then who . . .? Oh, Lord."

"Yeah, that's what I figure. Only person I know that'd have a hundred-dollar bill in her pocketbook would be Tootsie Turner."

"Oh, Lord," Ruby mumbled again. "It's just too much to deal with."

Sister walked to the stove. "Well, you don't have a choice because we're gonna be burying Pa here pretty quick." She set the teapot on to boil and took two mugs from the cabinet.

"That might be so, but he's gonna live and die on his own terms. We are *not* taking him off life support."

Sister measured cocoa mix into the mugs and filled them with water as the teapot began to spew. "I figure Nonny makes a good point about Grace's grave being a good sign." She carried the cocoa to the table.

"What are you saying?"

"I'm saying we can bury Pa next to Grace, just like he wanted."

"Next to Grace? Pa talked about being buried next to Bill and Jack, not her!" Ruby hesitated. "You think that's what he would've wanted?"

"Why do you think he wanted Grace to forgive him? Of course, he'd want to be buried next to her. And Bill and Jack's there, so it'll all work out just the way he wanted." Sister walked to the pantry, pulled out a bag of miniature marshmallows, and shook some in her cup. "Want some?" she asked, looked at Ruby.

"I better not." Ruby watched her weight closely. Women in the beauty profession needed to maintain their looks, keep up a professional appearance.

Professional appearance . . .

Ruby looked around the kitchen at the beauty paraphernalia she had accumulated over the years, then at the framed documents on the wall. She had considered her livelihood a profession once, but that was before her son had labeled her a "kitchen beautician" and her best customer turned out to be a fraud. Had all her customers come to her out of pity?

"Oh, why not," she said, holding out her cup so Sister could shake marshmallows into it. She used her spoon to sink them, waiting for them to melt. "So you think there's a chance the Turners will give us permission to bury Pa there?"

Sister sipped cocoa with a spoon. "Question is, what if they won't?"

"Lord have mercy, it's just too much." Ruby gave her hair another tousle.

"Pa ever own anything but that double barrel in the pantry?" Sister said.

Ruby stared at her a minute. "Not to my knowledge. Why?"

"Those slugs Mack found."

Ruby drew a quick breath. "Hunters, Sister. Those slugs were put there by hunters. Back in the old days, people hunted squirrel and rabbit for the table. Lord knows, we ate our share. And nowadays, city folks like to pretend they're hunters. We called the sheriff out a couple of times ourselves to chase trespassers off our land—*Mack's* land. If it was my land, we wouldn't be leaving it." Suddenly Ruby crossed her arms on the tabletop and lowered her head into them.

"Oh, straighten up, Ruby. Mack thinks he's doing the right thing by us, and who's to say he isn't. Speaking of which, what did Mack say about that realtor that called tonight? You think the place is sold already? I figure that's why she wanted to meet up with him so bad. Good thing we don't have a lot to pack up. Least I don't, you got all this beauty shop stuff . . ."

Ruby raised her head. "Sister, would you *please* stop your rattling? I just can't deal with all this! Why has all this has been dumped on me right now? I've done things by the book all my life. *It just isn't fair*." She cupped her face in her hands as deep uncontrollable sobs shook her body.

"Why, Ruby, no need for that." Sister shoved a box of Kleenex across the table.

"I'm sorry Sister. I just feel like I want to spit on someone. Or yell. Or *cuss*, cuss till I'm blue in the face."

"Well then, go ahead." Sister scratched at the mole on her arm again. "Get it out of your system if it'll make you feel better. Better than letting yourself come apart at the seams. I've let loose many a time."

"You have?" Ruby blew her nose. "When? I never heard you say a bad word in my life?"

"Out in the yard there." Sister pointed toward the back door. "I wouldn't be traipsing about in the dark right now, though. Could break a hip. Best stay on the porch."

"I couldn't . . ."

"I don't figure you'd say anything I hadn't heard before, so cut loose."

"I shouldn't . . ."

Go," Sister said, pointing at the door.

Ruby pushed her chair back slowly and glanced over her shoulder as she exited the room. "I feel stupid."

"You'd be surprised how much better you'll feel after a good bout of swearing."

Outside on the stoop, Ruby looked at a November sky that was so cold, earthly emissions hung like a shroud. The Milky Way was a pale ladder leading to a paler Heaven, casting an aura over the land. Even the night creatures talked among themselves timidly.

"Hell," she whispered.

"That's the puniest Hell I ever heard," Sister snorted from the kitchen. "You know what Pa used to say: If you're gonna do something, do it right—"

"Hell . . . damn . . . damn them all to a living hell . . ." Ruby paused, searching her mind for more blasphemies she could utter against those that had wronged her. Finding her blasphemy vocabulary limited, she repeated the same diatribe, word for word, twice more.

She stood breathless once she had used herself up, listening to her voice fade into the night, and waiting. She knew not what she waited for. Some sign, perhaps. Some indication that she had not just damned her own soul to everlasting hell. Some sense that her world had returned to a natural order, to predictable human activity. As the minutes passed, she openly received the late night benediction of frogs and crickets, inhaled the wet pungent smells of rotting leaves in the creek, noticed a ring around the moon that promised rain. Even now, she could feel moisture in the air, soothing as a balm.

Rain is good, she thought. It heals a drought, sets things right again. She returned to the kitchen, feeling subdued.

"You let go of your angst now?"

Ruby did not even question where Sister had come up with the latest term. She just rubbed her hand across her chest and said, "I believe I do feel some better. Yes, no question about it."

"Good, now let's get down to business. You think we got enough to blackmail Tootsie Turner into selling us Beulah Land to us?"

"What—?"

"Well, the way I figure it, Pa didn't drive Grace up to that bus stop, and he sure didn't keep hundred-dollar bills lying around. *And*, he never owned anything but a shotgun in his life. Those slugs Mack found came from a different gun. I don't know about you, but I'm not inclined to go begging the Turners to allow us to bury Pa on something that was rightfully his to begin with. I figure we can swing a thousand dollars between us, give them back just what they paid for it. I got half. You got the other half?"

"Why yes, I have the other half." Headlights raked across the porch. "Mack's home . . . Oh no, you suppose he sold the place?" They waited in silence for the door to open.

"Well," Sister said when Mack walked into the kitchen. "What's the scoop? Do we to start packing?"

"We got an offer . . ."

"*You* got an offer," Ruby said. "Not *we*. You're the one—"

"Shut up, Ruby," Sister snapped. "Give the boy a chance to settle down."

If Mack heard his mother's remark, he did not let it show. Given he was pacing the length of the kitchen non-stop, in all likelihood he did not hear her at all. Sister finally called him to a halt.

"You're pacing like a beetle on a hot rock. Tell us what that realtor wanted. Must've been important to call you out at night."

"Not much to tell." Mack walked to the refrigerator, pulled out a beer, and popped the cap. "They met the asking price."

"Does that surprise you?" Sister said. "You act surprised."

"It does at that. I mean, who the hell doesn't come back with a counter offer these days? Hell, wish I'd asked for more now."

"Who?" Sister asked. "Who bought it? Was it horse people like you wanted?"

He shrugged. "Don't know. Everything's being handled by an attorney."

"When?" Ruby asked. "How much time we got."

"Buyer wants to close in a couple of weeks, but said we could live here till the duplex is finished." He started pacing again. "I need to push on that builder there at that gated community. He's gonna have to move faster."

"Maybe he'll hire you to help him out," Sister said.

Mack paused. "Well now, that's a thought."

Ruby glared at Sister, feeling an impulse to ring her neck, but she focused on Mack instead. "What about your job in Texas? Can you hang around here that long? You could risk losing your job."

He considered the comment, then shook his head. "Got no choice. I'll call and check in tomorrow, see if the guy I work for's got anything lined up yet. Oh . . ." He looked between them. "You know of anyone that might be interested in buying the other side of that duplex, someone you wouldn't mind living next to?"

Ruby exchanged a glance with Sister. "I don't know of a single solitary soul that would want to move into town."

"Me neither," Sister said.

"Well, think on it. I'm gonna turn in, need some rack time bad. Can't believe you two are still up. Why are you still up?" Without waiting for an answer, Mack left the room mumbling, "Maybe I *will* look at helping out with that duplex. Could make sure it's done right that way."

Ruby sat staring at nothing after Mack left the room. She broke the stare a few minutes later when Sister rose from her chair and pulled a bottle of brandy from the pantry. She watched wordlessly as the bottle and two juice glasses were set on the table.

"Don't know about you, but I think I'll make mine a double tonight."

"I can't believe you actually suggested he help that builder." Ruby watched Sister measure brandy into one of the glasses.

"Spoke before I thought."

"Why didn't you tell him how you really felt?"

Sister looked at Ruby over the top of her trifocals. "That's your job. Your son, your job. I'm just hitching a ride." She held up the empty glass. "You?"

"Double up." Ruby took the glass from Sister. "So let's talk some more about this blackmailing business. How you see that working?"

Sister spoke without hesitation. "Work on Tootsie's guilty conscience, let her know we figured out the reason for the big tips, how they had something to do with Grace. Then bring up the hundred-dollar bill and the bus, how Grace would've got to Tulsa. And those slugs in the doubletree sure didn't come out of that scattergun there in the closet."

"Yeah." Ruby sipped her brandy. "Pa probably had the shotgun with him in the fields, now I think about it."

"In case he ran onto a rattler or badger. Pays to keep a gun handy out there in those fields."

Ruby looked toward the pantry door, which stood ajar. The old shotgun in the corner drew her eyes like a magnet. "Pays to keep a gun handy other places than the fields," she murmured.

CHAPTER THIRTY

Mack eyed the beanpole of a man, skin brown as a nut and tough as leather, thinking in another ten years he would be his twin. He extended his hand to the builder.

"Mack Barlow. We talked on the phone." Feeling the calluses on the hand the man extended, he realized how soft his hands had gotten in the time he'd been out of work.

"Walker," the man said as introduction. "Let's get one thing straight right off. I run the job. You'd be a carpenter, nothing more."

"I'm the one writing the checks."

"Understand that." The man narrowed his eyes. "But two roosters in the pen only leads to a cockfight. It's my crew . . ." He nodded toward a group of men reinforcing a wall at the back of the duplex. "I give the orders."

"Okay, you run the job." Mack hesitated as he strapped on his tool belt. "Mind if I use my own tools?"

"Most do," Walker said. "You'll be working with that bunch over there." He motioned to a group of carpenters getting ready to set roof braces in place. The sound of hammering punctuated the air like mortar blasts. "Follow me. I'll make your acquaintance."

Mack followed after the man called Walker, shook hands all around, and decided not to bother trying to remember names as it was a short-term deal.

"Well then," Walker said when introductions were done. "Let's get to it."

Mack worked, measuring, marking, cutting, pounding. Hoisting his twenty-two-ounce framing hammer, he nailed ring-shank nails in wood. The hammer an extension of his right arm, the vibration pounded through tendons and ligaments. He felt back muscles tighten as he lifted joists overhead, winced as fresh-cut wood snagged his palms, felt sweat bead on his forehead and tasted salt on his lips. Before long, however, he got into a rhythm. He had found his groove.

All day long, the man called Walker stuck to his side, putting in as good a day as the others. Both units were framed by the end of day and Walker speculated the shingles would be on and the place watertight in another couple of days.

Mack decided the contractor was an all right guy. "You move fast," he said as he removed his tool belt.

Walker stood next to him, doing the same. "Bid by the job, not the hour."

Mack nodded. "No need to drag your heels then. But I've known some that put time ahead of quality."

Walker straightened his back, giving him a look.

"Glad to see you're not that kind," Mack said hastily. "You do good work."

Walker gave a nod. "My dad was a builder, as was his dad. Can't get as good timber these days, but I do the best I can with what I got." He hesitated. "But I gotta tell you straight up, what you're doing here doesn't make a helluva lot a sense."

Mack loaded his tools into the back of the Bronco. "How's that?"

"Building a custom home here. This town's on its last legs, don't see it ever pulling out of it. Just throwing good money down a hole."

"It's for my mother and aunt. I want them to be safe." Mack gave a nod to the other duplexes. "Those cracker boxes won't withstand a big windstorm, much less a tornado."

Walker laughed. "Hell, not much withstands a tornado, it's a big one." He nodded toward the duplex they'd worked on all day. "You think that better lumber would withstand a three on the Fujita scale?"

Mack took in the extra bracing, the heavier timber and joists, and said, "It might."

"Well," Walker said, scratching his chin, "it might at that. But look at it this way. The people buying these places are on their last legs, probably won't live to see the linoleum wear out. Don't take me wrong, I know your intentions are good, but hell, think about it. Why go for the best money can buy when good enough'll do?"

Mack considered this. "A stout house would give me peace of mind. There's something to be said for peace of mind."

Another nod. "Yeah, there is, 'specially when you're not around to check on things." Walker stretched, his backbone plinking like a xylophone. "And this here work sure don't allow for that."

"So let me get this straight," Mack said, still chewing on the man's words. "It was your folks, you'd put them in one of those cracker boxes?"

"Hell, the place they live in now's a cracker box. No way my dad would leave the home place. He's retired now, lives out in Chickasaw County. We talked once about these retirement complexes and tornados, mobile phones, things like 'at. All I could talk him into was a safe room. You know, those reinforced rooms they're putting in houses now?"

Mack paused, looking thoughtful. "I heard about those."

"Rented a backhoe, didn't have a basement on the house, you see, so we dug a hole just big enough for a safe room. Folks don't even have to leave the house to get to it. Just walk down the steps and lock the door."

"That was a damn good idea."

"Got 'em a weather radio, too. You hear 'bout them? You program this radio to certain bands and it goes off when there's a storm coming."

"Guy I work for in the Panhandle has one," Mack said.

"Oklahoma Panhandle?"

"Texas. Sounds like you done right by your folks."

"Hell, who's to say. I mean, if a tornado comes in the middle of the night and they don't hear the radio, well . . ." Walker shrugged. "They take their hearing aids out at night, you see."

"Sounds like you did the best you could."

"I figure it's a coin toss. Any way to flip it, they got a fifty-fifty chance. Let's face it, that's all any of us got."

Mack nodded thoughtfully.

"Anyhow," Walker continued. "I finally stopped mouthing off about it. My Pa would look at me and say, 'You don't take a few chances, life would get mighty dull.'"

"Some truth to that," Mack said, tracing his bottom lip with his index finger.

Walker opened the door of his truck. "Told the guys I'd catch up with them at that bar out on 69. You're welcome to join us."

"Another time, maybe. Got some loose ends to tie up."

Walker dipped his chin. "You put in a good day's work, Barlow. I'd hire you on, you was interested. We mostly do this kind of stuff. Whole blasted country's getting old."

"Thanks, but I prefer the big and wide."

"And it's your dime," Walker added. "I like a man who respects his family. We'll do this place your way, you'll get no more lip outta me."

Mack watched the truck pull away, wondering what it was about this place that made boozers and philosophers of people.

Might it be those tornadoes? came the whisper in his ear.

Realizing that he was the last man standing on the site, Mack walked around the empty shell of a duplex, thinking on Walker's words.

"It's still the right thing to do," he mumbled. "It's different when your folks are women living alone and that far out of town." His thoughts went to Nonny Folsom then, and he shook his head. "She's not mine to worry about."

He walked into the second unit, which he had not yet found a buyer for, and thought again of Nonny. On an impulse, he decided to pay her a visit on the drive out to see if she had thought of someone who might be interested in buying it. Like it or not, she was his ace in the hole.

Ace won't do it, Pard, came the retort in his head. *You're trying to fill an inside straight.*

CHAPTER THIRTY-ONE

Mack pulled through the Popeye's drive-through, picked up an order of hot wings, and finished them off on his drive to Nonny's place. Driving down the dark tunnel of trees to her house, he drowned a greasy-gut feeling with the last of a diluted Pepsi, its ice melted by the Bronco's heater. He hailed the house as he saw her appear at the kitchen door.

"What are you doing here, Mack?" Nonny walked onto the porch, arms crossed.

Sensing her coldness, Mack stopped at the steps. "Thought I'd check to see if you thought of anyone to buy the other half of that duplex. Don't know if you heard or not, but I got a buyer for the home place."

"Uncle George mentioned it. He went in for a haircut today and Sister told him."

"I, uh, I interrupt something?" With the light to her back, Nonny's face blended into the shadows. Mack glanced beyond her to see if she was in the midst of making jelly or some other do-good project. A Mason jar sitting on the kitchen table glowed like a giant gold nugget.

"What the hell—" He pushed past Nonny and walked to the table, where he took the jar in his hands. He stared at the golden brew and then into eyes the same color. "You're not thinking on opening this . . ."

"You're intruding."

"You are, aren't you?" He pinned Nonny's eyes with his own.

"No, I'm not . . ." There was a pause in her eyes. "Well, yes, I'm thinking about it. It's been sitting on that table for two days and I haven't opened it yet, so I'm thinking long and hard about it."

"Why? Something to do with this business I got you involved in?"

Nonny rubbed the back of her neck. "I don't know, maybe in a way."

Mack walked to the sink, making movements to open the jar.

Nonny grabbed his arm. "Don't do that—I'll puke."

"What?"

"The smell makes me puke. I think that's the reason I haven't opened it yet. Because I know I'll puke."

"And after you get through puking?"

She paused again. "I haven't gotten to that yet."

He tightened the lid down on the jar. "What set you off? It have something to do with me or the stuff I had you look up for me?" When she didn't answer promptly, he pushed harder. "Spill it, Nonny, I've got a right to know."

"Maybe indirectly."

"Where's the coffee?" Mack picked the coffee pot up off the stove, pulled out the basket, and filled the pot with water. Giving her a look, he said, "Put some coffee in the basket, Nonny. I don't know where you keep it." As she opened a cupboard door and spooned coffee into the basket, Mack noticed the tremble in her hands.

"Indirectly?" he said. "What's that mean? I got no time to do this deconstruction stuff, so talk. Given your reaction to Grace's tombstone, I figure it has something to do with that. What? The stone? The inscription? The woman? Mama and Sister call her a hussy. You done something you're not proud of? You sleep around out there in Norman—"

"Shut up, Mack."

"Hell," he said, "you're a good-looking woman, only normal. Unless . . ."

Mack recalled Chester saying something about women students filing a complaint and began to question the man's assessment of Nonny's sexual preferences, wondering if the man had been wrong.

"Aw, shit," he mumbled.

Nonny glanced at him. "What?"

"None of my business."

"No, it's not. But you think you got something figured out, I have a right to know what it is. You started all this palaver."

Mack walked to the cane-bottomed chair across the room, took a seat, and tilted it against the wall. "I just never took you for a . . ."

"A what?"

He took a deep breath. "That fella Chester. He, uh, he said some of your girl students filed a complaint."

Nonny paused momentarily, taking time to translate the innuendo, then laughed. "What is it with you Barlows? All of you think I'm a lesbian. First your mother, and now—"

"Mama thinks you're a lesbian? Why?"

"Because I never married! Sister figures it's because I got *spoilt* like she did. Which is why she never married, in case you didn't know."

Mack raised his eyebrows. "I always wondered about that."

"For your information, I have lots of friends that *are* homosexual and they're good people."

"But you're not? Homosexual, I mean."

"For pity sake, what do I have to do with you Barlows? Sign in blood?"

"Then what? What's the connection to Grace?" Mack paused as he saw uncharacteristic tears fill Nonny's eyes.

"She gave up her children, dammit, just like I did. That's what Ruby can't forget—or *forgive*." Nonny wiped her nose on the sleeve of her shirt. "I'd like to think my daughter would forgive me for giving her up for adoption, but she might not. I mean, after all these years, Ruby still can't forgive Grace." She hesitated. "Then, when I learned I couldn't have any more children . . ." A harsh sound came from deep in her throat. "Mom and Dad always hoped for grandchildren and I'd thrown away the only chance they'd ever have like . . . like a piece of garbage in a trash dumpster."

Mack jumped to his feet and reached for Nonny. He felt her face pressing against his shoulder, heard himself saying things to try to make her feel better, then stumbled backward from the force of the stiff-arm blow she dealt him.

"Stop hovering, Mack! You know how I feel about that."

Mack stood with one hip cocked. "Yeah, I remember. Always Miss Independent, needing to stand on her own, didn't want help from nobody."

"That's right," she said, wiping her nose again. "Aw crap, coffee's ready." Walking to the cabinet, she took down two mugs and joined Mack at the table. She grimaced, watching him pick at a blister on his palm. "What the hell you do to your hand?"

"Started working on that duplex today. My hammering hand's got soft."

"Well, don't pick at those blisters. You could get an infection. I'll get some hydrogen peroxide and band-aids. You got any bag balm? Wouldn't hurt to work some into those hands."

"Yeah, I keep some in my truck, but that's not what I need right now. You got any alum?"

"Alum?" Nonny paused. "For making pickles?"

"Toughens up the skin. You got some, I'll make a soak."

Nonny rummaged until she found what she was looking for, then took a glass bowl out of the cupboard and filled it with water. Mack poured in alum until the water turned milky, then dunked his right hand into it.

Nonny grimaced. "Doesn't that burn?"

"Like hellfire and brimstone." Mack picked up his mug of coffee with his left hand, swished his right hand in the milky concoction, and resumed hammering on Nonny. "So, you started drinking because of your daughter, because she wouldn't forgive you?"

"Not exactly," she said, sounding irritable. "It's a long story."

"I got nothin' but time."

*****

Two pots of coffee later, Mack had pieced together the story of Nonny's life, at least since she had left town a blooming optimist and returned a recovering alcoholic. A lot of experimentation as a footloose freshman. An all-night kegger, lots of drinking and sex. A few weeks later, the realization she was pregnant. Some months after that, a baby put out for adoption.

"How'd you know it was a girl? Thought that kind of thing was kept from the mother?"

"Talkative nurses who didn't know I could hear them."

"What'd they say?" He watched Nonny turn away, stare into space.

"They, uh, they were talking about her eyes, how unusual they were. Making bets they'd end up the same color as mine."

Mack's mind went into overdrive. "So you started looking for her. When? Right away?"

"No, not until years later. One day at school, a girl passed me whose eyes were similar to mine, a student, and it occurred to me that my daughter would be about her age." She let out a long sigh. "After that, things just snowballed."

"You try the legal route to find out who adopted her?"

"Oh, yeah."

"I hear they're pretty tough about releasing that information to the birth mothers. You know, later."

"They are."

"So then . . .?"

Nonny blew out her breath. "So then, I became obsessed with finding her. Obsessions can make a person do dumb-ass things. I started looking for girls at the school who'd be about the right age, one whose eyes were colored like mine, hoping she'd been put into a decent home and sent to college." She pushed her hair from her face and tucked stray ends into the rubber band holding what was left of a ponytail. "Alcohol took the edge off."

Mack sat quiet for a spell, then said, "You never could hold your liquor."

"*What*?"

"Remember that high-school dance when in the tenth grade? Liquor makes you turn loose."

Nonny flushed slightly. "It was the eleventh grade."

Mack grinned and wiped his hand dry. The blistered skin had bleached out white and his hand had shriveled up like a dead carp washed onto a riverbank. He heard Nonny sniff and looked her way. "What's your thinking?"

"I'm thinking that looks awful." She pointed to his hand, then looked him in the face. "And I was wondering what you're thinking about all this? You know, the mess I've made of things."

Mack dabbed some more at the blistered skin. "I'm thinking I should've knocked you up in the eleventh grade."

"*What*?"

"We should've stayed right here, bought a little place in the country, raised a houseful of kids. That's what I'm thinking." He looked away from his hand and into her eyes.

Contemplating this, Nonny shook her head. "No, that would've made things worse than it is now. Our kids would've ended up not knowing you, because you stuff everything inside, and hating me when I ran off and left them because I felt unfulfilled. Not unlike Pa and Grace."

Mack grunted, wondering if she might not be right and thinking she was damned good at this deconstruction business. "Ever occur to you that she might be looking for you? Lots of adopted kids try to find their birth mothers."

She hesitated. "You think?"

"You don't put yourself out there, she won't have much luck. It's not all about you, you know." Mack got up from his chair, poured the alum water down the kitchen drain, and spoke over his shoulder. "Ever occur to you, she might be dead."

"It has." Nonny retrieved Mack's denim jacket from the doorknob where it hung.

Shouldering his way into the coat, he said, "I've done some things I'm not proud of that makes me throw-up, too. You know, when I dwell on them."

"Do you pee your pants?"

"What?"

"Do you puke so hard, you pee your pants?"

"No."

"Well then, you should thank Heaven for small blessings, Mack Barlow."

"Aw, hell," he muttered as her meaning sunk in. He picked up the Mason jar of homemade brew. "I'll take care of this."

"Thanks." Nonny stuffed her hands deep into her front pockets, looking like a child curling in on itself when it was hurt. "I, uh, I have to back off this one, Mack, for my own sake. Please try to understand. I mean, I'll come to Pa's funeral and all, but . . ."

"I do understand, Nonny." He stepped outside, then turned to look at her. "Still wish we hadn't used protection back in high school."

"What?"

"Don't take a few chances, life gets mighty dull." The door closed slowly and the light went off, turning the night inky black. He stumbled his way down the steps and made the drive home.

He gave Whitey a rub on the head when he reached the house. The dog followed him to the barrow ditch, watched as he emptied the Mason jar into the grass along its banks, and cocked his ears when Mack lofted the jar into the air. The remaining liquor spilled across a pale-moon sky like drops of liquid gold, and the clink of broken glass, sounding like a tambourine, caused the chorus of croaking and chirping night creatures to cease momentarily.

"Well, that's that." As he uttered the words, Mack felt a tightness in his chest that brought back a memory. A remembered pain from when he had suffered cracked ribs. Doctors had taped him back together so tight he could hardly breathe.

Just like now . . .

Sometime later, Whitey nuzzled his hand. Mack turned and followed him to the front door and, without further *adieu*, closed them both inside the dark house.

CHAPTER THIRTY-TWO

Ruby stood at the front door watching the road, her hand on Whitey's head. She breathed a sigh of relief seeing her car turn down the lane. She hurried outside, not even taking time to put on a sweater. She was talking before the engine stopped idling.

"How was he, Sister?"

The two had been taking turns sitting with their father since he had gone into a coma, structuring their day around Ruby's hair appointments. With Mack working on the duplex, there was no choice but to let Sister make the drive into town alone. Ruby did not know which she worried about the most, her father's coma or her sister's driving.

"Still out like a light. They said we don't have to sit with him like this, said they'd call us if anything changed. But I told 'em that's not the way we do things. You ready to go?"

"Almost. Just need to get my coat and purse. Made a pot of soup in between the perm and haircut. It's ready, in case you didn't eat."

"Ate some gumdrops that Mr. Carter keeps stashed in his dresser, but I could use something more substantial. The doctor came by to see Pa while I was there."

"What'd he say?" Ruby opened the door for her sister and the old white dog and followed them inside. "Did he give any kind of indication of what might happen?"

Sister shook off her coat and hung it on the coat rack. "Said the prognosis hasn't changed. Pa's no better, but no worse neither. He brought up again the idea of pulling the plug."

"Pulling the plug?"

"That's what they call taking someone off life support."

"I'm here to tell you," Ruby said, pulling on her coat, "there is *no way* we're pulling the plug."

"That's what I told 'em. Oh, and you'll never guess who came by to see Pa."

Ruby felt a hopefulness fill her chest. "Nonny? That girl hasn't stopped by in days, not since she picked up the last of those mailbags from you."

"What'd you expect? Can't go round insulting people and expect them to come calling."

"Well, I'm glad she went to see Pa."

"Wasn't Nonny came by."

Ruby wagged her head. "So *who*? I don't have time for guessing games, Sister."

"Tootsie Turner."

"You're not serious?"

"I wouldn't pull your leg, not on that score. You could've knocked me over with a feather. Her hair looks awful. Don't know who's doing it, but it looks like crap. Kept fiddling with it, too. I think she was ashamed of the way she looked. The color wasn't near as pretty as when you do it. And she must've got a perm, a bad one, 'cause it frizzed something fierce."

"Sister, I don't care what Tootsie Turner looked like. What'd she say?"

"Nothing much. I stayed right in the room, didn't see any reason to leave. She just stood there and looked at Pa for a bit, then mumbled something like, 'It's time to lay your burden down, Grover, so I can too.' Then she left. Didn't stay more than five minutes."

"Five minutes? Hardly worth the trouble."

"Oh, she did say something funny, right as she was walking out the door." Sister lifted her nose and sniffed. "Soup smells real good."

"*What*, Sister? What did Tootsie say as she left the room? I need to leave!"

"Well, it was something about, 'You and Ruby will be taken care of. I'll make sure of it, just like always.' What do you make of that?"

Ruby sighed. "Sounds like she was making small talk. You know how it is when you go see someone sick or who's just lost someone and you don't know what to say. She was just trying to be charitable."

"Tootsie Turner doesn't have a charitable bone in her body. None of the Turners do."

"Well now, that's not so. They did after Will was killed in that riot. Still, it's a surprise she showed up at all." Ruby stepped toward the front door. "I'll be home soon as Mack shows up to relieve me tonight."

"You forget? He said he had to go to the lawyer's office and sign papers after he got off work. Bennett and Brown, that's the ones handling it."

Ruby felt as though her life had skipped a beat. "I must not've been in the room when he said that."

"That realtor lady called this morning to remind him. Was real early, don't think you had pulled yourself together yet. Which seems to be the case these days. I didn't know better, I'd think it was purposeful. When you gonna get over being mad at that boy? What time should I look for you home?" She paused, waiting for a response. Getting none, she raised her voice. "Ruby, did you hear me?"

"What?"

"You haven't heard I word I said."

"I'm sorry, Sister, guess I'm still thinking about Tootsie's visit. She drive herself into town?"

"Must have, that or old Washburn stayed in the car."

"Well, I guess she was trying to be a good Christian. She's known Pa a long time."

"It was her guilty conscience acting up again, that's what it was."

"What?"

"Tootsie Turner. That's why she came by to see Pa. *Guilt*. Just one more thing we can use to blackmail her into selling us Beulah Land. When are we gonna spring that on her?"

"Lord help, Sister—I'm barely holding it together as it is, what with Pa's condition and trying to keep up with my customers."

"Can't wait too long. We need to talk about when to pay her a visit. Maybe now's a good time, her conscience bothering her and all."

"Go *there*?"

"She sure isn't gonna come to us! Though Lord knows, she ought to, the looks of her hair today. Maybe this evening when you get back home?"

"I'll think on it while I'm sitting with Pa."

"Need to strike while the iron's hot."

"I'll think on it." Ruby closed the door on Sister and walked to a sedan whose engine had not cooled down enough to stop ticking.

*****

In the thirty minutes it took to drive into McAlester, Ruby did think about Sister's suggestion. She also questioned her sanity for thinking they could buy back Beulah Land. Reminding herself that her father had made her the Assignee, she accepted that she had no choice and so began to think about a plan of attack.

"Best to get Tootsie when she's alone, without the old Mister there." Pulling up an image of Wash Turner's brooding countenance and hunched body, she shivered, recalling that he had looked the same to her since she had been a child. How were they going to get around him? No, around *them*? With Junior and Billy Joe living next door, there would always be somebody around.

"Lord help, there's no way this is gonna work."

Ruby slowed as she drove through the outskirts of town and shifted into a lower gear to make the climb up the hill to McAlester's main streets. The Masonic Temple shone brightly in the early December air, drawing Ruby's eyes like a magnet.

"Eastern Star," she murmured. "Tootsie belongs to the Eastern Star."

Eying the building, she began to think that catching Tootsie off her home turf might be a better plan. Wondering when the next meeting of the Eastern Star was scheduled, she turned down the street where the meetings were held to look at the bulletin board. The route took her past Bennett and

Brown's office, and she stared in surprise as Tootsie and Washburn Turner walked out the front door.

Why, they must have some business with their lawyer today, too, she thought. Now isn't that a strange coincidence?

Hunkering down in her seat, she pulled into an open parking space and refocused her rearview mirror so she could take in the scene. The Turners stood on the sidewalk talking with the attorney named Bennett, both dressed fit to kill. Washburn in a leather, knee-length trench coat, and Tootsie, a fire-engine red cashmere coat with a mink collar.

"Sister was right on one score," Ruby whispered to no one. "Tootsie's hair does look pitiful."

Even from three car lengths away, she could see magenta-colored streaks highlighting the blonde tresses. I'd need to put some green on it to get rid of that red, she thought. Glad I don't have to fix that mess.

As she watched, she began to wonder what the Turners were up to. Strange, she thought again, that they should be at the same lawyer's office as Mack would be, and on the same day. It took only seconds for the only logical reason to make itself known.

"No, it couldn't be . . . could it?" Ruby's heart began to pound in her chest. "My lord, I bet it is— I have to tell Mack before he signs those papers!"

Jamming the sedan into first gear, Ruby wheeled out of the parking spot. She looked at the bulletin board in front for the Eastern Star long enough to note the next meeting was scheduled for that evening at seven o'clock. Then made for the gated community.

"That's just like something Tootsie would do," she muttered as she drove. "Schedule the meeting with their lawyer the same day as the Lodge meeting. I would if it was me, what with the cost of gasoline these days. Why make the drive in twice when you can kill two birds with one stone?" The next thought jolted Ruby. "Make that *three* birds with one stone, Pa being the third bird."

She felt the surge of blood in her ears as her temper ignited, and she talked through gritted teeth. "Charitable, my ass. That hussy couldn't even make a special trip into town to see Pa, that's why she couldn't give him but five minutes. She worked him in between a lawyer and a secret clan meeting and probably dinner to boot. Why, I bet she makes Wash take her to the country club before the meeting for shrimp or lobster, probably lobster because it costs more. I've never had lobster in my life!"

Ruby's foot on the gas pedal grew heavier as her temper grew hotter and she almost drove through the gate barring entry to the gated community. Flustered when the guards surrounded her car, she could not make herself understood and so, was refused entry.

"But he's my son," she yelled. "He's buying one of these duplexes for my sister and me to live in. Not that we want to move to this God-forsaken place. It's nothing short of a tomb!"

"Ma'am, if you'd just calm down—"

"But I need to tell Mack something. He doesn't know what he's doing or he wouldn't do it. He'd never sell the place to the Turners. Don't you see? That's why the buyers wanted to remain anonymous. They're the buyers!"

When one of the guards mentioned calling the sheriff, Ruby decided it was time to take another approach. She wheeled into a bootleg turn and drove away, two guards running down the street after her. Skirting the perimeter of the subdivision, she found a dirt road along its backside and forced herself to slow down so she could look for new construction. When she spotted the duplex, she braked to a jerking stop. She considered laying down on the horn to get Mack's attention but decided not to, remembering that she was on the lam. Worried that patrol cars were looking for her already, she opted to climb through the barbed-wire fence.

She spotted her son sitting on the edge of a newly poured cement patio, pulling a fried-egg sandwich out of a bread wrapper. Figuring Sister had fixed it for him, she suddenly felt ashamed of the way she had treated a son who was only doing what he thought was right. As she stumbled to his side, she called out an apology with the breath that was left in her lungs.

"I'm . . . so . . . sorry . . . Mack . . ."

"Mama?" Mack came to his feet as Ruby stumbled through the stacks of lumber on the building site. "What's wrong? Is it Pa?

"No." Ruby was breathing so hard, she could barely talk. "It's the Turners . . . they're the 'nonymous ones." Seeing that he was not getting her meaning, she tried again. "I saw them . . . at that lawyer's office . . . just now," she gasped, fanning her face with one hand. "The one handling the sale of the house . . . they're the ones buying the place."

"Get hold of yourself, Mama. It was probably something else altogether."

"No—Tootsie paid Pa a call while Sister was sitting with him. Tootsie said something like, 'We'd be taken care of here soon enough.' Don't you see, that's why they wanted to remain—"

"Anonymous," Mack said, finishing her statement.

Ruby watched her son's face flare as red as hers felt. "You can't let them have the place, Mack. They'll just run it into the ground, turn cattle into Pa's pasture, maybe even tear down the house— And after we just painted the front room that pretty butter color."

"Slow down, Mama. Let me think."

"Okay . . ." But no matter how hard she tried, Ruby could not stop her mind from racing or her mouth from running. "I know you meant good, son, but . . ." Waving her arm in the direction of the duplex and gathering her wind, Ruby held nothing back. "I don't want to live in this damn place, Sister neither, we just couldn't bring ourselves to tell you to your face, it'd be awful living here, dull as dishwater, I'd die of boredom, and I don't want to give up being a kitchen beautician, I *like* being a kitchen beautician, and my shotgun, I *like* that shotgun—"

"Hush, Mama." Mack pulled her into the crook of his arm, muffling her face into his denim jacket. "No way in hell, I'm gonna let those Turners get our place, no way in hell."

Ruby pulled her face out of her son's shoulder. "Does that mean Sister and me don't have to move?"

"You don't have to move, that's what it means. Now calm down."

"Okay," she said meekly.

As her legs would carry her no longer, Ruby sank down onto the newly poured cement patio, and for the first time, noticed the leathery-skinned man standing nearby, one hand resting on a cocked hip. She knew she owed him an explanation and opened her mouth to attempt one, but when she noticed the grin on his face, she knew one was not necessary. He had heard everything.

"Name's Walker," he said, nodding at her. Still grinning, he turned to face Mack. "Like I said, why go for the best money can buy when good enough'll do."

CHAPTER THIRTY-THREE

"That's collusion," Mack said to Walker. As Ruby recovered on the patio from her wild race to the construction site, the builder had given Mack the low down on how the Turners and Roxie Komenski were working deals in the area. The realtor set the price low, the Turners stepped in quick and sealed the deal, and the two profited from the unsuspecting landowner's inexperience. "You got any proof?"

"Plenty," Walker said, "if you want to talk to those that got snookered. Some of 'em are still madder'n hell, just like you right about now. You like getting burned?"

"Hell, no." Mack rubbed his hand across his face, recalling on the day he arrived Billy Joe had mentioned something about a new enterprise they were into. It all made sense now. The buyers' need for anonymity. Roxie handling deals for which she got no commission. The lower asking price.

"Well, I'll tell you what," he told Walker. "It stops right here."

"What's your thinking?"

Mack pulled a long breath. "I intend to finish what I started. Not sure exactly how it's going to play out. You just handle the building end of it, I'll take care of the rest of it." As Mack loaded his tools into the back of the Bronco, he assured Walker he would make good on the deal. "You won't be the one made to pay, I guarantee."

"Good enough." Extending his hand, Walker grinned. "As for my part, I'll keep my ears to the ground for anyone dumb enough to buy a custom duplex in a down-and-out place in the middle of tornado alley."

Mack left Walker at the gated community and followed his mother to the nursing home to make sure she made it without further incident. He walked inside with her to check on his grandfather. The old man grew smaller every day, and he speculated he was not long for the world.

"I need to handle some business, Mama."

"You going to that meeting with those lawyers?"

"No, I'm not."

"But you signed them house papers, Mack. It's all legal."

"Haven't signed over the deed yet. Not legal until I take their money."

"It isn't? I thought once you signed a paper, you were obliged."

"All kinds of way to beat the law, Mama. Don't worry your head about it."

"I don't want to hear that again, Mack. I'm tired of you telling me not to worry. I worry because you don't tell me things. Does that mean you don't have to buy that duplex, does it work the same for that?"

He hesitated. "That might be a different story. Right now, I need to clear the slate on this Turner business. But you're not moving. You and Sister are staying right where you are, that's a promise."

"What's your plan then? You gonna drive out to the Turners and tell them off?" She shook her head, forehead creasing. "That might not be a good idea, Mack. You could lose your temper. Or old Wash might, he's got a bad one. Talking to them lawyers might be the best bet. Then again, lawyers are sweet talkers, they might—"

"*I'm* not talking to any of them. That ball belongs in a different court."

Ruby paused. "I don't understand."

"I'll explain later." He glanced at his watch. "It's getting late and I need to make a phone call. I'll be back soon as I set some things in motion." He paused. "You look tired. You feeling all right?"

"I'm feeling fine now. My heart was going a mile a minute there for a bit, but it's slowed down."

Mack looked at his grandfather again, then back to his mother. "Pa's not gonna hang on much longer, you best prepare yourself."

"I'm prepared, Mack. No need to worry about me. Pa's lived a good long life." She hesitated, looking at the person in the bed. "Well, maybe not a good life, given all we found out, but I'm prepared. It's you I'm worried about right now. Something's troubling you."

He drew in a breath. "It's just his final request about being buried with Bill and Jack. He might not hang on long enough for me to pull off that part of the deal."

Ruby's shoulders took a straight set. "I'm planning on taking care of that. You just get back here soon as you can. I need to pick up Sister. We have some business of our own to take care of."

Mack was surprised at the calmness in his mother's voice and puzzled by the coldness that entered her eyes. "What kind of business?"

"Nothing to worry your head about. Go make your call."

*****

Mack stopped at the Seven-Eleven on the highway to put gasoline in the Bronco and to use the pay phone. He pulled alongside a gas pump, set the lock on the nozzle so it would run unattended, and walked to the telephone. He dialed the number of the Henryetta realty by heart and waited for someone on the other end to pick up.

"Put Komenski on the phone," he said to the person who answered. "Don't care if she is in a meeting, pull her out of it." He started talking, low and even, the minute he heard the realtor's voice on the line.

"Deal's off. I'm not selling the home place." He listened to the woman on the other end begin to rattle about the terms and conditions of the sales agreement and stopped her mid-sentence.

"You snookered me, Komenski. I talked with people in the building trade. You've been working deals with the Turners for years. Finding acreage, talking people into selling cheap, making your bread on volume. No wonder this country's dying. People like you scamming honest people and ruining the land, just to put a few pieces of gold in your pocket."

Mack paused to catch his breath, just time enough for the realtor to say she would reduce her percentage if he would meet with the attorneys and go through with the deal. He cut her off again.

"Ball's yours, Komenski. Don't care how you handle it with that attorney or the Turners, but it's not happening. You push this, I'll hire a lawyer of my own to track down every one of your illicit deals, and you know I'll do it. Your days of working both ends against the middle are done."

The silence on the other end was a blessing to Mack's ears, but short-lived. The realtor got in one last punch before she hung up on him. Mack held the receiver in front of him and spit out his answer to the buzzing on the line anyhow.

"Yeah, I know. I'm still obligated to buy those two units, but you won't get a dime in commission from either of them or off the home place." He banged the receiver on the hook so hard, it ricocheted off the wall. Though the realtor could no longer hear him, he made her a promise. "You watch and see. I'll just sell *both* sides of that duplex."

Mack thought about his last statement on the way to his SUV. "Right, Barlow," he mumbled to himself. "Haven't been able to sell one, how in hell you figure on selling two?"

He looked up as a long battered Buick pulled alongside another of the gas pumps and a bent old woman got out. Recognizing Bessie Anderson, he hurried over.

"Let me help you there, Bessie." He fitted the nozzle into the Buick's gas tank and set it running.

She smiled. "Why, that's right nice. Don't I know you?"

"Yes ma'am. I'm Mack Barlow, Ruby and Will's son. You got your hair fixed not long ago out at Mama's. We're cousins, second or third time removed."

"You're the one helping Ruby find them mules."

"Yes ma'am. We found them."

"You did? Well now, that's good. Guess you found Grace, too. Knew that story wouldn't stay buried forever. You can bury a person, not their sad tale." The woman shivered even though she was dressed in a long wool coat.

"Getting right cold, idn't it? Think I'll just get on back inside the car."

"Yes ma'am." He held the door for her. "Want me to top off the tank, or stop at a certain number of gallons?"

"That'd be fine," she said, closing the door.

As he filled the tank, Mack ran Bessie's words through his mind again. "Bessie," he said, tapping the glass so she would lower the window. "What'd you mean when you said you knew that story wouldn't stay buried?"

Bessie turned eyes clouded with cataracts and magnified by thick lenses to him. "Why, Will borrowed my car to go chasing after Grace that night she died. Said he heard the gunshots and got out there in time to see Grace leave with that friend of hers, Tootsie Turner. I found him running down the road like a crazy man, waving that shotgun in the air and swearing he was gonna kill her. Wouldn't even drop me and the girls off at the house for fear he'd lose her. I had the girls in the back seat, you see. I babysat for them in those days. They fell asleep on the way to Tulsa, thank the Lord. We got there just in time to see Tootsie pull away, leaving Grace to catch that bus."

She shook her head, sighing. "Fool girl didn't have the sense God gave a goose. Soon as she saw Grover and that gun, she took off running, and he took off running after her." Bessie paused, looking at some distant place in a time long past. "Grover chased Grace right in front of that bus. Thing knocked her a country mile . . ." She shook her head again. "Before anyone saw us, I jerked the gun away from Grover and put it in the trunk, shoved him in the passenger seat, and took off. He was limp as a dishrag, poor thing."

Mack felt his lips go numb. "Pa chased her?"

"Grover never got over it. Wouldn't listen to me when I tried to tell him he wasn't to fault. 'Course, guess he was."

She looked at Mack. "He wanted to turn himself in, be punished. Said he deserved to get the electric chair 'cause he was a murderer. Guess if you look at it in a certain light, he did kill her."

She hesitated, frowning. "Always wondered if he would've shot her. You can bet your bottom dollar that the law would've seen it that way, what with that gun in his hand and all. Probably locked him up right out there at the state pen where he worked. Now wouldn't that've been a fine thing for those girls to grow up with?"

She sighed again. "I drove us back home and made him swear he'd never say a word. Told him it just wouldn't be right to take both a mama and a daddy away from those girls. I swore I'd never say a word either. I dealt with the cops that came around asking why Grace was up there. I told them Will was too distraught to question and fed them a line about Grace's frail state of mind—which wasn't really a lie if you think about it." She sighed. "But I never told them the reason why it was frail." She smiled at Mack. "Family's family, you know. And show me one that don't have its secrets."

Too numbed to speak, Mack looked up to see the station attendant racing toward the Buick. The man passed him up and began to tap on the passenger-side window.

"Mrs. Anderson," he called out, tapping furiously on the glass. As she rolled it down, he said, "You want to use your credit card today? Or pay in cash?"

"That'd be fine," she said.

Mack watched as Bessie rolled up her windows. Before he could blink, she was shifting into gear and pulling out of the station, leaving the attendant standing empty-handed and him holding a nozzle spewing gasoline on the pavement.

"Great God a-mighty," Mack yelled, fumbling to take the lock off the nozzle.

"Get the water hose," the attendant called to another person inside the building. He turned to help Mack shut off the spewing gasoline nozzle, saying, "She does that every time. Her sisters, too. Started a fire over at the Texaco a couple years ago. Drove off with the nozzle still in the tank, it struck the pavement and set off a spark. Whole damn thing went up in a blaze of glory."

Mack waded through the spilled gas to remove the nozzle from his Bronco.

"Don't start your engine," the attendant yelled. "Whatever you do, don't hit the ignition."

"Wasn't planning to. Anyone hurt? Over at the Texaco, I mean."

"No, thank the Lord." The attendant grabbed the water hose from a teenage boy who dragged it up and hurriedly sent the boy back inside to call the fire department. "But I tell you the truth, somebody ought to lock them three women up, just to keep them from wreaking havoc on society."

Mack stared at his gasoline-soaked work boots and swore under his breath. "You're right about that, pard," he mumbled. Then he considered what the man had said. "They *do* need to be corralled, don't they?"

He turned then to look down Oklahoma 69 where a big blue Buick weaved over the center line and took the turn down Peaceable Road with its tires squealing. And his mind went to weaving and wheeling just as fast.

CHAPTER THIRTY-FOUR

Ruby sat in the driver's seat of her car, shivering even though she was bundled in a wool coat, stocking cap, and mittens. She glanced at her sister who sat beside her, looking like an Eskimo. "You warm enough, Sister? I hate to start the engine. Could get carbon monoxide poisoning with the windows rolled up."

"I'm fine. What's the plan?"

Ruby pulled a long breath. "Well, I called Betty Winslow and she told me the Eastern Star meetings usually last about an hour and a half. So I figure we need to catch up with Tootsie right after it ends, corral her in a room there in the basement where the meeting's held, and have our talk with her there."

Sister looked at her. "That's the best idea you could come up with?"

Ruby returned the stare. She'd spent all afternoon thinking about how to handle tonight. "You got a better one?"

Sister turned thoughtful. "Well, Tootsie came by herself, so we could head her off on the road back home."

"She's not alone. Wash was in town with her earlier. I figure she dropped him off at the country club and plans to pick him up after the meeting." She reached a rag from under the seat and wiped the windshield. "All this talking's fogging up the windows."

Sister gave her another look. "You're the one doing all the talking."

Ruby sighed. "I'm just trying to fill the time."

Ruby focused on the silence, wanting its curative power to calm her nerves. Though the streets were empty, she could hear the throaty snarl of traffic from the turnpike. Television sets in the windows across the street flickered, but with the windows rolled up, the sounds were muted. It was a different silence than she was accustomed to. Alien. A silence that needed to be filled in order to keep it at bay.

"You glad Mack's changed his mind on that duplex business?"

Sister rolled her eyes. "Goes without saying."

Ruby rubbed at the windows some more, then reached over and turned the key in the ignition so she could check the time on the dashboard clock. "Eight-fifteen. They should be letting out pretty quick."

"This isn't the right place," Sister said. "Too many people."

"Well . . . where then?"

"Country Club road is a lonely one, can head her off at that S-curve and force her into that wide spot where the kids make out."

Ruby stared at her sister, wondering where she had learned of the local teenager's make-out spot. Then she considered maybe she didn't want to know how Sister would know that. "You really think that's a better plan?" she asked.

"No way we'll catch Tootsie alone here. She'll be palavering all the way to her car. You know how she is, likes to play at being high-n-mighty. She's probably the Grand Dame or Duchess whatever it is they call the head honcho. Gotta be the Country Club Road."

"Maybe you're right . . ."

Ruby paused, watching the back door of the Masonic Temple open and a troupe of women walk outside. Laughing and chattering, they traipsed after a shriveled-up piece of woman in a bright red coat like a brood of chicks after a mother hen. When the last of the women walked away, leaving Tootsie alone and unlocking a long sleek Lincoln, she turned the key in the ignition.

"We'll just ease up behind her and follow her out," she murmured.

"Leave a few cars between us. These other gals will drop out before we get to the Country Club Road. I speculate most of them live close by."

Ruby did as Sister instructed and within a few minutes found that she was the only car on the road with Tootsie Turner. "I don't drive this road often, not sure I know where that S-curve is."

"Just watch for the road sign."

Within another mile, Ruby saw the sign ahead indicating a sharp curve.

"You got to get closer, Ruby. That pull-off's just ahead."

Ruby stepped on the gas. "This is insane, Sister."

"It's now or never."

Ruby pulled across the double-yellow stripe in the road, caught up with Tootsie, and passed her. Wheeling in front of the big sedan, she slammed both feet on the brake. Holding her breath, she listened to the squeal of brakes and waited for an impact. She was surprised when she ended up in the turn-off, Tootsie's car wedged in behind her, without contact being made.

"Good Lord, it worked," she said. "Just like on the TV."

Sister began waving her hands, gesturing behind her at Tootsie's car. "Get out of the car, Ruby. She's doing something. She probably has one of those mobile phones. Let her know it's us before she calls the cops."

"*Oh*, right." Ruby stepped into the cold air and saw her sister following suit on the other side. She saw the lights come on in Tootsie's car and the driver door open, then the flash of chrome as the frowzy-headed woman stepped to the ground. Recognizing what it was, she reached behind the front seat.

"I've got a gun," Tootsie Turner yelled from behind her car door.

"Yeah, but mine's bigger," Ruby said, leveling the long gun at Tootsie.

"Ruby Barlow? What the hell you think you're doing?"

"What *are* you doing, Ruby?" Sister hurried around the car. "You brought Pa's gun? We didn't talk about this . . ."

"Need to talk some business, Tootsie." Ruby's voice wavered and her knees trembled. She had practiced what she would say to Tootsie all afternoon as she sat with her father so the words would become a script. But now, all she could see was the long barrel of the gun bouncing in the air as though it had come down with Saint Vitas Dance.

"What kind of business," Tootsie drawled. One hand rested on a cocked hip, the other waved a small gun.

"I wouldn't push her, I was you," Sister said. "She's stretched pretty thin, 'bout as thin as I seen her. I didn't know she brung Pa's gun with her."

Ruby listened to her sister's words and felt a sudden calmness engulf her. She slid off the safety, listened to the *click* resonate through the cold night air, and grinned at the woman across from her.

Instantly, the cockiness left Tootsie's face and skin sagged into folds around her mouth. "You saying that's the same gun— Hellfire, you're as crazy as that mother of yours." Tootsie pitched the small revolver into the car seat. "Now, what kind of business?"

"Land deal," Ruby said, walking closer. "*Beulah* Land deal."

"Beulah Land . . ."

Ruby watched Tootsie's jaws go slack.

"Hurry up Ruby," Sister said, giving Ruby an elbow to the ribs. "Lay it on her before she pulls herself together. We got 'er on the run."

"We want Beulah Land back," Ruby said, raising her voice.

"We're *taking* Beulah Land back," Sister yelled. "Was ours all along, Pa's anyways."

"You forgot your pocketbook, Sister," Ruby whispered. "Go get the check."

"Oh, yeah." Sister hurried back to the car. She pulled her purse from the front seat and out of it, a crumpled check. She walked back to where Ruby stood, waving the check in the air. "Me and Ruby figured that all you deserved for Beulah Land was what you paid for it. *One . . . thousand . . . dollars.*"

"No way in hell." The snort Tootsie let out was ugly. "So Grover told you about Beulah Land, huh?"

"We did more than that," Ruby said. "We *found* Beulah Land—and Bill and Jack."

"And *Grace* too," Sister said. "You remember Grace?"

"Yeah," Ruby said, noticing the shaken look come over Tootsie again. "You remember the woman you gave a hundred-dollar bill to, then dumped off on the side of the road to get killed?"

"Wasn't like that." Tootsie took a step forward, waving a finger in front of Ruby and Sister's faces. "I did not drop her off on the side of the road."

"Then what?" Ruby stepped forward too, feeling her blood pressure rise. "What're you hiding, Tootsie Turner? What were those big tips for all those years? Pay-off money? Leaving that five-dollar bill on the edge of the table like I was nothing more than a cleaning lady in a motel you never met face to face. Never once a 'Thank you, Ruby.' Not once in *twenty . . . some . . . years*."

"And what about those slugs in Bill and Jack's doubletree?" Sister said. "All Pa ever kept was a shotgun, that very one Ruby's holding in her hands right there. You seen that gun before, Tootsie? Something tells me you seen that gun before."

Tootsie's knees buckled and she began to stagger.

"Oh Lord, grab her." Quickly, Ruby propped the shotgun against the front bumper of the Lincoln and made a move to catch the older woman before she fell. Tootsie slumped against her shoulder like a rag doll.

"You know what I think," Sister said, standing up close to Tootsie's face. "I remember my mother as well as anyone does 'cept Pa, and you being her best friend and all. I figure Grace wasn't the one shot those mules. My mother didn't have the spunk to do it. But you did. I heard tell how you carried a gun in your pocketbook." She pointed to the front seat of the Buick. "Proof of the pudding's right there."

"Oh my God." Tootsie Turner cupped her face in trembling hands and leaned against the car.

"You think that's what really happened?" Ruby whispered to Sister.

"Get the bill of sale out of my purse." Sister gave Ruby a nudge in the ribs. "She has to sign that bill of sale."

Ruby let loose of Tootsie, stumbled to Sister's purse, and pulled out a wrinkled, hand-written bill of sale with a line drawn at the bottom for a signature.

"Here," she said, laying the paper on the hood of the Lincoln. "Sign right here, Tootsie."

"Use this." Sister pulled a ballpoint pen from her coat pocket.

As soon as Tootsie finished scrawling her name on the bottom of the document, Sister pulled it from her hands. "I'll take charge of this. Ruby, give her the check."

"Oh, right." Ruby forced the check into Tootsie's hand and watched the woman stare at it dumbly.

"It wasn't supposed to happen like that." Tootsie's voice quivered as badly as her hands. "Things got out of hand, you see."

Ruby swallowed hard, not sure she wanted to find out more, but she had come too far down a long, dark road to turn back now. "So," she said, "what happened after Pa beat up Grace?"

Tootsie looked startled. "You know about that, too?"

"We figured it out. Go on, what happened?"

"Well," Tootsie said, talking slow. "Grace settled down too young . . . Hell, she didn't even know enough to practice birth control. Parents died young, she grew up with a widowed aunt that didn't teach her such things." She turned to Sister. "You wasn't planned for, in case you ever wondered."

"Never gave it any thought," Sister said.

"You neither, for that matter," Tootsie said, looking at Ruby. "Always felt short-changed, Grace did. She said Grover was more married to that piece of land than he was to her. He was a good-looking man but poor as a church mouse and didn't have an ambitious bone in his body. All he ever wanted was just a little piece of land." She laughed, sounding bitter. "But not Grace. She wanted to live in town, join the Eastern Star, own a little dress shop."

"Dress shop," Ruby said. "She wanted to own her own business?"

"Yes, she was a good seamstress."

"Well, I swan," Sister said. "I never knew that."

"Grover wouldn't have none of it though, refused to live in town." Tootsie paused. "Then after the war, he come back . . . I don't know, changed."

"The nightmares?" Ruby said.

"Nightmares? Well, don't know about that. Grace said he'd go crazy. She'd come whining to me and I'd tell her to leave him. Just hop a Greyhound and go back to Georgia, I'd say. She was from over round Marietta, you see. But she was too lily-livered."

"The war caused those nightmares," Ruby said. "He wasn't like his sister. Ida was crazy as a bedbug."

"All I know is he used to hit Grace in the middle of the night and she just got fed up. When I come over that last time, she looked like the devil. Busted lip, black eye, mad as hell and swearing she was gonna get even. I tried to get her to listen, but . . ." She shook her head. "Things just got out of hand. She took that double barrel and walked out to Beulah

Land, found those two mules tied up to a couple of hickory saplings. Grover did that when he wasn't using them. She unloaded both barrels on them, right in the head."

"Oh my Lord," Ruby murmured. "She *did* kill Bill and Jack."

"No, only wounded them. She slung that double barrel to the ground when she realized what she'd done and took off running down the road. Y'all was living at that old place on Tannehill Road back then, next door to Bessie Anderson. That's where you kids were. I finished Bill and Jack off with my pistol."

Tootsie nodded toward the chrome-plated twenty-two pistol on the front seat of the Lincoln. "That big revolver I used to tote, not that pea-shooter there. It was awful. Mules hurt bad—blinded 'em, you see. Squealing at the top of their lungs. Jumping around so's I couldn't get a good bead. Blood everywhere. Lord help, I never seen so much blood."

"It was the right thing to do," Ruby said. "End their suffering, I mean."

"Explains the slugs in the double tree," Sister said. "That when Grace run off?"

Tootsie nodded. "She was beside herself, just knew Grover would put her in the ground when he found out. And who's to say he wouldn't have? He loved those mules most near as much as you kids, maybe more than Grace. So the short end of the story is I drove her up to Tulsa there on the highway where the Greyhound picks up, give her all the money I had in my purse, which was enough to get her to Georgia. It got late and she began to worry about me getting back home, told me not to wait around. I didn't see no need to either, so I left."

"And the bus hit her," Ruby said.

"And the bus hit her," Tootsie repeated. "That's what the paper said. She was crazy out of her head that night, probably got scared it wasn't gonna stop."

"That when you decided to buy Beulah Land from Pa? So he could buy a coffin and headstone?"

"What?" Ruby faced Sister. "*Tootsie* bought Beulah Land?"

"I figure that's what Tootsie was implying at the nursing home today when she said we'd be taken care of like always."

Ruby faced Tootsie. "It was *you* bought Beulah Land, not the old Mister?"

"Had to! I wanted to give Grover the money flat out, but Wash has a miserly soul. Insisted Grover sign over the deed." She shook her head as if trying to dislodge something too ugly to look upon. "Grover didn't have money to bury Grace proper, you see. Nice casket's what I told him to get. I figured he'd bury her out there at Hugh Low Cemetery. But the damned fool buried her right next to those mules and put up that tombstone with that saying on it. I just couldn't bring myself to allow Wash to run cattle over her grave. I put my foot down on that one. Land's just laid there fallow all these years . . ."

Tootsie's voice faded and Ruby stood for a good bit without saying anything, long enough to grow chilled. She noticed the needles on the pines beside the road had curled in on themselves from the cold and realized Sister and Tootsie were doing the same thing.

"We'll catch our death, we don't get someplace warm," she said.

"Guess all's said can be said." Sister folded the bill of sale into her coat pocket and looked at Tootsie. "I aim to take this here paper to the lawyer first thing in the morning, make sure the deed's transferred to Ruby and me proper like."

"Let's get you inside your car." Ruby took Tootsie's arm. "We'll follow you to the Country Club so you can pick up Wash."

"What? How do you know these things . . ."

Tootsie's voice trailed off as Ruby helped her into her car. She studied the old woman sitting dumbly in the front seat, then tapped on the window. As the glass rolled down, she leaned forward. "You come by the house next week, I'll fix that hair. A little green tint will do the trick. You look like hell, you know."

"I know." And as she rolled the window up, Tootsie whispered, "Thank you, Ruby."

CHAPTER THIRTY-FIVE

Grover Cleveland Anderson died a week before Christmas, passing over at first light. Mack refused to leave his side in the last hours. He talked nonstop in those last minutes, hoping his grandfather had enough consciousness left to understand what he was telling him.

"We found your buddies, Pa. You didn't leave them behind. Beulah Land is yours again, Grace is there waiting for you. It's done with now." When Pa drew his last breath, he was thankful it was a peaceful one.

Chapman's Funeral Home came out and dug a hole between Grace's plot and Bill and Jack's. George Folsom drove his International tractor over before the graveside service and mowed the grass underneath the two hickories. Mack used a weed whacker to trim up around the tree trunks and stumps. Eying the gravesite, he sensed the irony of the situation. A man might lay claim to a piece of land, he thought, but in the end, it was the land that claimed the man.

There wasn't much of a turnout at the funeral. Old friends had become few and far between with the passing of time. Mack saw Nonny sitting with George Folsom at the church and then afterward at Beulah Land. He'd been thankful her eyes were clear and bright, which he hoped against hope meant she was sober and sound. She said her condolences to his mother and aunt, but only nodded his way. He figured that was only proper given she had come close to committing self-annihilation because of the mess his good intentions had wrought.

Right before the funeral, Mack talked Bessie Anderson and her sisters into buying the duplex, on the condition Walker would put a door between the two units. Walker complied without batting an eye, saying "It can always be closed up when the old sisters give up the ghost."

When Mack expressed a concern that his cousins might not get their money out of the place, Walker dismissed it, saying, "A fool's born every minute, ready to pour good money down a hole." After Mack learned the Anderson sisters had no children and the property would fall to a television minister, he didn't give the matter another thought.

He had finished up the duplex sale that morning as well as a couple of other loose ends. Two boxes of fresh ammo lay on the front seat along with an amended deed to the home place. He'd put the home place in joint tenancy with his mother and aunt, with rights of survivorship. In addition to Beulah Land, they were now as much the owner of it as he was.

Driving straight back, he laid the deed to Beulah Land on the kitchen table, along with an amended copy of the deed on the home place. He carefully positioned the documents between their two coffee mugs and used boxes of shotgun shells as paperweights to keep them from blowing away. He debated hanging around long enough to witness the expression on their faces when the impact of joint tenancy sunk in, but the day was getting short and the road was long. Time to pull up stakes, head for the big and wide.

He loaded his gear into the back of the Bronco, gave the place one last look, and headed for Beulah Land where his mother and aunt were tending to some business of their own. He spotted them under the hickories as he pulled into the dirt track, laying out wooden stakes on the ground.

"Everything go all right with the lawyer?" Ruby asked as he walked up.

Mack nodded. "Left the deed to Beulah Land on the kitchen table. As for that duplex, both units now belong to the Anderson cousins. Bessie and her sisters seem real satisfied with the place, plan to move in soon as Walker puts the finishing touches on it."

"Hate like everything I'm gonna lose them as customers. Still don't see why they can't drive out here to get their hair fixed."

"That was part of the deal, Mama. Would you rather see them get sued for property damage or get killed in a car wreck? Worse yet, kill someone else?"

Mack had decided not to share with his mother and aunt what Bessie had told him about the night Grace was killed. They had been sheltered from the truth all these years. It didn't make sense to expose the grisly details now. To his thinking, worse crimes than his grandfather's were committed every day. Land swindles. Crooked realtors. Governments turning boys into killing machines. And living with the memory of that night had been a harsh enough sentence for his grandfather to serve.

"Water under the bridge anyway," he told his mother. "The Anderson cousins already surrendered their driver licenses."

"Well, guess they can just walk across the street there, and they'll get a senior discount. Still and all, sounds like blackmail to me."

* * *

Sister straightened from her work and gave Ruby a look. "You're a fine one to be talking blackmail," she snapped.

Mack did not push for an explanation. He still felt bewildered that the Turners had signed over Beulah Land to his mother and aunt. But in spite of his probing, neither of the two would divulge the particulars of how that deal had come to pass. All they would say was Tootsie had turned over a new leaf in her old age. He had laughed at that, but let the matter drop. Some questions were better left unanswered.

"What you doing there, Sister?" Mack watched as the little woman picked up a small rubber mallet and began to pound one of many stakes into the ground.

"Marking off a place for myself. This here's my spot, right next to Grace. She was a seamstress, too." She waved toward two other stakes. "Those are for Will and Ruby."

"Will? You mean, Dad?"

"Guess I should've talked with you about it," Ruby intervened. "You know how your daddy always wanted a place and . . . Well, it seems only right to bring him here. Come spring, I plan to move him, headstone and all. You're not upset, are you?"

"Not a bit. I think he'd like that. You decide on a headstone for Pa yet?"

"No, I just don't know what to put on it—what *he'd* want put on it."

"Seems to me he took care of that right there." Sister pointed at Grace's marker. "Nonny said at the funeral she'd clean it up if we wanted."

"Not sure that'd be a good idea," Mack said hesitantly. "We troubled Nonny enough. Besides, I don't figure it matters no one else can read it. Those words Pa put on it was meant for just him and Grace. I'm inclined to just let it stand like it is."

"That would suit me just fine. You, Ruby?"

"I don't know. Grace caused a lot of heartaches."

"Now Ruby," Sister said. "Grace had a lot put on her, especially there at the end."

"I suppose." Ruby took a deep breath. "Well, guess even sane people are entitled to go a little nuts now and then. And she sure didn't deserve to die the way she did."

Hearing the change in his mother's attitude toward Grace, Mack knew that a door had opened. His mother was looking forward, not back. He turned toward the road where a pickup pulled in and parked beside his Bronco. "That George Folsom?"

"Yes, he's here to talk business with me." Ruby combed her hair with her fingers, shook hands with the old man as he walked up, and led him towards the back of the property.

Mack looked at Sister for an explanation.

"She's negotiating to have a fence put around the family plot, set it off from the back pasture. We've arranged for Luther Winslow to drill in alfalfa come spring. I think Pa would approve of that, don't you?"

"Yes, I do." Mack watched his mother mark a line for a fencerow with a can of bright orange spray paint. "Mama's in her heyday, isn't she?"

Sister raised her eyebrows. "Goes without saying. She likes being an independent businesswoman. Never owned a thing in her life and now she does. We *both* do." Sister smiled at Mack. "Feels real good, being a landowner."

"It's long past due."

"Better late than never." Sister hefted the hammer in her hand again. "If you want to be planted here, you better pick a spot. Ruby's putting most of the land into horse hay to pay the taxes."

Mack looked at a stake that had been placed near his parents'. "I figured that one over there was for me."

"That one next to Ruby? That's Whitey's. Ruby picked out his spot herself."

"Whitey!" Mack grinned and looked at the old white dog stretched out next to a stump. When the old dog heard his name, he twisted his sides in pleasure and pounded his scrawny tail *whump, whump* on the ground. "Well hell, just stake me out there next to Whitey."

"All right then." Sister wrote his name on a stake with a felt-tip marker and pounded it in the ground next to the dog's.

Mack sobered as he watched the wooden picket bite into the soil. Ordinarily, it would be the sign of an ending, but in his line of work, a stake in the ground meant new construction.

"Well, that's it," Sister said, looking around. "We're all accounted for."

Mack gave the little old woman a peck on the cheek and walked to his mother to say his goodbyes. "It's time for me to go, Mama."

"I wish you could stay, son, but I know you can't."

Mack saw a change in his mother, not just in outward behavior, but inward too. For the first time ever, he knew that she truly understood why, all those times past, he'd had to leave. Giving George Folsom a handshake, he left the congregation to handle Beulah Land.

*****

Mack pulled to a rolling stop at the Y in the road, hesitating. He knew taking the northern route would get him on the Indian Nation Turnpike faster. In spite of that, he turned south toward McAlester.

Questioning his sanity, he steered the Bronco to the Ace Hardware. He left a few minutes later carrying a plastic bag holding a deadbolt and window-lock replacement. Driving to the old part of town, he pulled up at the old storefront on Choctaw Street that now housed the homeless shelter.

Seeing Nonny's Jeep sitting alongside the building, Mack sat a moment, thinking about the wisdom of his being there. Climbing out of his Bronco, he tried the Jeep's doors and found them locked. As he glanced hesitantly toward the back door, the voice in his head said, *You've come this far . . .* Inhaling deeply, he walked to the kitchen where he figured Nonny would be working and found Chester handling duties instead of her.

Noticing him peering around the doorframe, Chester said, "Soups on, Mack. You hungry, go on out front. Plenty for everyone."

"Thanks, but I need to hit the trail." Mack slipped inside the back door. "Got a call from the guy I work for out in the Panhandle. He got the contract on a big job at the college in Canyon, little town west of Amarillo. New dormitory going up. I'm heading out right now."

Chester wiped his hands on a tea towel. "You come by to say your farewells to Nonny? She's out front."

"Yes and no." He paused. "Would you give this to her. It's some things I noticed she needs."

Chester took the bag. "Sure thing." He gave Mack another look. "That it?"

"Yeah, that's it." Mack noticed the man was grinning again. "Well, maybe I'd like to get a look without her seeing me. Just to see if she's, you know, okay."

"Take a peek then."

Mack saw Nonny wearing a long white butcher's apron, ladling soup into bowls. He studied what he could see of her face, which was mostly a profile, but it was enough to see that she was looking straight into the faces of the people in line. He also noticed her hands were trembling a bit, but not bad enough to be deemed unsteady.

Backing away from the door, he turned to Chester and said, "Well hell, she's putting herself out there."

"You the reason?" Chester said, laying slices of day-old white bread on a platter.

"Me? No, I can't take credit. She's got an independent streak big as Texas. But I'm glad for it, whatever the cause."

"Me, too."

"Think she's gonna make it?"

"One day at a time, Mack." He grinned. "But I'm an optimist."

"She's got a lot of grit in her craw."

"Hard to keep a good woman down." Chester extended his hand.

"That it is." Mack loosened his grip and made to pull his hand away, but when Chester hung on, he waited.

"'Quaint and curious war is, you shoot a fellow down, you'd treat if met where any bar is, or help to half-a-crown.'"

Mack blinked. "Afraid I didn't catch all of that."

"Thomas Hardy. He wrote a poem about a hundred years ago about a man who went off to war to kill the enemy. After he got back home, he speculated if he met the same guy in a bar, he'd probably buy him a beer, maybe loan him a buck." He turned loose of Mack's hand. "War's hell, isn't it, Mack? Screws with your head. Take care of yourself, kiddo."

"You too, pard." Mack hesitated at the door, then turned to face Chester again. "Next time I'm in town, I'll buy you a Bud."

"We'll have to sneak off, not let Nonny know what we're up to."

"There's this little bar out on the highway . . ." He hesitated, taking note of the scar on Chester's head. "But it's mostly good old boys that hang out there."

"Salt of the earth," Chester said, grinning. "Make it sooner rather than later. You better beat it now. Nonny's probably close to being out of bread."

Without further adieu, Mack left. He hadn't done exactly what he had set out to do on this trip, but it had ended well. The people he had upended had righted themselves and were looking forward, not back.

Retracing his path down Choctaw Street, he headed toward the interstate. Forty-five minutes later, he was doing the speed limit and then some on the Indian Nation Turnpike, trying to make the best of the daylight remaining in the short winter day. A much-needed job that would put money in his pocket waited at the end of the road. Though they set him back a bundle, the improvements he'd made on the home place were worth every penny. But he'd have to keep an eye on that roof, he reflected. A warranty wasn't worth the paper it was written on.

As the country rushed past, he glanced in the rearview mirror, sensing something inside was settling. Rolling down his window, he let the rich smell of wet earth and fresh air flush out the staleness. Though barren now, the monsoons would come soon and the country would become a mass of green. Hardwood trees would fill the space between the short-leaf pine, and the underbrush would become so thick, a man couldn't see a foot in front of his face.

A jungle . . .

Even as the thought entered his mind, he corralled it. If he'd learned one thing on this trip, it was life was a coin toss. Some days would be winners, some not. The biggest loser was the person who lived in fear of flipping the coin.

Lu Clifton writes adult novels set in Oklahoma and Texas Panhandle, with a mingling of Native American cultural beliefs and traditions thrown in. She became interested in those cultural traditions while tracing her mother's Choctaw roots. She was born in and spent her early childhood in southeastern Oklahoma, then moved to the Texas Panhandle with her family. She completed an associate degree at Amarillo Junior College in Texas and a B.A. and M.A. in English at Colorado State University. She now resides in Illinois.

Writing for adults and children, she is a member of the Oklahoma Writers Federation, Mystery Writers of America, and the Society of Children's Book Writers and Illustrators. The first book in the Sam Chitto mystery series, *Scalp Dance,* was a finalist for the 2017 Oklahoma Book Award in Fiction and the second book, *The Bone Picker,* was a finalist for the 2018 Oklahoma Book Award in Fiction. She has three middle-grade novels in print. Her middle-grade novel, *Freaky Fast Frankie Joe,* received a Friends of American Writers Award for Juvenile Fiction in 2012, and *Seeking Cassandra* won the 2017 Oklahoma Book Award for Young Adult Fiction.

DISCUSSION GUIDE:

Seeking Grace in Beulah Land by Lu Clifton

1. Discuss the double meaning of the title. What does the term Beulah Land mean to someone in the Bible Belt? What did it mean to Pa? How does this relate to Mack's view of the Panhandle? To his father's reference to the region as "heaven on Earth"? The word *grace* can also mean absolution. How does this alternate translation relate to the people in the novel?
2. At the beginning of the novel, Ruby's obsession with genetics makes her weak and needy, but she rises up to take control of finding Beulah Land. Nonny is seen as strongly independent in the beginning, yet crumbles after she becomes obsessed with Grace.. And Mack's memories of military duty are an obsession that locks him in the past. Discuss Nonny's view that "obsessions can make a person do dumb-ass things." Discuss the need to face the dark night of the soul before consolation can be found.
3. Discuss the strong family ties in the novel. Pa once stole his sister from the asylum in Vinita and brought her back home. Ruby wanted to do the same for Pa, taking him out of the nursing home. Cousin Bessie kept the secret of the fateful day Grace disappeared hidden for years because "family's family." How has the sense of family changed

now that the extended family has all but disappeared in this country? What has been lost . . . or gained?

4. Nonny defines deconstruction as "picking apart words and the meaning behind those words to get at the truth of things long dead." When she tries to explain what the term means to Mack, he interprets it in terms of what he knows, saying, "I'm in construction . . . Not salvage." Discuss the theme of deconstruction and salvage in light of the missing Grace. In terms of the story as a whole? Is the entire novel a story of deconstruction? Of salvage? Discuss.
5. The retired philosophy teacher Chester asks Mack as one point if he had given any thought to laying down his sword and shield. What did he mean by this? What did he mean when he talked to Nonny about invisible tattoos on Mack that accumulated under the skin, "permanently separating the person from others." Do all soldiers who've experienced war return with invisible scars that separate them from the rest of society? Other characters also bear invisible scars. They apply balms to ease the pain caused by external scars, but not the invisible. Discuss the difference between physical and emotional wounds and the difficulty healing those not visible.
6. The construction boss Walker challenges Mack's need to build a custom home for his mother and aunt, saying, "Why go for the best money can buy when good enough'll do?" Does his rationale make sense? Does the story prove Walker or Mack to be correct? Should adult children follow the desires of their parents, even if it isn't the safest solution?
7. The novel opens with a description of the Staked Plains, described by Francisco Coronado as a place "with no more land marks than if we had been swallowed up by the

sea ... there was not a stone, nor bit of rising ground, nor a tree, nor a shrub, nor anything to go by." [Wikipedia] Why do you think thc author chose to begin the novel with this reference? What characters in the book have lost their landmarks? What stakes did the main characters find that led them to a safe place?

Made in the USA
Middletown, DE
30 August 2019